Cover Illustration by @alilyushka

Cover Design by Elliana Maggetti

Developmental Edits by Kay Morton @kmortonedits

Copyediting by Bailey Suttle

Proofreading by Katrina Hirsch

Inside Art: @badeyart

MORETTI
RACING
MORETTI
RACING
VIP

SPARKS FLY SERIES

# Heart Racing

## A FORMULA ONE ROMANCE

# ELLIANA ROSE

*For the ones who feel deeply, give endlessly, and have ever wondered where they belong. You are meant to be here, exactly as you are.*

# PLAYLIST

Honey Whiskey – Nothing but Thieves
Karma – Taylor Swift
Dress – Taylor Swift
Achilles Come Down – Gang of Youths
Do I Wanna Know? – Arctic Monkeys
Die For You – The Weeknd
Dazed & Confused – Ruel
I Found – Amber Run
You Are In Love – Taylor Swift
Silver – Nic Nim
Caramel – Sleep Token
I Don't Even Care About You – MISSIO
I'm Yours – Isabel LaRose
Leave Me Alone – Reneé Rap
False God – Taylor Swift
Bad at Love – Halsey
Maison – Emilio Piano & Lucie

# GLOSSARY

- **Chicane:** A series of sharp turns that alternate directions, used to slow down cars
- **Downforce:** The aerodynamic force that pushes a car down at high speeds, which helps the car grip the road
- **DRS:** Short for drag reduction system, which allows a driver to increase the car's top speed by opening an adjustable flap on the rear wing
- **Halo:** A cockpit safety structure that was introduced to Formula 1 in 2018 and has already been credited with saving the lives of several drivers. Resembling a horseshoe, the halo consists of a bar that surrounds the drivers head and is bolted to the chassis at three points.
- **Overcut / undercut:** Race strategies that involve a driver attempting to pass the car in front during a pit stop window
- **Paddock:** The area behind the team garages (or pits) at every Formula 1 circuit that is home to the teams' technical staff and equipment, catering, media, race officials and other important functions that contribute to the successful running of the race weekend.

- **Parc Femme:** Literally translated from French as 'closed park,' this is a secure parking area where Formula 1 cars must be left after qualifying.
- **Pole Position:** The first position on the grid at the start of the race. Pole position is earned by the driver recording the fastest time in the final period of qualifying.
- **Free Practice:** Open practice time on track for all teams
- **Qualifying:** The one-hour session on Saturdays (or day before the race) that determines the order in which drivers start the race.
- **P(x):** Position or ranking in the race. P3= third place.
- **Typical Race Weekend Structure:**
  - Day One: Free Practice / Media
  - Day Two: Qualifying
  - Day Three: Race

# DEAR READER

Welcome to the *Sparks Fly* series—a collection of interconnected standalones. While each book can be read on its own, I do recommend reading them in order!

To catch you up or as a little refresher: book one, *For the Thrill of It All*, is Lucia and Alexander's story. It follows Lucia as she joins the remainder of the F1 season after summer break. She joins the travel schedule with her daughter, after her brother, Matteo, convinces her to come along. The timelines do slightly overlap—specifically during vacation! I've also sprinkled in many future characters throughout this book, so have fun finding those little crumbs. This book dives into Matteo's story and can function as a standalone, so if you haven't read book one, that is okay!

While these are sports romances, the series also explores heavier topics. One of my favorite things about the romance genre is its ability to address the beautiful mess of being human—life experiences, trauma, and how they affect our lives, as well as the highs and lows of growth and healing.

The *Sparks Fly* series is inspired by Formula One. I've loved Formula One for years and grew up watching races with my dad. That said, you do *not* need any prior knowledge of Formula One to enjoy this book. I do my best to describe everything in an easy, accessible way, and I hope you enjoy the fast-paced, spotlight-driven world. There are also some changes to racing rules or structure to better serve the storytelling, as this is a work of fiction—and a love story first.

## <u>Content Warnings</u>

*Heart Racing* is a contemporary romance filled with sweet and spicy banter, tension, and swoon.

Content warnings include explicit language, multiple explicit sex scenes, on-page mentions of a car crash, masking one's true emotions as a coping mechanism, high-functioning anxiety, and body image insecurities.

I know these topics are complex. If they aren't something you wish to read about, please take care of yourself. As always, protect your heart first. If you have any questions, my DMs are always open.

This is an open-door romance intended for an 18+ audience.

# CONTENTS

# 1

## NICOLA

There was a time when I thought the man crowding my space next to me in the back seat of the limo was cute. The dimples, the floppy hair, the charm – it made him hard to ignore. And I maybe had a tiny little crush on him at the beginning of the season. Now? Now, there was no crush, no admiration. His dimples were infuriating, and his hair was always messy like he never bothered to brush it or owned a hair product. His whole face actually was rather stupid.

Matteo DeLuca was the most annoying person to exist. He was a driver of my family's Formula One team: Moretti Racing. My best friend's older brother.

And I hated him.

I sat in the car with his whole body pressed next to mine, making my skin buzz with annoyance. Lucia, his sister, was across on the other side of the limo with Matteo's best friend, Alexander. A year ago, I wouldn't have thought I'd be here, squeezed between two Formula One drivers and my best friend. A year ago, I was on a beach in Monaco, not paying attention to my family's company events.

That had all changed when I had waltzed into my father's study with a frustrated (albeit slightly dramatic) sigh, and plopped into the cold leather chair across from him. An oversized deep walnut-stained table sat between us. One his grandfather had built, sanded, and stained with his own two hands. He reminded me of that fact more than he needed to. We came from a hardworking, breaking-their-backs, rooted Italian family. We had made the name Moretti all by ourselves. Not born into the legacy, but one that was made.

*Carved.*

Carved a damn long time ago. Moretti Racing debuted in 1930, but it was my grandfather who'd made Moretti into a name. My father had taken up the helm and brought them into world championship titles and top of the line sponsorships.

*"I'm very busy today, Nicola." My father had sighed, not looking up from his computer.*

*"Fine, then I'll cut to the point." I crossed my arms over my chest. My cashmere sweater was a deep green and flowed over a leather skirt, tights, and high-heeled black boots that reached my thighs. I tapped said heeled boot rhythmically onto the hardwood floor beneath me.*

*"I'll be joining you on the circuit this season with the team. I'll help with whatever needed, but if you think Michael gives a fuck about your world, he doesn't. And I do. Which you know. So I'm done waiting for him to step up, and you should be too." I felt out of breath by the time all the words toppled out of my mouth. My anxiety wafted over me, but I kept my face even and confident, reminding myself of the goal.*

*Father wanted Michael, my brother, to work for the family company, but he was off wrapped up in his own life. He had little to no interest in the Moretti empire. I, however, did.*

*I stared my father down, shoulders back, pin straight posture, manicured fingertips now clasped on my knee. Calm but firm. He had been the one to teach me to be fierce, to not take no for an answer, and that if I led with facts and fortitude, I could do anything I wanted. Much to mother's dismay, I wanted this.*

*The silence stretched on, my father dragged his attention from his computer, his gaze meeting mine. Eye's softening slightly. Copper brown eyes that were a near mirror to my brother's whereas I got my mom's blue shade instead. However, we shared the same deep brown hair and olive skin, and other than the eyes, it was obvious I was his daughter and a Moretti.*

*He had rings on his fingers, and his suit was pressed to perfection, as it always was. Gianfranco Moretti was not to be tried. Except maybe by his daughter, because after a short moment he did the unexpected.*

*"Very well." He agreed with soft eyes and a nod. "If this is really what you want."*

*I smiled brightly, fidgeting with my charm bracelet. The one I had collected each and every charm for, the small race car gifted from my father was one of my favorites.*

*"It is."*

*"Alright then. I'll add you to all the flight information and make some introductions for you." He typed away on his computer.*

*I stood, pressed my hands against my skirt and squared my shoulders again. Only the click of my heels on the hardwood accompanied me as I walked out the door.*

*"You really want to live on the road?" my mother said, looking up from her book as she sat on the plush living room couch. She loved nothing more than to lounge in her favorite room and read a trait I had inherited. Our house was cozy but decadent: high vaulted ceilings, huge windows letting the sunlight stream in, original impressionist paintings were on many walls of the house, my mother's favorite.*

*"You're the one that always told me to chase my dreams."*

*"Hmm," she hummed her approval before going back to her*

*book. I smiled to myself. My parents were such opposites, but even after being married some thirty years, they were inseparable. Father's steely exterior was softened by only two people, two women: myself and my mother. Looking like an actual replica of my mother helped. He had never been able to say no to her, and by default rarely said it to me.*

*That was the beginning of it all. When I decided to take my fate by the damn horns and carve my own path. Great grandfather would be proud.*

I shook away the fond memory. We were now more than halfway through the season, and I had managed to make some new friends along the way too. My favorite of the bunch was none other than Matteo's sister, Lucia DeLuca. Her and her daughter Gianna had joined in on the season not long ago now, and we had become fast friends after summer break when Matteo brought them back with him. From the moment I met Lucia, I knew we would be friends. She was all warmth to my icy exterior. I was more like a dark cloud;my resting bitch face and dark hair really solidified the fact. Lucia said we were like the sun and the moon: one light, one dark, both bright. The downside was more time with the other DeLuca. Regardless, life on the road has been a bright new experience.

This season felt like it had flown by. I'd been helping with odds and ends jobs around the paddock: shooting content for the marketing team, helping organize events and meetings, and occasionally being a liaison for the drivers and the upper management. My father was letting me figure out what side spoke to me the most. Tonight, we were on our way to a charity gala thrown by the Moretti Foundation. I had grown rather fond of the philanthropic side of the Moretti business over the first half of the season, helping out as much as I could. I loved it all – the rush of it, how many moving parts contributed to make the team function and thrive.

There were two Moretti drivers. Carlos, who I had known for

years, his family always in the same circles as my own. Then the other one, the overly irritating one who'd just plucked my phone out of my hands.

"Matteo, give it back," I seethed, trying to keep my voice down. I was wearing a glittering black gown, one that hugged my every curve and ended in a flare of black, sparkling gauzy fabric. I had sky-high silver heels to match, little bows on the back that made me deliriously happy when I found them while shopping with Lucia. A pair of sheer black gloves that Lucia had insisted would be perfect for tonight trailed from my palm to the middle of my upper arm, small pearls scattered along them. The Moretti Racing team had a longstanding sponsorship with Terra Mia, a diamond jeweler, so my neck, wrists, and ears were adorned with sparkling diamonds. I felt amazing, and I looked damn good too.

But here to ruin it was my least favorite Moretti driver. Matteo's espresso eyes narrowed on me, his gaze heavy as it always was. Unfortunately, he looked downright edible in his tailored Armani suit. For Christ's sake, he matched me, down to the glimmering threads on his suit jacket that lined the inside and sparkled as he shifted in his seat. His thigh was flush with my own. Regardless of the fabric between us, it felt like an inordinate amount of heat coming from the contact. Irritation bloomed as he dangled the phone out of my reach like he wanted me to press up against him. *Infuriating.*

"I swear to God Matteo, I will push you out of this moving car," I threatened in a whisper, reaching for my phone again. Much to my dismay, he was unfazed by my threats, if not entertained by them. It had been like this since I arrived on track at the beginning of the season. I knew he did it to annoy me, I knew my reaction was what he was fishing for, but I couldn't help it.

Matteo DeLuca got under my skin.

"Take a break, enjoy the view." He raised a brow.

"I'm going to a work event. I'm *actively* working, DeLuca." I glared and he glared back, half-heartedly.

"I was there when your father said to relax and enjoy." He crossed his arms, trapping my phone.

"Moretti's don't relax."

"What a shame. You should really try it sometime. Hugely positive feedback from those that do."

I only rolled my eyes and crossed my arms, leaning back in the seat, purposely pushing my chest out. The low-cut front did wonders for me, and I was not above being petty. I knew for a fact he was maintaining eye contact a little too much since the moment I'd walked into the lobby. Leave it to him to be all straight-laced and polite when I was the one who wanted a rise out of him. My boobs looked amazing; it was rude not to look.

"What do you have to do for work tonight?" he asked, tone softer. This stupid man and his stupid ability to read my emotions. Lucia had mentioned it was one of her favorite aspects of her brother: how he gave everyone his full attention, noticed little details and seemed to commit them to memory, but I couldn't stand it. Lucia's laugh floated through the back of the car. She looked stunning in a light pink satin gown, a stark contrast to my black one and exactly so very us.

"I promised some of the marketing team I would help take photos and content tonight," I told Matteo, squeezing my arms together. His eyes faltered, glancing down for only a second, before snapping back up to my eyes.

*Mission accomplished.*

He swallowed hard, his eyes glued to my own again. His annoying pretty eyes that seemed to twinkle under the dim lights in the back of the limo. I hated them.

"I'll give it back..." he started, and I sat up straighter. "If, and only if you have a drink with me," he smirked, revealing his stupid dimples.

"In your dreams, DeLuca." I scoffed and rolled my eyes. He met me with just as stubborn of a look before sliding my phone under his left thigh, knowing I wouldn't reach for it. Reminding me of the same cocky attitude that had annoyed me from the very first day we had met.

The morning I had met Matteo was everyone's first day back for preseason testing. I remembered how sticky it was, how the blouse I had specifically picked out for the day felt like it was plastered to me, and how my nerves were ricocheting around inside of me like a pinball machine. First days had always made me slightly sick to my stomach. I woke up too early, before my alarm even rang through the hotel room. I re-ironed my shirt twice, despite ironing it the night before. I triple checked that I brought a pair of backup shoes, that my laptop was stored in my bag, with the wall charger and a portable one just in case. I went over every scenario or version of things that could happen and preemptively mitigated it. I made a list. I crossed off each item as I put it in my large leather bag. I was ready to face the day and make a good first impression.

Throwing on my mask to perform all day as my work self left my cheeks tired from smiles and feeling touched out from handshakes and unsolicited awkward side hugs. There were too many chances to say the wrong thing and have someone decide who I was before I even opened my mouth. But I knew this dance well, growing up in an important family that had been running a Formula One team for decades came with many events, and many important first impressions.

So, I spent the entire morning doing what I did best: performing. Polite, professional, and put together. I greeted everyone with the kind of warmth people expected from a Moretti, a charm I had perfected over the years.

Inside, though, my nerves were coiled so tight I could barely breathe. Only the Moretti Racing drivers were left to say hi to.

Carlos was easy. I knew him well already. He gave me a thumbs up and a grin that said 'You've got this.' I didn't entirely feel like it, but it was nice to pretend.

What felt like the biggest meeting was with the other driver. The new one. Fresh off his rookie year and apparently already everyone's favorite golden boy.

I'd seen his face on enough screens to know what to expect—cocky smile, messy curls, that 'I don't take anything seriously' energy that made sponsors drool. Still, knowing didn't prepare me for him in person.

He walked in like he owned the place, sunglasses pushed up on his head, sun-kissed and smiling like the world had never told him no.

"Matteo," he said, offering a hand. "You must be the famous daughter."

I blinked. "Nicola, nice to meet you."

His grin widened, like I'd said something amusing, it made my nerves fray. "Right." He dragged out the word, like he was already fitting me into some mental box. Then his gaze flicked down my outfit—cream trousers, silk blouse, and my standard heels. I was unfortunately not blessed vertically and hated feeling small, especially in a business setting. Two things were a must: my armor of red lips and high heels. I watched his expression shift, the spark of mischief landing before he opened his mouth.

"Careful where you step, or you might get dirty. We wouldn't want that for the new paddock princess."

The words hit like a slap dressed up as a joke.

Everyone around us laughed—quick, easy, like he'd said something harmless. I forced a smile, the kind I used for sponsors and distant relatives. The mask slipped over me automatically.

"Oh, don't worry," I said lightly, "I'm used to steering clear of messy things."

That earned me a few chuckles of my own, but it didn't matter. The nickname had already landed.

And Matteo? He looked far too pleased with himself, like he'd just won something.

The worst part was how fast it caught on. One lunch break later, someone called me Princess in passing. By the end of the day, it was

*Paddock Princess on half the crew's lips, said with that teasing affection reserved for someone not to be taken seriously.*

*All my effort, every polished smile, every calculated step to prove I wasn't just a name was reduced to a punchline made by the golden boy.*

*I told myself I didn't care. That people would see through it eventually. That I'd make myself indispensable, the way I always did.*

*But when I caught Matteo across the garage that afternoon, still grinning, still golden, I knew it wasn't going away anytime soon.*

*And I hated that some small, stupid part of me envied how easy he made it look. Like he wasn't scared of anything at all.*

*I couldn't admit it at the time, but I was the one scared. I was scared to prove myself in this world that had always felt reserved for my brother and father, and seeing a driver with too much charm and not enough care made me angry. Made me hate him for treating my family legacy like it was just a paycheck, just something fun. That's where it had all started. And sure, months had passed, and I had tried my best to endure his sarcasm and jabs here and there. But Matteo DeLuca fucking annoyed me.*

So when he looked at me with his pompous smirk and raised an eyebrow and said, "Weird that you would bring up dreams, Moretti. You dreaming about me?" I wanted to throttle him.

"Fuck right off," I spat out, staring out the window, feeling too hot and too trapped in this car.

"Hey—" Matteo started, a finger reached out and brushed my arm. I jolted away from him in response. "Okay, okay I'm sorry." A moment of silence passed between us.

I huffed, narrowed my eyes and let out a groaned, "Fine."

"Sorry I didn't hear that."

"I said fine."

"Why yes I will have a drink with the most handsome driver on the circuit," he mocked in a high-pitched voice. I rolled my eyes.

"Never mind, keep the damn phone." My voice was harsh. I

got up from the cramped seat and sat down next to Lucia. Everyone shuffled around, Alexander coughing a little to cover up a laugh. I shot him a glare for good measure, and he held up his hands in surrender, then immediately started chatting with his best friend. Once seated next to Lucia, I let out a sigh.

"Planning my brother's murder?" she asked me.

"It's become quite elaborate at this point."

# 2

# NICOLA

Cameras flashed as I exited the car. I plastered on a rehearsed smile as I walked, head held high and shoulders back. My father was at the doors, his own team surrounding him, when his eyes met mine. His usual stoic and cold facade melted, and he let out a smile. The cameras and shouting from the paparazzi became frantic as Alexander and Lucia exited the car behind me. The media was obsessed with them, just as they had expected with the fake dating scheme they cooked up to help Alexander repair his image and for them to control the narrative of the media. It was a rather difficult task, but they seemed to be succeeding at it. I had never seen any two people denying obvious feelings more than the two of them. They'd figure it out eventually.

I walked ahead to my father.

"*Ciao, Bella.*" He greeted me with a kiss to each cheek. I smiled. Gianfranco Moretti was a force. He was nearing his seventies, but nothing could slow the man down. He was dressed and polished, no doubt overseen by my mother's own expert eye. His eyes softened as he took me in.

"Thank you," I replied. He gave my arm a gentle squeeze and

motioned for me to enter the large hotel doors. The event was better than I could have imagined. Amid the last few months, I'd found a bit of a sweet spot with the events team, so when the opportunity to help with one of our biggest charity galas of the year, I had jumped right in. I found myself drawn to the Moretti Foundation side of the business more and more.

"You did good." My father leaned down, and I looked up to him, pride filling me. I hadn't realized he knew I had a hand in the event, but nothing really got by him. Even when I thought he was too busy to notice things, he always did.

"The events team is really remarkable," I nodded. He hummed a noncommittal agreement and looked at his watch then to me. I smiled and bumped his shoulder gently.

"Go be important," I whispered, knowing he had many people to speak with during the event. Morettis never rested.

"*You* are important, my darling. Remember to have fun tonight." With that, he walked away to a set of older men greeting him. I looked around, taking in the moment: the clinking of glasses, a live band playing in the back on a decked-out stage. Tables lined the room, a dance floor in the middle, and ahead of me, a rather extravagant golden glittering bar. Just where I wanted to go.

"Looking for me?" a cocky voice spoke from behind me. I turned on my heel, those dimples on full display.

"No," I glared, "I was looking for alcohol."

"Me too," he said and walked ahead of me toward the bar. I let out a huff and followed him after a moment.

"Nicola!" I heard a woman's voice, turning to find Carlos and his mother, who was beaming at me. I smiled back, pausing my stride to talk with them.

"Oh, how are you?" I reached out, a hand going to her arm, and kissed both her cheeks.

"Oh, you know dear, good as always. You look beautiful!

Carlos, darling, tell her how beautiful she looks!" She fussed over me. I glanced over to Carlos who was trying not to laugh.

"You look beautiful, as always, Nicola." He said warmly, his accent seeping through each word, looking rather dapper tonight in a tailored suit. I did my best not to roll my eyes at him and how he was the biggest mama's boy around. I'd poke fun at him later.

"You look very handsome, Carlos." I smirked back at him. He hated these events, but like me, he grew up around them. Galas and charity events, plastered-on fake smiles and our family's friendly feuding with who can win charity auctions. We were used to it. When we were teenagers, we would sneak away into the hallways and pay off the servers for a smoke. We were too old for that now though. Plus, for once, I was rather excited to be at a gala. Being a part of the planning had shed new light on it. The charity tonight was for local animal shelters, one I'd offered up at one of the board meetings. The cause was dear to me. My dad had rescued a golden retriever mix about a year ago after much convincing from myself and my mother. I loved him with my whole heart—at this point I had shared custody of Monty since I loved having him with me.

After saying goodbye to Carlos and his mother, I only made it a few steps before another voice called out over the low hum of conversation.

"Nicola, dear!" I turned, already straightening my posture out of instinct. Henrietta. She was the chairwoman of the Moretti Foundation, industry legend, and the closest thing Formula One had to female royalty. Henrietta glided toward me with effortless confidence. I'd met her a handful of times over the years, always in passing, always thinking the same thing: *This is the kind of woman I want to become.*

She commanded every space she entered, not with volume but with presence—the kind that made men twice her size step aside and listen. For decades, she'd been a fierce advocate for women in motorsport, pushing doors open and holding them there for the next generation.

"Henrietta, it's so good to see you," I said, closing the distance between us. We exchanged a kiss on each cheek in greeting. She wore a deep navy gown, the high neckline sweeping into draped sleeves that trailed behind her like a cape. Tiny glass beads shimmered as she moved, catching the soft light of the room.

"Likewise, my dear." Her eyes sparkled as she took in the event space—the auction tables, the overhead installations, and carefully curated room. "I heard you had a hand in this fantastic event. When I found out, I must say, I was very eager to see what you would do with it." She paused with a look around again and added, "I am rather impressed."

The words hit me so hard my lungs forgot how to work. Praise from the chairwoman of the Foundation was not something people earned easily. She had run the Foundation for decades; her approval was deeply coveted.

"Thank you so much," I managed. "I really enjoyed helping out." I'd poured weeks into this event between the branding mockups on flights, charity coordination between races, late-night calls with organizers, and layout and decorations for the ballrooms. It was the most passionate I had ever felt about any type of work.

"Are you interested in this side of the company long-term?" she asked casually.

My eyes widened before I could stop them. Was I interested? The Moretti Foundation was quite literally the top of my mental list of where I wanted to work within the company—the dream spot I'd always convinced myself was too ambitious to voice out loud.

I swallowed hard, trying not to sound like an overeager intern. "Very much so," I said smoothly. Or as smoothly as possible when my entire bloodstream was fizzing. "Working with the Foundation has been the highlight of my season."

Her smile deepened warmly, like she'd expected that answer.

"That's wonderful to hear. Your idea of partnering with local charities along the race route? It's brilliant. Truly. I think you might be onto something quite special."

My cheeks actually hurt from how hard I was smiling. I wasn't normally this smiley—not in public, not around people who weren't my family—but Henrietta's praise was like sunlight straight to the soul.

"I'll be in touch," she said, tapping my arm with a soft pat. "I'd like to hear more of your grand ideas." She started to move toward another cluster of donors, and I—God help me—waved.

Why did I wave? Who waves at the chairwoman of a philanthropic organization? Mortified, I lowered my hand and exhaled a breath. I knew how to present myself, how to be professional. I was raised by a motor racing family. I knew how to do this. But at the prospect of working more seriously with the Foundation, my true excitement burned away the normal firm and stoic mask I had in place at these types of events.

Reorienting myself, I headed back toward the bar, offering polite nods and smiles to guests who stopped me with compliments or questions about the event. But my mind wasn't on them.

It was still replaying Henrietta's words, over and over. *I'll be in touch.*

By the time I reached the bar, my jaw ached from the effort. I caught the bartender's eye and leaned an elbow against the polished oak, tilting my head the way I knew got immediate attention.

"You're about to be my best friend," I said, voice syrupy with relief as I flashed him a smile.

His brow arched, mouth twitching like he had a clever response ready.

"Fancy seeing you here."

That voice. That maddening, familiar voice that grated on me like sandpaper on glass.

I snapped my head left, startled that I hadn't clocked him the moment I walked up. Matteo leaned against the bar like he owned it, dark curls falling onto his smug face, looking altogether too comfortable in a tux. He pushed a crystal glass toward me across the bartop, the deep red catching the low amber lighting.

"Here," he said, like he was doing me some sort of favor.

The bartender, sensing his services were no longer required, gave me a knowing grin and slid away. Traitor.

I narrowed my eyes at Matteo, rolling them for good measure as I dragged the wine toward me. My burgundy nails glinted under the chandelier light. An unintentional match to the liquid inside that made me smile. "Jealous, much?"

His smile was infuriatingly easy. "Popular, much?"

I sighed, resisting the urge to throw the wine in his face.

"Thank you," I muttered begrudgingly instead, lifting the glass.

The moment the wine hit my lips, my stomach turned. Not from the taste—it was perfect. A Vienella Reserve Cabernet Sauvignon, full-bodied and smooth, the kind of thing I would have ordered without hesitation. Of course he knew. Of course he'd noticed. And somehow that ruined it for me, the perfection soured by the thought of Matteo watching, cataloguing, remembering.

"Damn," he said after watching me take a slow swallow, eyes trained on me again. "Didn't think you had it in you."

I tilted my head, pretending innocence. "What?"

"Saying thank you."

"I say thank you all the time," I said, indignant, sitting up straighter. "I'm a *delight*."

"True," he conceded with mock sincerity. "But usually not to me. Kinda rude, actually."

"Please." I rolled my eyes again, the motion starting to feel habitual around him. "I've thanked you before."

Had I?

My brain came up short. No specific instance, no recollection of extending him even the most basic courtesy. The realization was a little mortifying.

It wasn't that I *tried* to be cruel—I wasn't that kind of person. Usually, I could smile through anything, smooth over tension, turn prickly situations into polite exchanges. That was what I was good at, my skill, my *reputation*.

But something about Matteo cracked through that veneer. Around him, my filter dissolved. The truth—sharp, unpolished, and often harsher than I intended—slipped out before I could catch it. He pulled it from me like a tide dragging loose stones, exposing everything I wanted neatly buried.

"Actually," his smirk curled, slow and deliberate, as he lifted his glass of whiskey. The amber caught the light, his throat working as he swallowed before speaking again. "You don't have to ever say thank you to me."

I narrowed my eyes, suspicion pricking sharp. "Why?"

"Because," he said, voice dipping lower, rougher, like the single word had weight, "*please* was so much better."

The flush hit me before I could armor up. Heat spread across my skin, traitorous and instant, as if my body had decided to betray me without running it by my brain first. Matteo was—God, he was always *too much*. Too close, too smug, too loud. His flirtation was relentless, a constant hum in the background of every room he entered.

But this, his voice wrapped around that word, was different. It struck low, sharp, pulling something tight in my chest I absolutely refused to name.

I straightened in my chair, spine a steel rod, and rolled my eyes as if that could douse the fire licking up my neck. "Fuck off," I snapped, my glare a shield, a lifeline.

I stood and turned on my heel before he could see the crack in my composure. The slit of my dress skimmed high against my thigh as I walked, and maybe I let my hips sway more than necessary. I didn't have to look back to know his eyes were still on me, fixed and unblinking, tracing every step like he couldn't help himself.

*Good.*

LUCIA:

SOS

NICOLA:

What?

LUCIA:

Nathaniel is here

Want me to shove my heel into his foot?

I can spill wine on him

WAIT. What about a whole tray of food??

My skin itched at the mention of my ex boyfriend, like bugs under my skin. I knew he came to events during the season, but I usually only visited a few times unlike this year, where I was at every race. I chastised myself at the anxiety bubbling up. I should have seen this coming, should have mentally prepared. But there was no time for that. My anxiety waned at the thought of Lucia brought to violence in her want to protect me.

NICOLA:

Not surprised he's here but ugh.

I love your viciousness. I'm so proud.

LUCIA:

Love YOU!

By the silent auction table

Alex said not to cause a scene but if you want
me to I will gladly

"Nic!"

I heard my name first, then the familiar timbre of Carlos's voice. He appeared through the crowd, steady as ever, his hand hovering at my back before tipping his chin in a silent cue. *'Come with me.'*

I followed him through the throng and into a quieter alcove at the edge of the ballroom. Floor-to-ceiling windows loomed, their doors cracked open to a balcony outside. The cool night air rushed over me like a balm, soothing the spike of my pulse.

"*Stai bene?*" Carlos asked, his accent curling over the words, so much like my own.

But my mind was elsewhere, already drowning in memories I didn't invite—sharp edges of a relationship that had imploded back in January, right before the season began. I'd told myself to be ready, to expect him at some point, to prepare for polite hellos and colder silences.

I exhaled, shoulders tight. "Nathaniel is here."

Carlos hummed low, leaning forward onto the railing. His suit pulled at the seams as he settled, unbothered.

Of course he knew. We all knew Nathaniel. His family's empire stretched across Formula One like greedy fingers. Big energy money, sponsorship deals, backroom power plays. I'd been foolish to hope this year might be different, that he wouldn't attend events. But it had only taken a few months for him to resurface, as bold and smug as ever.

"I know it's stupid," I muttered.

"It's not."

"It's been almost a year," I pressed, dragging a hand across my forehead. "And yet here I am, flustered over a stupid man." My voice pitched, sharp with irritation, but Carlos's lips twitched like he was seconds away from laughing. I caught it. "No offense."

"None taken; men suck." His shrug was easy, used to my antics. "Don't let him mess this up, Nicola. This is *your* night. Don't give him that power. He doesn't deserve even the corner of your thoughts."

A reluctant smile tugged at me. "You know, you do have flashes of wisdom every now and then."

"Few and far between." His grin broke wide, warm, before he draped an arm around my shoulder. "Now come on. You need another drink, kid."

"You're literally two years older than me," I shot back.

He arched his brow. "And who bailed you out when you tried that awful fake ID at sixteen? Who covered when you snuck out of boarding school to see that band you were obsessed with?"

I groaned, throwing a hand up in surrender. "Okay, okay. I get it. What would I do without you?"

Carlos barked a laugh, nudging my shoulder as we turned back toward the ballroom.

"We need alcohol. Now," I announced, draining the last sip of my wine.

"Something stronger than wine," he agreed, steering us back into the light and noise.

Carlos and I were well into our second round of vodka sodas when he was snagged by a group of late arrivals. He gave me one last look over his shoulder, lips jutting into an exaggerated pout before disappearing into the crowd. I snorted into my drink, nearly spilling it, the laughter bubbling easy. That was Carlos—always able to pull it out of me. He'd had tunnel vision even back then, talking about engines and tracks. He always wanted to be a racecar driver, following his own father's footsteps.

I lifted my glass for another sip, relishing the cool bite of vodka and lime—when suddenly the air shifted. The overly pungent scent of a cologne I now hated invaded my personal space.

Nathaniel.

I looked over to him in annoyance. He wore a perfectly tailored suit that I was sure cost a small fortune. Seeing Nathaniel here burned something hot and ugly inside me. Rage, unfiltered. He didn't belong in this space I'd built, this night I'd shaped with every ounce of effort and control I had.

"Nicky!" Nathaniel's toothy smile grated on my nerves as much as using a nickname I despised. My name, from his mouth, was enough to sour the drink on my tongue. Nathaniel, standing there like he belonged, like his presence was a damn gift to the world. "Good to see you."

I inhaled sharply at the exact wrong moment, the vodka catching in my throat. Smooth, Moretti. Real smooth. I tried to play it off, aiming for cool and breezy—instead, it came out as a mangled sound halfway between a choke and a greeting. My coughing fit was rewarded with the lift of his eyebrows, that smug flicker of satisfaction across his face.

Very much not breezy.

*Stupid, stupid man.*

My gaze darted desperately across the ballroom, searching for escape, for backup, for literally anyone I could drag into this nightmare. Across the way, I spotted Alexander's unmistakable frame beside Lucia, her back turned toward me. Too far. Too loud in here. My silent pleas went unnoticed.

Fine. Cordial. Polite. I could manage this.

"Hello, Nathaniel." My voice steadied after I cleared my throat, every syllable sharp as glass. "How're you?"

Inside, my brain was screaming one word, over and over, louder and louder—

*Leave. Leave. Leave. Leave.*

"I'm *really, really* good."

Of course he dragged it out, hitting every syllable like he was auditioning for the role of walking red flag entitled douchebag.

"That's...fantastic," I said, stretching a smile across my face so tight it could've cracked porcelain. Meanwhile, my brain was busy mapping every possible escape route out of this personal hell.

"Are you here alone?"

Not '*How are you?*' Not '*You look well.*' Straight to the jugular, as always. His words dressed themselves up in charm, but every syllable was a blade, slicing neat and intentional. Nathaniel never wasted a chance to remind me how precise he could be when he wanted to cut.

I pictured it—my drink arcing gracefully through the air, splashing across his smug face, his perfect suit ruined. God, the satisfaction it would bring.

But before I could mentally commit to my fantasy homicide, a hand slid around my waist. Warm. Steady. Possessive enough to make me jump.

"You really think Nicola Moretti would be alone at an event?"

The voice cut through the noise, smooth and familiar, slipping into the tight little bubble Nathaniel had cornered me in. Normally, I'd roll my eyes, slap his hand off my waist, and mutter a scathing '*as if.*'

But right now? Right now I could've kissed Matteo DeLuca for his timing.

"Well—" Nathaniel started, tone poised to pivot into whatever smug line he'd been rehearsing.

"She's the type of woman men fight over." Matteo's smirk was all teeth as he tugged me closer. My hip collided with his, and I did my best to ignore the electric buzz ricocheting through me at the contact. Every nerve firing like I'd stuck my finger in a socket.

"You must be Nathaniel," Matteo said, extending a hand like they were old pals. His skin was tanned, rings glinting on his pointer and pinky, a woven bracelet resting against the expensive weight of his watch. Casual but calculated. "I should really be thanking you, my man."

Nathaniel blinked, thrown, but took his hand anyway.

"For letting someone like her go." Matteo's grin widened, dimples flashing like camera-ready weapons. "Seriously. Massive fuck up. But lucky me, right, *Baby*?"

*Baby*. My heart stuttered at the word.

His gaze swung to me then, pinning me in place. I could practically feel the heat of it against my skin.

Before I could process—before my brain could catch up to my body—he was already steering me away, hand firm at my back.

"Well, we better be going," Matteo tossed over his shoulder. "Such a *displeasure* to see you."

And just like that, Matteo guided us away.

I let myself be led away, half in a daze, unsure if any of that had actually happened or if the vodka sodas were finally catching up to me. Because if I was hallucinating, damn—my subconscious had a mean flair for drama.

"Did you say displeasure?" I asked once Matteo had guided us back to the bar and ordered two fresh drinks.

"Yup." He popped the P like it was a performance, then took a slow sip. Sliding the second glass across the counter to me, he added, "Alcohol helps with the aftereffects of seeing a shitty ex. Trust me."

"Oh, you have experience in this department?" I arched my brow. I'd never once seen Matteo in anything resembling a serious relationship. Week-long flings, maybe a couple of weeks if someone was lucky, but that was the extent of it. Matteo was a flirt, a man who flashed those dimples and got whatever he wanted. Infuriating didn't even cover it.

"Wouldn't you like to know." I was met with a taunting spirk, grading on my nerves..

"Yes. That's why I asked," I deadpanned before huffing into my glass. "Also, *Baby*? Really?"

"Thought it was a nice touch. Not your thing? Maybe Darling. My love. Sweetness. Oh, I know. My Duchess."

"Do you have a fucking off switch?" I glared, but he only leaned in farther.

"Want to search for one?" His dimple cut deep as the chaos glinted bright in his eyes.

"You're the worst."

"Hmm," he hummed, eyes never leaving mine. "Keep being mean to me. I fucking love it."

"I loathe you." The words slid out sharp, my voice low as I pushed closer to him without realizing. The alcohol hummed in my veins, hot and restless, and judging by the flush at his throat, it was doing the same to him. I was drawn to Matteo like a moth to a flame. I should walk away. I should *really* walk away.

"Keep going, *Baby*." His voice rasped low, rough, scratching over my skin like static.

"Fuck off," I muttered and turned on my heel, walking away before he could see what that voice actually did to me.

Of course, he followed like a persistent dog. "Okay, okay, sorry. I'll lay off." The words tumbled out, quick and unconvincing.

I stopped and turned, catching him too close. Matteo's cologne was soft and warm, and it wrapped around me. I could see the flecks of gold in the center of his irises, distracting, irritating, dangerous. His smile had slipped into something softer. I was gravitating to his light again, something low in my stomach humming at me. His lips looked soft, stretching into a thin line, eyebrows scrunching an imperceptible amount. But it didn't get past my visual analysis of him.

"He really got to you?" His voice was quiet now, annoyingly gentle, cutting right through the shield of my annoyance and landing straight in the place I didn't want him to see.

The perceptive bastard.

"It's fine." I waved it off and took a long swig of my drink. The icy burn slid down my throat, instantly making me feel better. Healthy coping mechanism? Absolutely not. But that was a problem for my therapist, not this drunk version of myself that felt like her skin was flushed and hot, and focusing too hard on the beautiful man in front of me.

"If there's one thing I've learned from having a sister," Matteo said, giving me a pointed look, "it's that '*I'm fine*' actually means you're one thousand percent *not* fine."

"I *am* fine. Just great, actually."

"Hey..." He reached out, eyes soft again—

"Nic!" His sister swooped in, tipsy and glowing, breaking the moment. "This event is stunning. Literally perfect. I made Alexander bid on the yacht!" She dissolved into a giggle as Alexander steadied her from behind, his hand at her elbow, watching her with an indulgent glint in his eye.

"We should go check the auction table, see what the highest bids are!" Lucia announced, grabbing my hand before I could respond.

"Your timing is impeccable," I told her as she tugged me away.

"Saving you from my brother is a full-time job at this point," she laughed, then tilted her head. "So...did you see Nathaniel yet?"

"Yeah. He came over and talked to me."

Her gasp was scandalized. "No!"

"Yes. But your brother kind of swooped in and saved me."

"Yay!" she squealed.

"How drunk are you?" I whispered, leaning closer.

"Drunk. Definitely drunk. You?"

"Getting there, but another won't hurt."

We burst into laughter. A nearby table turned to look, and we both straightened immediately, smoothing our faces into faux composure as we tried to keep walking without cracking up again.

"Ooooh!" Lucia waved me over to a clipboard. "A million on this one!"

"Check the original Bayani painting!" I said, glancing over the cards. I heard Lucia curse under her breath.

"Over six million for the highest bidder!"

"Really?" I gasped. I had pulled some major strings to get the owner to donate it to be auctioned off for the event. Honestly, I'm still shocked she agreed to it, but it turned out the ninety-year-old Scottish woman had a soft spot for charity work and had no children to hand down the painting to. She herself had been friendly with Bayani himself. The painting was made for her as a gift when they were young, long before his art took off, making it rarer and sought after.

"Ladies and gentlemen, the silent auction winners will be announced in ten minutes. Please grab your drinks and make your way to the tables," A foundation member announced over the microphone at the front of the stage. I steadied myself, sobering as much as possible. Lucia and I linked arms, walking together in a bit of a haze to try and find our table. I worked on the damn seating chart; this should not be so hard.

"Table is this way, Angel." Alexander appeared with Matteo in tow. Lucia looked up to him with stars in her eyes, her arm leaving mine and going to him. I felt the small pang. While I was not one for physical touch, watching them was something else.

Matteo cleared his throat and held out his own arm. I replied with a glare, taking a step forward on my own. I didn't need him. When I ignored his offer, I caught the tug of his lips in a poorly concealed smile. He walked by my side instead, Alexander and Lucia falling behind us. I'd sat us all at the same table with a few other drivers who'd attended as well. Theo Bauer was sitting already with his date, a pretty redhead I didn't recognize. Anna was typing away on her phone. She looked particularly spectacular tonight in a deep blue satin gown. As both Alexander's and Matteo's manager, she was probably the most impressive woman I had ever met—another surprising friend I had gained in my time on the road with the team. An empty chair sat next to her, which was meant to be her space for a date, though I couldn't remember if she RSVP'd for one.

"Hey, mate," Alexander greeted Theo. Lucia bounded over to introduce herself to his date. They easily slipped into conversation as I slid into the open chair next to Anna.

"You look stunning." I rested my head on my hand.

"I better, I'm wearing a contraption under this thing, and I cannot breathe."

"Who's..." I looked at the name card occupying the seat I was sitting in. "Dante?" Anna grimaced. "No!" I whispered in shock. Not *the* Dante. The one who was some tech wiz and helped out Alexander, and who Anna hated with pure fiery vengeance.

"That would be me," a deep voice interrupted. I looked up slowly, hoping my mouth didn't drop open as well. In front of me stood a wall of muscle, suited without a tie, the top buttons of his shirt undone, with dark tattoos that creeped up his neck on display.

"Oh good, you're back," Anna said, rolling her eyes, sarcasm dripping from every word.

"I don't want to be here either, Barbie."

*Barbie?* I mouthed at Anna who shook her head looking a mix between mortified and heavily annoyed.

"Buzzkill Barbie, technically," Dante corrected, crossing his hands over his chest, still standing directly behind Anna looking like a damn tower.

"Seriously, how did Alexander get you here?" Matteo asked, sitting down in his assigned seat.

"Lost a bet," Dante gruffed.

I looked wide eyed around the table. Alexander smirked and nodded confirming.

"And they won't share what the bet was," Lucia added.

"Who's the buzzkill now?" Anna glared. Dante replied with a grunt. A literal grunt. I moved over, giving him back his seat next to Anna, though that didn't seem like the best idea.

"Fancy seeing you here." I realized I was now sitting next to Matteo. That was wrong. I spent hours on the seating charts, and I very specifically planned it to not sit next to him, actually. My head snapped toward him.

"Did you switch the cards?" I seethed. He just smiled, dimples revealing themselves, much to my dismay. Before he could answer, the announcer was at the mic. Each item was described, and the winner with the highest bid was announced. The last would be the Bayani painting; it really was the prize of the night. We'd already raised more than our goal. When I first saw the number on the board in our first planning meeting, I thought it was a stretch, but here we were.

"Last but certainly not least is the original Bayani painting, graciously donated by Madame Marie Steward."

The crowd went silent, all waiting on pins and needles to hear the results. A few whispers here and there, surely hoping they would win the bid.

"Mr. Zaiella, congratulations, you are the highest bidder at six-point-five million pounds." Heads whipped around the room, waiting to see who secured the painting, whispers snaking around. Dante cleared his throat and pushed his chair back. The room silenced. Anna stared, mouth agape.

*What?* I mouthed to Lucia across from me who shook her head in disbelief looking at Alexander who only smiled to his friend. Good God, how much was Wright paying this man for his work? He had to do something else too—over six million pounds, on a painting, on a whim. *Holy shit.*

Anna's hand gripped Dante's sleeve, an unreadable expression there. He reached out, patting her hand awkwardly.

"I like art," he said gruffly, getting up and walking to the stage to shake the announcer's hand.

"So Dante is a millionaire..." Lucia broke the silence.

"I'd say billion," Alexander cut in, "by now anyways."

"What—" Anna was slack jawed. "I need a damn raise."

"Sure, send me what you want." Alexander shrugged. Lucia looked to me, to Anna, to her brother, to the man sitting next to her.

"So, working for you is not his main job?"

"Uh, no," Alexander replied as if it was the most obvious thing in the world.

*Huh.*

# 3

## NICOLA

The evening unfolded with a plated dinner, each course more decadent than the last. The place settings themselves shimmered under the glow of crystal chandeliers, dripping with elegance. Once the final course was cleared and coffee had been poured, the evening transitioned into something more heartfelt.A woman who helped with the spotlighted animal shelter took to the podium in turn, offering a rather moving speech about how this money would save so many lives—reminders of why they were all gathered here beneath the chandeliers and candlelight.

A set of double doors at the far end of the ballroom slowly swung open. Beyond them lay an entirely different world. The second room pulsed with soft amber lights and golden uplighting that washed the walls, transforming the space into something intimate and electric. A polished wood dance floor stretched out, with a stage tucked into the corner hosting a local DJ. As guests filtered in, laughter grew louder, jackets came off, heels were kicked aside, and the room came alive.

"You did an amazing job, Nicola!" Lucia came over hugging my side quickly. "Everything has been perfect!"

"I had a very small hand in it all," I brushed off her praise.

"I can't believe the painting sold for that much, or that *Dante* bought it. Or that we met Dante," Lucia rambled cheerily, her cheeks flushed and her blonde hair sparkling under the light. She was a burst of energy at most times, between her golden hair and her permanent smile.Add in her adorable daughter Gianna, and they really were sunshine incarnate.

"Let's dance!" she shouted over the music, grabbing my hand, and then looked at Alexander and eyed her brother. "You too!" We all followed Lucia onto the dance floor. Anna joined after a few songs, leaning in near me and Lucia.

"I think I'm going to head back!" she shouted over the music.

"We can all go!" Lucia replied, looking around. Anna shook her head.

"No, no. You guys enjoy it! Nic, you did a wonderful job, the event was perfect! So proud of you."

"Thank you!" I shouted back.

"Text us when you get back to your room, so we know you're safe," Lucia said, reaching out her arm. Alexander looked behind us.

"Make sure she gets back safe?" Alex asked. We turned to see Dante nod silently.

"Bye! Love you!" Lucia shouted, hugging Anna. Anna smiled saying she loved her right back. Instead of hugging me, she waved and then followed Dante.

"I cannot stress this enough; you look so hot in this dress. Nathaniel's probably kicking himself," Lucia said, ending in a little drunk giggle.

"He better fucking be." I rolled my eyes, the alcohol clearly sinking in. Nathaniel was standing across the way, his smug smile faltering for a second when his eyes raked over me, landing on my curve-hugging dress like he just realized what he gave up. Good. I hoped it stung.

"*Amore,*" Matteo purred like we'd been attached at the hip all night, leaning in as he mumbled the term of endearment. "Play along, shithead is watching you."

I didn't miss a beat, leaning into him and whispering back, "You sure are aware of who's staring at me."

Nathaniel eyed Matteo warily, sizing him up. Matteo in turn leaned into me and kissed my neck, then my shoulder, and looked up to me with overly adoring eyes making tiny explosions of goosebumps overtake my body and my breath hitch. I was enveloped fully with that warm spiced cologne that Matteo favored. I hoped he never used another one. I wanted to drown in it. I tried to remind myself that I didn't like Matteo, that I found him annoying and irritating and bothersome. That this was for show and he was making a point, staking his fake claim. I should be mad.

My eyes glanced up and out of the haze of Matteo this close to my body. Nathaniel scowled toward Matteo before slinking off, his ego in shreds on the marble floor.

As soon as he was out of sight, I elbowed Matteo. "*Amore?*"

He smirked. "I was improvising."

I barely had time to exhale before Matteo's still-too-warm hand rested on my lower back. A possessive touch that shouldn't have made my stomach flip the way it did.

"I didn't need saving," I muttered, stepping slightly to the side. His palm fell away.

"Didn't say you did," he said, tone maddeningly casual. "But I wanted him to watch and suffer."

I glanced up at him. Matteo's profile glowed under the chandelier light—sharp jaw, annoyingly perfect cheekbones, hair pushed back in that '*styled but not really*' way that screamed effortlessness. He looked good. *Infuriatingly* good.

"I can handle Nathaniel."

"I know." He handed me a fresh glass of champagne from a passing tray, and then added with a little smirk, "Still. No harm in watching him squirm, *Amore*."

My grip on the glass tightened. The word sank into my bloodstream like a shot of something warm and heady. He said it like it meant nothing, like it was just part of his charm, but the way it rolled off his tongue? Yeah. No. *Nope.* That was not allowed.

"You're the *worst*," I said with a forced sip.

"Not tonight," he replied. "Tonight, I'm your hero in a tux."

"And tomorrow you'll be back to being the arrogant pain in my ass."

He leaned in slightly, eyes gleaming. "Can't I be both?"

Before I could reply, the music changed to something slower, strings and elegance pulling over the room like velvet. The dance floor began to fill. Couples swirled in practiced rhythm, all champagne-laced laughter and candlelit romance. I took another sip, just to avoid looking at him.

Matteo offered his hand. "Come on, dance with me."

I hesitated.

"It'll make Nathaniel jealous; he's still watching," he added, too smoothly. I looked over and saw that he was right. Nathaniel had moved but was glaring daggers at Matteo, and something thrilled inside me at the thought of making him miserable the whole night.

I never said I wasn't petty.

I rolled my eyes, said pettiness winning out. "Fine. One dance."

His hand wrapped around mine, warm and sure, and I didn't know how *one* dance turned into *that*—his palm pressed against the small of my back, our bodies closer than they should have been, the scent of his cologne clouding my thoughts.

I hated how well he moved. How we moved *together*. His hand shifted just slightly, his thumb brushing skin where my dress dipped low—and it was nothing. *Nothing.* Just a touch. A respectable touch at that. But my whole body reacted like he'd set a fuse to me.

"I thought you hated me," he murmured near my ear, voice

low, velvet and sin wrapped together in a way I'd never heard from him. My brain stuttered at it, and I tried to push through.

"I do," I tried to pull back up my guard, lock my walls in, but then his thumb began moving in a painfully slow swipe across the skin on my back. It was a live wire to my core.

His chuckle vibrated against me. "Then why are you shivering under my touch?"

I didn't have an answer. I wasn't even sure I *could* pull away. But his touch left me, and he nodded toward the bar, giving me the option for a reprieve. I took it because God knew I needed another drink and maybe some fresh air before my body betrayed me into being attracted to Matteo. I tried to repeat to myself that he was a shameless flirt and had been a permanent annoyance since the start of season, but I couldn't think much under the haze of his light touch.

The rest of the gala blurred after more drinks. I found myself laughing too easily at his regular teasing. He brushed a strand of hair from my face, and I swore his fingers lingered longer than they should. Our elbows touched at the bar. Our knees bumped beneath a cocktail table. He kept calling me *Amore* with this soft smirk, loving that we had this little inside joke and I kept pretending I wasn't letting it dig under my skin into places it shouldn't reach.

We slipped away sometime past midnight. I don't remember who suggested it. Or maybe we just drifted to a quieter space. The hallway was quiet and dim, the hum of the party fading behind thick walls and heavy doors.

"I should go," I said, leaning against the cool plaster, trying to ignore the spinning in my head. From champagne. From proximity.

"Okay," he said, voice low again, stepping closer to me as if he felt this pull between us and couldn't help himself.

"Why are you looking at me like that?" I asked.

His gaze dipped to my lips before returning to my eyes. The

pause was painful, it felt like minutes or hours passed before he answered, barely saying the words out loud as if afraid to make them real. "I think you want to kiss me, Moretti."

I did. God help me, I *did*.

His fingers caught my jaw, tilting it up, and for a half second my pride flared—ready to shove him off, to tell him he'd had the wrong idea if he thought I'd melt just because he looked at me like that. But the fight didn't come. Not when I could feel his breath warm against my mouth, not when the room was spinning from too much liquor and too much wanting I shouldn't have felt. I should have pulled back. I should have stopped it before it started.

But I didn't. I couldn't.

Instead, I leaned in.

Our lips brushed, just the faintest, teasing touch, and it sent a sharp jolt down my spine. Sparks raced beneath my skin. My stomach twisted, a molten ache pooled low, and suddenly nothing in the world mattered but the half-inch of space left between us.

Then he closed it.

Matteo didn't kiss like any normal kiss, he kissed me like it was his life's breath. The kiss landed with the weight of something breaking open, the snap of a taut thread finally giving way. His hand stayed cupped against my jaw, steady, grounding, fingers sliding back until they skimmed the skin behind my ear and dove right into my hair, holding on as if I'd disappear. He kissed me like it had always been inevitable. Like this whole time we'd been destined for this moment. My body pulsed with anticipation.

His other hand found my waist, firm and certain, fingers biting into my hip as he dragged me into his chest. The shock of it ripped a gasp from me, and I used it as an excuse to clutch him back, curling my fists in his shirt as if I'd fall if I let go. His mouth moved against mine, greedy and sure, and I hated that I matched him, that my body betrayed every sharp word I'd ever thrown at him.

The wall caught me before I could stumble, the cool plaster

pressed at my back, his body a wall of heat and strength pinning me in place. I felt caged. I felt alive.

And it should have been all wrong.

He was wrong for me. The last person I should want.

But with his mouth on mine and his hand dragging fire down my side, I couldn't seem to conjure the list of why I shouldn't want this.

"Tell me to stop," he whispered against my skin, breath warm where his lips dragged down the line of my throat, then hovered and waited for my answer. Then a door opened somewhere in the distance, the loud thrum of music and reality slammed back into me. I pulled away, taking space and shaking my head. I watched his eyes sadden for only a moment before I grabbed his hand and tugged him with me.

Because against all odds, I wanted Matteo DeLuca.

By the time we reached the sleek black town car waiting outside, the air between us was a live wire. Matteo opened the door, and I slid in. The silence inside the car was thick, broken only by the sound of our breaths. His thigh brushed mine as the driver pulled away from the curb, and I swear I stopped breathing altogether. I didn't look at him. Couldn't. I just stared ahead, my pulse thrumming in places I was too proud to admit. The ride was filled with stolen touches, as if not wanting to break the haze. I wanted nothing but to have my lips on his again. It was the only thought rattling around in my brain.

*Kiss him again.*

*Again.*

*Again.*

His knee pulled away for a moment then tapped mine, my attention immediately snapping to him. His eyes were soft, in that tender way he reserved for big moments I'd seen him share with his inner circle of friends. It shocked my system with warmth all over again. He leaned in slowly, eyes on my mouth like he was giving me a chance to change my mind. I didn't. Our lips met in the hush of the leather seats and tinted windows. The kiss was slow at first, like he was trying to learn every curve of my lips, every fiber of my being. His hand brushed my knee, then up, fingers tracing the edge of my dress. Every inch of me buzzed under his touch. My breath hitched as his palm slid to my thigh, anchoring me to this moment.

His voice cut into the quiet, low and warm. "Kissing you is pure sin, Moretti."

His expression was dark and heavy, fixed on me, jaw tight, his other hand curled on his knee like he's trying to hold something back.

My heart trips over itself, and with a roll of my eyes, I said, "Shut up."

His eyes alight, dimples on display, he said two words, "Make me."

I found myself wanting to prove him right.

We walked next to each other through the hotel. Our rooms were booked across from each other as they usually were. Ever since Lucia and Gianna joined us halfway through the season, we'd all become a bit of a unit. My best friend's brother being around was usually rather irritating, but now I wanted to pull him into a room and forget about that.

The stale light of the hotel was too bright above us, buzzing with anticipation. I wanted his hands back on me, needed them on me. His eyes darkened like storm clouds rolling in, and before I could blink, he grabbed my hand and pulled me through the quiet hallway, past the art and the velvet chairs and the hushed staff pretending not to notice. Neither of us said a word. It was reckless, and I was completely breathless at the look of him so enthralled with me. I could barely keep up with the thud of my heart. We were falling now, right off the cliff.

In the elevator, he was still looking at me like he was trying to memorize this version of me—the tipsy, sparkling, unguarded one. I giggled as I tripped out of the elevator on our shared floor and his arms enveloped my waist, steadying me immediately. He was laughing too. I should have stopped it. I should have pushed him away. But the headiness of kissing him had stripped my armor clean off, and under it, I was raw with want.

"This is a bad idea," I admitted, once we were in his room. The soft click of the door filtered through the otherwise silence of his hotel room. I was standing in the entryway and that was the final moment we could go back, pretend it never happened, stop it before we went too far. *You don't want that,* my head argued with me.

"I know," he agreed.

"Tomorrow, I'll hate you for this."

He smiled like he'd already accepted it. "You hate me already."

I let out a sound—half laugh, half sigh.

And then I said it. The words that tipped everything off the edge.

*"Fuck it."*

His hands were on my waist, then sliding up my back, then tugging the zipper of my dress with careful fingers. The fabric slipped down my arms, pooling at my feet. I should have been embarrassed. I was not. His eyes trailed over me like he was seeing something sacred.

When he touched me again, it was reverent. Like he was there to worship me, savor every touch, every minute. I felt the heat gather, my pulse quickening. And I was pushing him back, onto the cool sheets and climbing on top of him. He let me take control, let me tease him, kissing down his neck and chest, unbuttoning his own shirt as I went. He pulled us up, me still straddling him, my legs on either side of his waist, pressed all the way into him. I pushed off his shirt the rest of the way. His mess of brown wavy hair was disheveled in that post-race way, and I ran my hands through it, tugging and being rewarded with a moan. I'd never be able to look at his post-race hair the same again. I'd think of this moment. How it was my hands that made a mess of him, how his hands felt feverishly running over me.

While all drivers were in peak athletic form, and I'd seen drivers shirtless—I'd even seen Matteo shirtless—but nothing prepared me for this version of him under the dull night lights outside the hotel making the dark room glow slightly. I probably was drooling. I was only brought back to reality by a hand slowly caressing my cheek, and pushing back into my hair, before he tugged me to him. He began exploring with his hands as he kissed me deeply, more harshly that time. Exactly how I craved it. One roll of his thumb over a peaked nipple had my eyes fluttering closed, a gasp on my lips. Then his lips left mine and he was looking at me with that same heaviness.

"You are so beautiful." His voice was edged and strained, like he was begging. My entire body heated. His chest was rising and falling, matching the same ragged breath that I had. He peppered kisses from the curve of my lips, my nose, my cheeks, to behind my ear then down my neck, and I felt the mix of laugh and groan escape me. He mapped me like a racetrack he had studied a thousand times and still found new ways to take the corners. I arched into him, needing the friction, needing our bodies to meld together and to forget everything but the feeling of his skin against mine. Of his name on my lips, soft and ruined.

When we were tangled in the sheets, sweat cooling on our bodies and the world gone quiet, he brushed a strand of hair from my forehead and pressed the softest kiss to my temple.

It was the gentleness that undid me—more than anything. And when I finally drifted to sleep, I didn't think about what this would mean tomorrow.

# 4

## MATTEO

The first thing I noticed was the smell of a familiar perfume.

It was faint now, like it had faded into my sheets and my skin, but I'd know it anywhere. Something floral, expensive, but not too sweet. Like *her*. Sharp edges and a hidden softness you only get if she lets you close enough. Something I'd noticed from afar because Nicola would never let me that close. I relentlessly flirted with her any chance I could because I craved any response from her, irritation included. I was addicted to her eye rolls, the pointed finger, and counting how many times she would mutter *Fuck off* in any given day to me. Despite her being the most off-limits person I could be interested in, it didn't stop me. Nicola was the boss's daughter. Not just the boss, the boss's boss. Mr. Moretti of Moretti Racing himself. I would be a fucking idiot to try anything, but I couldn't help it; I was drawn to her over and over again no matter the absolute havoc she would wreck on my heart.

I kept my eyes closed for a second longer, wanting to stay in the dream. Inhaling the dream, the perfume, *her*. I cracked open my eyes, sun gleaming in through the haphazardly closed curtains in my hotel room. I wracked my brain for the ending of the night.

The gala was a huge success, flashes of Nicola in that sinful black dress, my hands on her waist. Then flashes of a bare waist, of skin touching skin, of lips and alcohol. I sucked in a breath, feeling weight in the bed other than my own, the mattress dipping next to me. *How drunk did I get?*

It was a slow movement as I looked over to see who was in my bed. Long dark brown hair and that damn perfume.

*Fuck.*

Nicola Moretti was in my bed.

It was still early—the kind of soft light that makes everything feel quieter than it should. She was curled on her side, facing away, hair a mess across my pillow. The sheets barely covered her back, and all I could see was the curve of her shoulder, the dip of her spine. My fingers twitched.

Last night flashed through me like a match struck too close to dry skin. The hallway. The car. The way she said *Fuck it* like she was saying yes to more than just one night. The way she kissed me like she hated herself for wanting it—and maybe hated me more for making her feel it.

I shifted, pulling my arm back, slow and careful. Like she might wake up and punch me in the throat for daring to still be here. But she didn't move. Her breathing was steady, soft.

She looked...peaceful like this. Unburdened.

Not like the Nicola I knew—the sharp, sarcastic, high-heel-wearing ice queen who'd been rolling her eyes at me since she walked into the paddock on the first day of the season. She looked at me like I was an insect then. She still did. Except last night she looked at me like I was something else entirely.

My chest tightened.

This would be chalked up to a bad decision. A mistake we'd both laugh off and pretend didn't mean anything.

But now that it was quiet—now that she was here and not looking at me like she was already halfway to regretting it—I couldn't help but wonder what the hell I'd done, whatever tiny shot I ever had died here. Hell hath no fury like Nicola when she was mad, and there was no chance she would be happy about this.

I sat up slowly, scrubbing a hand over my face. My head ached, a dull reminder of champagne and whatever the hell we opened from the minibar after we got in. There was a faint lipstick stain on my chest. Her lipstick. Her mouth.

*Jesus.*

I glanced at her again.

We weren't supposed to end up here.

Nicola and I? We flirted like it was a sport, fought like we were in the ring, and orbited each other like something was always just about to catch fire. But this? This was past the line.

And if she woke up and looked at me like it meant *nothing*—

I didn't know what I'd do with that.

I stood, slipping into a pair of boxers, and moved toward the hotel's floor-to-ceiling window. I pulled the curtain back slightly. Morning traffic moved sluggishly below with people going about their normal lives.

Meanwhile, I was trying to figure out how the hell to breathe next to a woman who'd been under my skin since forever, since the day she walked into the paddock and in my bed for exactly one night.

Behind me, I heard her shift. A faint sound. Sheets rustling. Breath catching.

My pulse spiked.

She shifted again. This time, the sound was sharper—like she'd sat up quickly, tugging the sheets with her.

"Shit." Her voice. Groggy, hoarse, still thick from sleep. And panic.

I turned slowly. She was sitting up in bed now, clutching the duvet to her chest like it was a lifeline. Her hair was a mess cascading down her like a midnight waterfall, mascara faintly smudged beneath one eye, as strikingly beautiful as ever.

Her eyes went wide when she met mine.

"What the *hell* did we do?"

I blinked. "Good morning to you too."

Her mouth opened. Closed. Opened again. "Matteo."

She said it like a curse. Her screaming my name came back to me and went straight to my cock. I was hard just thinking of it again. The images alone were already burned into my eyelids.

I crossed my arms, leaning against the window frame.

*Play it casual.* Be disarming.

I'd perfected that look. The lazy smile, the easy charm. She didn't need to know I'd been staring at her like a lunatic for the last twenty minutes trying to figure out what the hell last night *meant.*

"You don't remember?" I asked, cocking a brow.

"I remember *enough,*" she snapped, voice tight. "I remember the gala. And the drinks. And—God—your hands."

I bit the inside of my cheek to keep from smirking. That would not help right now, but the blush creeping up her cheeks was so damn cute.

"Right," she muttered, dragging a hand down her face. "This didn't happen."

The inevitable crush was there, but I didn't let it show. I kept the same mask on as I always did.

"Pretty sure it did, Princess." I gestured vaguely at the bed, at *us.* "Happened all over this room, in fact, and over that table." I smirked. "Twice."

"Don't call me that."

"I've always called you that." The whole crew called her the paddock princess, and I was pretty sure even when she acted annoyed, she loved the endearing nickname from the crew. It also always made her roll her eyes at me, sometimes even the tiniest of blush crept up her cheeks before she would slam down her designer glasses to block it.

I craved that reaction like a drug.

She glared. "Well, you don't get to now."

She was angry. Not really at me, I think—but at herself. The way she was holding the sheets tighter, not meeting my eyes. Embarrassment. Shame. It twisted something in my chest. This was worse than what I expected. I'd rather her rage be focused on me.

I wanted to tell her she didn't need to feel any of that.

That last night was *fucking amazing*. That she was a literal dream.

But if I said any of that, she'd run.

So I forced a shrug. Forced the smile.

"It was just a night, Nic. You're allowed to have a little fun."

*Wrong move.*

Her head snapped up, her expression icy. "Fun?"

I nodded, slow, trying not to flinch. "Isn't that what it was?"

She didn't answer. She just slid out of bed, sheets tangling around her as she fumbled for her dress from last night. Her back was to me, and I caught the line of her spine, the faint trail of my fingerprints I was almost sure I imagined. My mouth went dry.

This wasn't what I wanted. Not like this. I dragged a hand through my hair, jaw tight.

"Nicola—"

"Nope." She held up a hand without turning. "We're not doing this."

"Doing what?"

"The post-disaster debrief. This was—" she paused, found her dress, and pulled it on over her head with a violent tug "—a lapse in judgment. One I'd really like to forget."

I laughed, short and sharp. "Right. Because sleeping with me is so unthinkable."

She spun to face me. "Matteo."

I met her eyes. "Nicola."

And then we just...stood there.

I wanted to go to her. Wanted to kiss her again just to prove that last night wasn't a fluke. That there was something *real* under all that hatred and history and heat.

But I didn't.

Because she was already rebuilding her walls, brick by brick, and I could see it happening in real time.

So I backed off.

"Fine," I said, voice too light, too easy, "It never happened."

She blinked at that. Like she wasn't expecting me to say it. Like maybe a small part of her *did* want me to fight her on it.

But I was not going to beg her to feel something she was not ready to admit.

So I let her walk out of my hotel room with her chin high, heels clicking, and armor locked back in place.

And when the door clicked shut, I sat down on the edge of the bed she had just left.

Her perfume clinging to the sheets, I fell back into them, deciding today was shit. I would try again tomorrow.

Smiling was second nature by now.

Not the real kind—the ones that creased your eyes and made your chest ache with something close to joy—but the practiced version. The one that felt like muscle memory. Easy. Effortless. Automatic.

It was what people expected from me, after all. The chill one. The funny one. The driver who didn't take life—or racing—too seriously.

And maybe that was the problem.

I stood in front of the mirror in my hotel room, tugging on my team jacket, the embroidered Moretti Racing logo catching the morning light. The day's schedule was already pinging on my phone, and Anna had sent a cheerful reminder about being "camera ready." Which—in my head—was code for, '*Be the version of you people like.*'

"Big smiles today, Matty boy," I said to myself. *Gotta make 'em forget you're running on three hours of sleep and a heart full of anxiety.*

I ran a hand through my hair for the third time, fixing it again. I'd learned early on that people got uncomfortable when you weren't smiling. They started asking questions. So I became the guy who filled the silence with jokes, with stories, with noise.

Laughter was easier than honesty.

Honesty was messy. It looked like 3 a.m. nights replaying races I should've won. Like the constant ache in my chest every time I wondered if I'd ever be enough—not just for the team, but for myself.

I'd made a name for myself in my rookie year. Fast, reckless, magnetic—*the media's favorite new toy.* But the thing about being everyone's favorite is that you can't stop being it.

*Can't slow down.*

*Can't mess up.*

*Can't let them see the cracks.*

So I smiled. I laughed. I told stories in interviews that made people think I was just some happy-go-lucky kid from the Italian countryside who lucked into speed and stardom. No one wanted to hear about the stress or the insomnia. About how, some nights, I woke up gasping from dreams of spinning out on a track I couldn't escape. No. They wanted charm. They wanted easy. They wanted *Matteo DeLuca.*

And maybe if I said it enough—if I played the part long enough—I'd start believing it too.

I grabbed my phone, keys, and sunglasses. Another day, another performance.

When I stepped out of the hotel, the cameras were already waiting. Shouts of my name, flashes, smiles I didn't feel but gave anyway. I waved, cracked a joke with a reporter, did that stupid wink that always went viral.

The crowd laughed. The cameras loved me. And somewhere behind all of it, I could still hear my heart pounding, whispering doubts of not being enough. Lately, the only time my head was silent was around Nicola. I was way too preoccupied trying to get her to like me. After our drunken night together, I might have made that part even harder.

I spotted her the second I stepped into the paddock.

She was impossible to miss—blazer perfectly tailored, sunglasses too big for her face, and her walk fast enough to make a grown man sprint just to keep up. Most days I'd call it a challenge. Today? She didn't even glance in my direction. It had been one week since the gala, a week of me dreaming of her screaming my name.

I adjusted the collar of my racing suit and grinned, purely on instinct. Catching up to her, I cleared my throat and lowered my voice. "Avoiding me doesn't erase the fact that you moaned my name loud enough to wake up half the damn hotel."

Her shoulders stiffened for a fraction of a second. Blink and you'd miss it.

But I never missed *her*.

She kept walking, fast and clean, ignoring me like I was a fly buzzing around.

I fell into step beside her, not bothering to hide my amusement. But I needed something from her, needed a reaction like it was a drug, so I kept poking. "C'mon, don't be like that. You'll hurt my feelings."

"You *have* feelings?" she muttered, not even looking at me.

"Ouch," I clutched my chest, feeling some type of way about the bite in her tone. "Right in the heart." Some may have called me a masochist. They'd probably be right.

"I'm sure you'll survive with your obnoxious positivity."

A smile spread slowly across my face. There she was.

Still, she wasn't flirting. No smirk. No sass beyond that sharp tongue of hers. She was trying to shut me down.

"You're so grumpy when you repress our sexual tension," I offered cheerfully.

She stopped walking. Whirled to face me. "Matteo."

"Nicola."

"Not now."

I leaned in a little, voice dropping just enough to make her blink. "You're going to have to stop saying my name like that, Princess. People might start thinking you like the way it tastes."

Before she could throw something at me—clipboard, radio, small fire extinguisher—I heard my niece's tiny squeal and my attention immediately pivoted to the little hurricane.

"*Zio!*"

A blur of blonde curls and red Moretti Racing gear barreled toward me. I crouched and scooped her up effortlessly, tossing her into the air as she giggled. Gianna was by far my favorite person to exist in the world, close second being my sister Lucia who walked up just as Gia curled into me, hugging me with her little arms.

"Look at you! You're a proper team mascot now!"

Lucia strolled up behind her, sunglasses perched on her head, wrist with a collection of friendship bracelets, and one of my team shirts fashioned in a cut-off way with a skirt—very Lucia.

"Figured we should make an entrance."

"Mission accomplished." Lucia had been on the road with us for a bit now; I didn't fully expect her to agree to my idea this last summer when I asked her and Gia to join us for the rest of the season. But watching my sister wither and lose her spark after she had been through hell and back was my own personal hell. I would do anything in my power to keep a smile on her face, to help keep her from that dark place from three years ago after she left her dirt bag ex. It had taken some time, but since she came here with me and my best mate Alexander who raced for Belen's Formula One team, she seemed to be finding herself again. She and Nicola actually hit it off right away, much to my own delight because Nicola was around us more and more these days. My eyes gravitated toward Nicola as she muttered an excuse to my sister and slid out of the moment like she was never here at all. She disappeared behind the hospitality curtain, leaving my sister with a frown.

"She okay?" Lucia asked quietly, watching her go.

"No idea," I answered, plastering on another smile for Gia's benefit. Lucia gave me a look, one only a younger sister can give, the '*I know you're fucking lying*' look. I just shrugged and refocused on Gianna who started telling me about how after the race we were all getting ice cream. I tried to focus on my family, I really did, but then I saw it, out of the corner of my eye.

Carlos talking to Nicola.

And not just talking—leaning in close, probably telling her something about his villa in Barcelona or how stunning she looked in navy.

And she was laughing.

Not polite. Not fake.

The kind that reached the corner of her eyes.

I felt the sudden urge to stomp over there, to rip something in half, it was like I'd been possessed.

*Get it together*, I told myself, shifting Gia on my hip. Carlos was my teammate. And Nicola was not mine.

Not my anything.

Except last weekend she was mine in every way that counted. And now she was letting him stand that close? I'd never been the jealous type, but something about Nicola made me lose all sense of sanity.

Carlos said something else, and she touched his arm.

*Fuck this.*

I sat Gia down gently, crouching to kiss her forehead. "I need to go get ready but cheer extra loud for me, okay G?"

She nodded seriously. "Oh-tay! Good luck Zio!"

"Hey, I saw your old manager is Theo's manager now?" my sister asked. I tried to hide the grimace. My old manager, Matt, was the worst. Besides being a bad manager, he was petty and constantly doing things for his own gain. Happy to throw me to the sharks to get a payday. I hoped it was different for Theo. Alexander had asked Anna if she could double as mine after I fired Matt with no notice when I found out he was leaking my location to the tabloids.

"Uh, yeah. Guess so. Theo goes through them fast." I shrugged, trying not to make it a big deal. The last thing I wanted was to add to my sister's stress. It was in the past now. Theo hated basically every single manager he had and was not one to mess around. He was known for his '*I don't give a shit*' attitude. So all in all, I was not worried about it. Matt could only fake being a good manager for so long. My mama taught me that bad karma was bound to catch up to those who deserved it. And, quite frankly, Matt didn't deserve any space in my thoughts, let alone my sister's. So I brushed it off and muttered, "See you after," to her with a hug goodbye.

"Try and beat Alexander today, hmm? He needs an ego check." Lucia smirked and I rolled my eyes at her. The two had been awfully close lately, agreeing to some crazy fake dating scheme where they were both totally not faking anything, and they were both just idiots. But who was I to talk anymore?

"Sure thing, I'll just jump ten grid spots, no problem," I sighed. Today was not the best start after qualifying for thirteenth position today.

"I believe in you," Lucia said simply, as if it was that easy. I waved goodbye to the pair and tried not to look over to the dark-haired siren of a woman that had obviously put a damn spell on me.

I retreated to the back of the garage. Everything was humming. Crew was moving like clockwork. Tire blankets were warming, radios crackling. It smelled like rubber, oil, and adrenaline.

I ducked into the quiet of my driver room, the one spot where I could breathe.

I closed the door, went through my rituals.

Tapped my helmet, then my gloves.

I sank to the floor, ignoring the couch and crossing my legs then putting my headphones on.

Three deep breaths. In through the nose, out through the mouth. One for calm. One for focus. One for every stupid, messy feeling I had no room for right now.

The rituals helped. The stillness before the storm.

I reached into the duffel by the wall and pulled out the same silver chain I'd worn since karting—my nonna's medallion. I tucked it under my suit, hiding it since we were not supposed to wear any jewelry while racing. But hey, it was my good luck charm.

I pressed play on my playlist. Same first song every time. Something that reminded me to move fast, stay loose.

Still, all I could see when I closed my eyes was her laughing at Carlos's joke.

She looked happy.

I clenched my jaw, stood, rolled out my shoulders and let it all slip away as I got into the car and rolled out into formation.

Helmet on.

Visor down.

Emotions out.

The lights above the grid ticked down like a heartbeat.

Five.

Four.

Three.

Two.

One.

*Lights out and away we go.*

I slammed the throttle. Gripped the wheel tighter than I should've. The roar of the engine was the only thing loud enough to drown out the buzzing in my skull. The car jolted forward.

Wheels worked hard. I cut inside on Turn 1, threading the needle between P12 and P11—two rookies too soft on the brakes. I wasn't. Two positions up before we hit Sector 2.

*That's more like it.*

My engineer's voice crackled in my ear. "Great start, Matteo. Let's settle into pace."

But I wasn't there to settle, I was going to score some damn points today. Every corner was sharper today. Every overtake, just on the edge of clean. I was driving like a man trying to prove something. Trying to chase a ghost in a navy dress with a wicked mouth.

**Lap 4 — P10.**

Carlos was a few seconds ahead, just visible in the dirty air, his rear wing flashing our team logo like a dare. I pushed to close the gap.

My engineer's voice sounded again, "Head down. Tires looking good."

"Copy."

I didn't tell them my jaw was aching from clenching it. That my gloves felt too tight. That every time I blinked, I saw Nicola's smile when she looked at *him.*

**Lap 9**

I was ahead on Turn 7, snatched P9 from a veteran who didn't see me coming. He tried to fight back, but I owned the inside line and squeezed him just enough to shut the door.

**P9.**

Clean. Aggressive.

Controlled chaos—my specialty.

"Nice move. Let's cool the tires a bit."

I didn't answer. I just breathed.

The rest of the race was steady. Couldn't crack P8 without sacrificing tire life, and Carlos finished P4—not a podium, but higher than me. Again.

Still, I clawed four spots up in the midfield. No penalties, no damage, and some good points for the team.

Back at the garage, the crew clapped my back, offered water, high-fives. I went through the motions, smiling where I should, nodding at the right people.

And then I saw her.

Arms crossed, lips tugged up with Carlos who was standing next to her, his track suit pulled down around his waist, running a hand through his hair. He leaned in and said something. She laughed again.

I swore I'd rather DNF than see that twice in one weekend. Someone handed me a bottle. I pretended to drink it. She finally glanced my way and our eyes locked. A flash of something I couldn't read—guilt? Tension? Defiance? I smiled, wide and slow, all teeth. She didn't smile back.

But she *looked,* for a second too long.

And that's all I needed to keep the shit-eating grin on my face.

# 5

# NICOLA

The restaurant was low-lit and gleaming, tucked into a cobbled side street with just enough flash to impress the sponsors and just enough history to satisfy my father. We arrived together, after staying too long on the track. My father was always very involved, at the heart of it all because he loved this world and everything that went into being a team owner. He worked closely with the principal, upper management, and admins. He was already changed into a tailored navy blazer when I walked into his office earlier. My own dress was hanging in there to change out of my day outfit. I opted for wine-red tonight. Sharp lines and bare shoulders, a simple diamond necklace adorning my neck. Red-bottomed black heels paired with a hint of subtle revenge.

It wasn't for anyone in particular, just for myself. Or at least I'd repeated that mantra to myself. But getting a little rise out of Matteo would just be a cherry on top.

The team was gathered around a long table, already half-filled with noise and wine. Matteo wasn't there yet. And I couldn't help myself watching the entrance for him.

Carlos spotted me first and waved me over with that too-handsome grin that always made him look like he was about to charm his way into trouble.

"*Ciao, Principessa*," he teased, pulling out my chair. "Finally gracing us with your presence after disappearing this week?"

"I've been busy," I said, letting my fingers trail over the rim of my wine glass.

Carlos arched his brow. "Too busy to respond to my texts?"

"I'm sorry," I sighed, and I was. I loved Carlos like family, but I was busy between self-care in the form of shopping and spending time with Lucia and Gianna, and working with the Moretti Foundation team on new ideas for upcoming campaigns. After speaking with Henrietta, I had this new determination brewing; I wanted to keep doing more. To prove myself. However, memories of a drunken night with the devastatingly handsome driver who I was supposed to hate kept flashing in my head. I mean, sure, he was annoying, but I also wasn't blind. His hands on my hips, the swallow tattoos on his thigh that I had never seen before. I was frazzled. And I didn't do frazzled. I prided myself on being composed, but here I was feeling uneasy at the team dinner. Carlos leaned in, dropping his voice so only I heard. "Funny. You were never one to get flustered. But lately...you're twitchy."

I rolled my eyes and sipped the wine. "Twitchy?"

He grinned wider. "You've had the same drink in your hand for ten minutes and haven't even made your rounds charming everyone."

I tilted my head. "You're the only one worth talking to."

He chuckled but didn't let it go. "So what's going on?"

"Nothing."

He stared at me.

I gave him my best '*I'm a Moretti and you don't get to pry*' smile.

Carlos leaned back, unfazed. "It wouldn't have anything to do with my teammate, would it?"

That made my stomach tighten. Not in panic, but in frustration. And a little guilt.

"Matteo?" I said, careful to keep my tone airy. "Why would it?"

Carlos shrugged, lazy and perceptive all at once. "Because you're staring at the door and he's the only one who has yet to arrive."

I opened my mouth to respond, but—

He arrived.

Late. Loud. Charming.

*Of course.*

Matteo strolled in, clad in denim and a shirt clinging to his chest like it was sewn on. Silver chain around his neck, shirt unbuttoned at the top. His curls looked slightly damp, and when he saw me—

His smile changed.

Subtle. Slow.

Like he already knew he'd win tonight, even if it was just in a game I swore I wasn't playing anymore. My father stood to greet him. "Matteo. Solid race today. You fought hard."

Matteo shook his hand, polite. "*Grazie, Signor* Moretti. We'll fight even harder next weekend."

My father clapped him on the shoulder and sat. "That's what I like to hear."

I sipped my wine and avoided looking at either of them.

Carlos leaned toward me again, smug. "So...nothing, huh?"

I elbowed him under the table. He just laughed. Matteo sat directly across from me, not letting me escape his gaze while each course was served, but not engaging with me once, setting my nerves on fire. If Matteo was anything, it was chatty. He never stopped talking. He always had something to say and was usually flirting with me while he was at it. And granted, we were at a team dinner, my father on one side of me and my oldest friend on the other, but still, I oddly missed his charmed smiles and words.

After the courses had been cleared, I excused myself from the table, heading for the bathroom, heels clicking as I went. The air in the hallway was cooler, quieter. My reflection in the mirror looked like I was in control. The mask was back in place.

But I didn't *feel* like it. My insides were screaming a different story.

I lingered a little longer than necessary, dabbing under my eyes, smoothing my dress.

When I stepped back into the hallway, I felt him before I saw him.

Leaning against the opposite wall, arms crossed, expression unreadable—except for the fact that his gaze *burned*.

"Stalking the hallway now?" I murmured, brushing past him.

He didn't move. Just stayed leaning against the opposite wall like he owned the damn place, arms crossed, ankle kicked over the other. A curl from his espresso-colored hair falling down the middle of his forehead. I wanted to push it aside.

*Infuriating.*

His eyes trailed over me with slow deliberation, and I swore I felt it, like heat crawling up the hem of my dress. I forced my chin higher. I wouldn't give him the satisfaction of stopping to give him the attention he wants.

"You don't run away from people when it meant nothing, *Princess*," he said, voice low and rough with whatever game he's decided we're playing.

My spine stiffened.

God, that nickname. The way he said it—all teasing and intimate, like it belonged to just the two of us. Like he knew exactly which nerve to hit.

But my feet...didn't move.

I hated that I liked the way his voice sounded when we were alone. Darker. Unpolished. It made something unsteady twist inside me.

"I didn't run," I said, keeping my tone even, bored. Safe. I didn't turn around. Couldn't.

"Then what do you call this week?"

He was closer. I heard the subtle shift of his body, the soft scrape of his shoe against the floor. My breath hitched before I caught it.

"I was busy," I snapped, sharper than intended. I could feel him watching me. The air between us practically vibrated.

Then, softly—dangerously close, he said, "You keep playing cold, and I might believe it...if your eyes didn't keep following me."

My blood pulsed so hard I felt it behind my knees. I whirled to face him, heat and irritation bubbling up in tandem.

"Not everything's about you," I bit out.

But he just smiled.

Slow. Dangerous.

Like he knew exactly what he was doing to me.

"You wore red."

My stomach flipped, traitorous. I wanted to slap him. I wanted to drag him back into that dark hallway from last weekend and kiss him until I forgot why I hated him. I hated that he noticed things like that. I hated that I *wanted* him to.

"I always wear team colors," I said coolly, refusing to let my voice waver.

I moved to brush past him, but instead of simply letting me— Matteo stepped aside with theatrical grace, a mock bow that brought his mouth just a little too close to my ear.

I didn't say anything. I didn't *look* at him.

I just walked.

Because the last thing he got—the *very last thing*—was the last word.

The air outside the pâtisserie smelled like butter and powdered sugar. Gianna's hand was wrapped around mine as she dragged me toward the next window display—a tiny boutique with glittery tutus and impractical toddler sunglasses.

"Look, the pink one!" She pointed at a frilly monstrosity of a dress.

"You already have three of those." Lucia laughed.

"I think she's eyeing number four," I said, glancing down at Gia. "Very fashion-forward of you."

Lucia grinned as we fell into step again, strolling the cobbled alleyway. It was a beautiful day, and the serene views of a small-town shopping day was just what I needed.

"I forgot what this felt like," Lucia said after a beat, her voice softer. "To have a normal day."

I nudged her gently. "That's why you have me. And pastries."

She smirked. "And fake dating a five-time world champion?"

"Minor detail."

The park was quiet, probably because half the city was working on a Monday. But we needed it. A breather. Something soft.

Lucia was sitting beside me on the bench, her sunglasses pushed up into her hair and her eyes on Gianna, who was toddling her way through a patch of wildflowers with one shoe half-off and zero concern for personal hygiene.

She was humming. I think it was a princess theme song. Crazy that I knew that now, but in the last few months with Lucia and Gianna, I went from knowing nothing about kids to being rather fond of the mini version of my best friend.

"I used to think I was done," Lucia said suddenly. "Like... maybe love was a thing I already spent. I had my chance and it didn't work out; I picked wrong."

I glanced over at her. She wasn't looking at me—her eyes were still on Gia. But there was a heaviness in her voice I hadn't heard in a while.

"Then this whole fake dating thing started," she continued, twisting the strap of her bag in her fingers. "And I thought I could handle it. Just press and PR and pretend smiles for the cameras."

I arched my brow. "You two don't look like you're pretending too much anymore."

Lucia smiled faintly, the corners of her mouth trembling just enough to betray her. "That's the problem," she exhaled, looking down at her hands. "He kissed me. It wasn't for show, no cameras, no one was watching, and it felt..."

"Dangerous?"

"Like I could do anything," she whispered. "Like I was invincible. And that...scares the hell out of me."

We sat in silence for a second, only the sound of Gia's little giggles and a bird rustling overhead.

I nodded slowly. "You're falling for him."

Lucia swallowed.

God, I knew that feeling. I had fallen for the wrong men over and over again. It was like I was a magnet for them. I understood the ache of wanting something to be safe and good, but being terrified that it can't last because it never had for me.

"He makes me feel seen, Nic. But also...I keep thinking, what if I'm wrong again? What if I've got no business trusting my heart after what happened with Josh?"

At the mention of her ex's name, a slow heat built in my chest. Rage—protective rage at anyone who would make Lucia feel small or unworthy.

"I let him in, and it tore me apart," Lucia said, voice smaller now. "He made me believe love meant sacrifice. Silence. Shrinking."

She blinked hard, looking up at the sky.

"And now, when Alexander says something kind, or when he's just there...when he remembers my coffee order or reaches out to hold my hand when I need steadying, God, I don't know what to do with it. It's so easy to give love, Nic. I can do that all day. But receiving it?" Her voice cracked. "That's harder. Like I don't know how to hold it without dropping it. I'm broken when it comes to relationships."

I bit the inside of my cheek. Then softly said, "You're not broken, Lucia."

She looked at me.

"You're cautious. And you have every right to be. But just because one man made you doubt yourself doesn't mean every man will."

"I'm scared he'll change," she said.

"Alex is different, he's the type of good not many men are," I replied gently. Alexander Wight was a good man, a responsible one at that, despite whatever the media was spinning. It felt rare out in a minefield of dating men in the motorsport world. But if anyone was worthy of my best friend, it was him. "Besides, you're trying so hard to be invincible, you forget that the strongest thing you can do is let someone love you while you're still healing."

Lucia's eyes glistened.

"I don't want to need anyone," she whispered.

"You don't *need* anyone, but it's okay to *want* someone."

She leaned her head on my shoulder, and we sat that way for a long time, watching Gia run through a patch of sunshine, arms wide, hair flying behind her like a little comet made of joy.

Lucia sighed again, softer now. "I wish I believed in forever the way she does."

I smiled faintly.

"Maybe we don't have to believe in forever yet," I said. "Just... today. One good day at a time."

Lucia squeezed my hand.

We met up with Alexander at our hotel before their planned fake dinner date, and Lucia looked every inch the PR fantasy—glossy hair, radiant smile, the kind of dress that made Alexander stare at her with those soft eyes. Gianna clung to her leg, then made a beeline for Alexander, who scooped her up to say hi.

"You sure you're okay watching her?" Lucia asked for the third time as we traded off the diaper bag and an emergency snack pouch.

"She's basically my godchild at this point," I said, ruffling Gia's hair as she beamed up at me. I lowered my voice. "Go on your fake date and get dessert and maybe accidentally kiss while you're at it."

Lucia rolled her eyes, but her cheeks flushed. "We'll be back before midnight."

Back in the hotel suite, Gia and I played a high-stakes game of *Stuffed Animal Royal Court*. She appointed me as the queen and then immediately overthrew me in a surprise coup led by a sparkly giraffe. By the time we got to bubble bath negotiations, I was winded.

"Okay, okay," I said, toweling her hair. "Time to relax. Maybe we put on a movie, hmm?"

She nodded, yawning as she curled into my side with a juice box like a tiny dictator at peace. I had my laptop out doing some research on charities along our racing route when a knock sounded at the door.

I frowned. Lucia wouldn't be back this soon, would she? I slid off the couch while Gia sat glued to the princess movie and walked to the door.

When I cracked the door open, I was met with a familiar soft scent of warmth and spice.

*Matteo.*

With takeout bags and that smug little tilt of his mouth like he knew I'd open the door and wouldn't slam it in his face.

"What are you doing here?" I whisper-shouted, glancing over my shoulder.

"Feeding my niece," he said, breezing past me without invitation. "Also, checking on her captor."

"Sure, yeah come on in." Sarcasm dripped from each word.

"You're welcome," he said, tossing a bag on the table. "Got those truffle fries you like."

I hated that he remembered that. I hated that I was hungry. I hated—

"I'll grab plates."

By the time Gia was asleep—snuggled between us in a sea of plush animals and holding the juice box like a teddy bear—Matteo and I were sitting on opposite ends of the hotel couch, the leftover fries between us. It was quiet and almost pleasant.

"Lucia looked happy today," I said eventually.

He nodded, face turned toward the dark TV screen. "Yeah."

"You've been watching her like a hawk."

"She's been through hell." His voice was lower now. His honesty was giving me pause; I hadn't heard him like this before. Something ached under my ribs at the emotion rolling off of him. "I thought...maybe bringing her here would help. You know, remind her who she is when she's not stuck at home."

I blinked.

That was not the Matteo I was expecting tonight.

He ran a hand through his hair. "I just want her to laugh again. Like she used to. When we were kids, she was always the brave one."

"She still is," I said quietly.

He looked at me then. *Really* looked.

The air shifted again, heavier now. Warmer. Threaded with tension but no longer sharp.

"You're good with her," I added, looking down at Gianna who was fast asleep, because I didn't know how not to say it. Matteo with Gia was enough to make any girl's heart do summersaults. It was sickening.

His gaze softened. "She's my favorite."

I rolled my eyes. "Charming."

"I have my moments."

We sat in the silence that followed, full of things neither of us knew how to say.

Eventually, I reached for another fry. Our fingers brushed.

I should have pulled away. Rolled my eyes at the sheer ridiculousness of it, he probably placed his damn hand there on purpose. I should have said something sharp, maybe, or tossed in one of my usual jabs to keep the distance exactly where I liked it.

But I didn't.

I just let it happen. His fingers were warm. Steady. Not lingering, not purposeful. But the contact left a spark in its wake that crawled up my arm and lodged somewhere stupid, like my throat.

He didn't say anything either. Just let me steal the fry.

The glow from the hotel room was soft and gold, shadows curling around the corners. Gianna was a little bundle of sleep on the couch, her stuffed bunny tucked under her chin.

"I used to think," Matteo said, voice quiet now, "that being a good brother meant protecting her from the world."

He exhaled, leaning back against the couch.

"But lately...I don't know. I think maybe it's about standing beside her when she faces it. Not stepping in front all the time."

I glanced at him. He was looking at Gianna again, his jaw tighter now. There was a kind of grief in his eyes I wasn't ready for.

"Is that why you wanted her to come on the road for the rest of the season?" After summer break, when Matteo had returned with his sister and niece in tow, he told everyone on the paddock that they were a part of the racing family and to look out for them.

He nodded, rubbing the back of his neck. "Yeah. I thought maybe if she saw the world again—saw herself in it—she might start to feel like she could take up space again. Not just survive, but...breathe."

There was a thud in my chest. A slow, aching resonance with

what he said—a part of me that recognized the weight of trying to be okay for everyone else and forgetting how to be okay for yourself.

"She's lucky to have you," I said, and I meant it.

But Matteo shook his head.

"She's the one who saved me first, you know? When I was a dumb kid with a bad attitude and no real direction. She kept me grounded. It reminded me who I was." He paused. "Sometimes I think I drive the way I do because I'm always chasing the version of myself she believed in."

I studied him, lips parting, because I didn't think I'd ever heard him talk like this. Not the cocky, swaggering Matteo DeLuca the world saw. Not the one who called me princess just to get a rise out of me. This version was quieter and more open in a way I hadn't seen. Everything felt like a performance with him because he was all charm. Seeing that sadness linger, feeling it in his words, it struck something deep in my chest, pulled at a damn heart string. Because that picture I kept of him made me not like him. But that man in front of me was different. Like I was seeing him for the first time.

"You're a better man than you pretend to be," I murmured, seeing the cracks of someone who also put on a mask for the world.

His gaze snapped to mine, and I immediately regretted saying it. Not because it was untrue. But because the look he gave me in return felt like an unraveling.

Matteo leaned forward, elbows on his knees, eyes still locked with mine.

"Why do you hate me so much, Nicola?"

I blinked.

"I don't hate you."

He smiled faintly. "Could've fooled me."

"It's easier," I admitted before I could stop myself. "To pretend you get under my skin for all the wrong reasons. To write you off as a reckless driver with too much charm and not enough substance."

He didn't flinch. He just waited.

"And is that still what you think?" he asked, voice soft now.

I looked away. "No."

A beat passed. Two.

"But that's what scares me."

The confession left my mouth like it'd been waiting there all night, and for the first time, the space between us didn't feel charged—it felt fragile. Like if I breathed wrong, the moment would slip through my fingers.

Matteo shifted beside me, his voice low. "I don't want to scare you."

I didn't answer, too lost in thought till he looked over to me. Gianna was still asleep in his lap between us.

"Have you ever been in love?" he asked.

My breath caught.

He said it casually, like he wasn't asking this huge momentous thing. Something I didn't talk about freely.

I leaned back against the couch, folding my arms.

"I thought I was once," I admitted, voice quieter than I meant it to be. "But I think I was just in love with the idea of being wanted. Or maybe just mattering to someone. Guess I know how to pick 'em since the only long-term relationship I ever had was with a man who was cheating on me the whole damn time."

Matteo didn't say anything, instead his jaw ticked, and I watched him swallow. But he gave me the space, waiting for me to finish.

"Turns out," I whispered into the night, voice cracking, "love shouldn't make you feel smaller."

"No one deserves that." His voice was low, brows creased.

I only shrugged, shoving back down the emotions that rose too quickly. "What about you?"

He let out a breath, running a hand over his mouth.

"I think I've come close," he said after a moment. "But I always held something back. I told myself it wasn't the right time or the right person. Maybe that's on me. But I think I might trust too easily. I've been burned a few too many times now by those I thought I could trust."

I studied him then, the curve of his shoulders, the dip of his brow. It was like the weight of his own honesty surprised him. And something deep inside me ached because we were two people who learned how to survive first and love second—if ever.

"Maybe it just hasn't been the right kind of love," I said, surprising myself.

He looked at me.

And whatever was in his eyes, it made it hard to breathe. Not because it was intense, but instead shocking me yet again with that softness.

"I think..." he started, then stopped, glancing down at Gianna's tiny fist curled in sleep against his arm. "I think the right kind of love makes you feel like more of yourself. Not less."

The only sound was the hum of the city outside and the gentle tick of the heater. Matteo was maybe the only person I had ever felt comfortable with in companionable silence. When he quietly hit me with this rather poignant remark, it showed me that Matteo DeLuca had layers. That there was something beneath that mask of the ever-smiling golden boy.

I thought about what he said earlier—about chasing the version of himself his sister used to believe in. About how he's trying to stand beside her now, instead of shielding her from everything.

He was proving that he wasn't the same man I rolled my eyes at across the paddock garages. He wasn't just the fast-talking charmer behind the wheel. He was complicated and messy and unexpectedly gentle.

God help me, I think that might have been *worse*. Because I could handle the version of Matteo who flirted just to get under my skin. I had armor for him. Sarcasm. Sharp edges. But this version? I was not prepared for it.

"Matteo," I said quietly, not even sure what I'm going to follow it with.

But he cut in first, voice softer than I'd ever heard it. "You're the most frustrating person I've ever met."

I blinked, caught off guard. "What?"

He was smiling then. "And you're also the one I think about when I can't sleep. Which, for the record, is extremely inconvenient."

My lips parted. I tried to form words. But they scattered like birds in a storm.

I swallowed, eyes darting down to Gianna, like she was some kind of anchor.

"She's asleep," he said, noticing. "You can say whatever you want."

But I couldn't.

I didn't know how.

Because part of me wanted to tell him not to look at me like that.

And the other part—the dangerous part—wanted to say *look at me more.*

So instead, I did the one thing I could manage.

I rested my head on the back of the couch, just slightly closer to him now, and whispered, "It's becoming rather difficult to find reasons why I should hate you when you're over here sharing things like this."

He laughed softly—and just for a second, we existed in that delicate balance between something almost and something real. Gianna shifted in his arms, letting out a tiny sigh, and the spell broke.

"I'll put her to bed," he said, getting up and scooping her into his arms. She snuggled in closer to him. My heart squeezed in response.

When he came back, he shut the door to the bedroom where Gianna's crib was and plopped down on the couch and smirked at the ceiling.

"You wore red again."

I rolled my eyes, and a reluctant smile tugged at my mouth. "If I knew you were going to turn that into a thing..."

"It is a thing," he said, grinning. "You wore my team colors."

I tossed a pillow at him. He dodged it with obnoxious ease. "It's *my* team, actually. Don't make it weird."

"Too late." His laughter filled the room like sunlight through curtains, and I hated how good it felt. How easy it was. How right. I reached for one last fry, but he'd already taken it.

"Asshole," I muttered.

He stretched, grabbing the empty takeout bags and headed toward the door. But just before he reached it, he paused.

Turned back.

And smirked.

"Give me your phone."

I blinked. "Excuse me?"

He wiggled his fingers. "Phone. You know, the small computer you are practically physically attached to?"

I narrowed my eyes. "Why?"

"So I can put my number in it."

I let out a dry laugh. "Why would I want your number?"

He shrugged like it was the most obvious thing in the world. "In case you ever want to talk again. Or yell at me. Or invite me over to babysit and bring you fries."

I glanced at the empty container between us on the coffee table. My stomach flipped, stupidly. "I'm not calling you."

He smiled wider. "That's fine. But now you *can*."

I hesitated. "You don't think that's a little...presumptuous?"

Matteo just held out his hand. "Come on, Princess. Don't make me beg. Or do. I would love being on my knees for you."

I gaped at him, heat rushing to my face. "You're—"

"Inappropriate? Charming? Irresistible?"

"Insufferable."

"And yet..." He wiggled his fingers again.

I sighed, exasperated, fishing my phone from my back pocket. I passed it to him with a scowl I didn't fully mean.

He typed something quickly, then handed it back.

"There," he said. "Now if you ever get tired of pretending you don't like me, I'm just a text away."

I snorted. "That's assuming I would ever text you."

He was already backing toward the door, eyes glittering with that infuriating confidence.

"I told you, Moretti," he said, grinning as he pulled the door open. "Ball's in your court."

# 6

## MATTEO

*I* was halfway through trying to convince Alexander that karting with me tomorrow at a local karting warehouse would be more fun than whatever sponsor meeting he was trying to avoid when my phone buzzed on the table between us. We were both half-slumped on chairs outside the gym post-training. Our trainers pushed us extra hard today. If I saw another tennis ball for hand-eye coordination practice after reps on the damn row machine, I'd probably scream. My phone buzzed again, reminding me I had a text.

I glanced at it, ready to ignore it—until I saw the message and I knew exactly who it was.

NICOLA:

Don't get too excited, DeLuca.

Another message came through a second later:

NICOLA:

Lucia wants to go out tonight. Some underground club. You and Mr. Down Bad are apparently invited. Anna's got Gia.

My brows lifted as I sat forward a little, thumb already typing before I could help myself.

MATTEO:

So this is your way of begging me to spend time with you? Bold move, Princess.

The three dots appeared immediately.

NICOLA:

By force not by choice.

I can tolerate you, I guess.

I grinned.

"She texted you?" Alexander asked, raising an eyebrow.

"She did."

"Damn. She must be desperate."

"Careful," I muttered, but I was still smiling as I replied.

MATTEO:

Tolerable. I'll take it. Underground club, huh? Should I wear all black and prepare to be judged by your impossible standards?

Her response came so fast it had me chuckling before I even finished reading it.

NICOLA:

Wear whatever. Just don't embarrass us.

And no sunglasses indoors.

I looked up at Alexander, shaking my head as I finished my drink.

He smirked. "You look like someone just handed you pole position."

"She said I'm tolerable now."

"Wow. Proposals must be next."

I flipped him off lazily and typed back one more message:

MATTEO:

Careful, Moretti. You keep inviting me places and I might start thinking you like me.

NICOLA:

Don't push it, DeLuca.

But I would, and if she thought I wasn't going to show up tonight looking like her next bad decision, well—she wasn't paying enough attention.

That night, Alexander appeared in the doorway of my room, already dressed in dark jeans and a perfectly fitted navy shirt. Of course he looked effortlessly good, the smug bastard.

"Going with the black, huh?" he said, leaning on the doorframe like he was there to deliver judgment.

"It's a club," I replied, buttoning the shirt halfway and turning to check myself in the mirror. "And Nicola Moretti will be there. I'm not showing up looking like a clown."

"Didn't stop you in Monaco," he said under his breath.

I glared at him in the mirror. "That shirt was a limited edition."

He shrugged. "It was lime green."

"It was bold."

"It was offensive."

I shook my head, grabbing a watch from the nightstand. "At least I don't look like I'm going to seduce someone's mum at a yacht party."

Alexander raised an eyebrow. "You know, for someone who claims not to care, you've been really concerned about impressing Nicola lately."

"She said I'm tolerable now."

"She also called you insufferable."

"Balance," I replied coolly, fixing my hair with the kind of precision I pretended not to care about but absolutely did.

Alexander watched me for a second longer before speaking again, this time more thoughtful. "You like her."

I glanced at him. "She's—" I shook my head. "She's infuriating."

"That wasn't a no."

"She's also sharp. Funny. She doesn't fall for the usual charm."

"So you have to work for it." He smirked. "You love that."

I didn't answer because, yeah, I did. I loved the way her eyes narrowed when she tried not to laugh. The way she argued like it was an art form and glared at me like I was her least favorite secret.

She was all fire and control and backbone. And she'd been in my head since that damn gala.

"She's not the kind of girl you mess around with," I said eventually.

Alexander shook his head, pulling his jacket on. "No, she's not."

"She deserves someone serious. Stable."

He looked at me with one brow raised. "You think that's not you?"

I paused.

Then exhaled. "I think I want it to be."

The silence lingered for a beat. Then he clapped a hand on my shoulder. "You're either about to have the best night of your life or make the biggest mess in the paddock."

I grinned. "Can't it be both?"

Alexander laughed. "Let's go, Lover Boy."

I grabbed my keys and followed him out.

Let the games begin.

The second we stepped out of the black car, the flashes started. Paparazzi lined up outside the underground club like wolves, eager for a bite of whatever staged moment Lucia and Alexander were feeding them that night. And they delivered—Alexander had his hand at the small of her back, Lucia leaned into his shoulder.

I lagged behind with my sunglasses pulled low even though it was well past sunset, hands in my jacket pockets like I didn't care. But I was scanning.

Looking.

And then I found her, midnight hair down in loose waves and all I could think about was running my fingers through the strands.

She was already inside, standing near the velvet rope of the VIP lounge, half-listening to a security guard while her eyes flitted across the room. Like she was casing the place for exits. Classic Moretti.

But it was her outfit that damn near knocked the breath out of me.

Black leather pants hugging her hips. A red, backless top tied at the nape of her neck, dipping low enough in the front to make me dizzy. And heels to match—scarlet, sleek, lethal. She turned slightly as she laughed at something Lucia said, and I swore to God—

My heart actually hammered.

Hard.

Like it was trying to punch its way out of my chest.

We moved past the crowd, ushered into the private lounge with ease, drinks already waiting at the table. It was all dim lighting, bass thumping, lights flashing in time with the music, like the place was alive and hungry. Lucia threw back a shot with a grin. Alexander saluted the table before tossing his down. I sat down beside Nicola, close enough that our knees brushed when she shifted.

She glanced at me, that familiar mix of suspicion and challenge in her gaze. "You're staring."

I smirked. "Hard not to when you wear red, Princess."

Her eyes rolled, but her lips twitched. "It's the Moretti color."

"Then I'll need to see this outfit in the garage next weekend."

She scoffed and lifted her glass. "In your dreams."

I leaned in, letting my voice dip lower, just enough for her to hear over the music. "Fuck, I hope so."

Her breath caught, barely—but I caught it. Every little flicker. Because I was watching her like she was the only one in this entire place. We drank. Laughed. Someone ordered another round of shots and Nicola made a face but took one anyway. Her cheeks were flushed, her pupils blown wide, and there was something in her smile that was looser than usual. Unrestrained. Alexander and Lucia went to the dance floor, getting consumed by the crowd.

The music shifted, bass thick and rolling through my spine as I stood, holding a hand out to her. "Dance with me."

She hesitated.

But then—God, those eyes.

She finished her drink, set the glass down, and placed her hand in mine like a dare. "Don't step on my shoes."

I pulled her into the crowd, the lights swallowing us whole. Bodies swayed around us, a pulse of heat and noise and motion, and when I slid my hands to her waist, she let me. Her hands found my shoulders, fingers brushing the back of my neck like it was nothing. Like she wasn't slowly setting me on fire. We moved with the beat, chests close but not touching—until we were.

My hands drifted down, thumbs brushing over the curve of her hips. She leaned in just enough for her mouth to brush my ear, the scent of her perfume sending my already weak self-control into freefall.

I pulled her closer, our hips aligning and the music drowning out everything but the heat of her against me. I felt the glide of her fingers up my chest as the dance became something else. It was a slow, deliberate kind of torment. Our hands roamed under the cover of the crowd. Her nails scraped lightly under the collar of my shirt. My fingers slid over the bare skin of her back.

Everywhere I touched, she shivered.

I was a man possessed, wanting to memorize every curve of her body. It took everything in me not to take her chin in my hand and pull her in to kiss her. Right there.

"Nic!"

My sister's voice sliced through the moment like a bucket of ice water. She grabbed Nicola's wrist, breathless, laughing, tugging her toward the lounge for more drinks.

Nicola glanced back once. Her eyes met mine. Wide. Lit.

But she went. And I stood there, fists clenched at my sides, still tasting her heat like it was seared into my skin.

*I need to fucking relax.*

# 7

## NICOLA

ours passed, and I didn't even know how I made it to the alley, heels clicking on cobblestones, breath uneven, adrenaline swirling through me like poison, like something was wrong. Too many shots was what was wrong. I didn't love the whole *'feeling out of control'* thing, couldn't stop thinking about Matteo and his hands. His goddamn hands. The cool night air slapped me in the face, slicing through the haze of alcohol, but not enough to clear it. Not enough to stop the ache behind my ribs at this *want*. I didn't ask to feel this way, I didn't want to feel *anything* when Matteo DeLuca touched me. All I could focus on was getting out of the club.It felt too small and too hot. I just needed some air to get my head on straight.

"Nicola?" Matteo's voice cut through the music still thumping from the club behind me, before the door slammed shut behind him.

I spun around. "Go away!"

He stopped, chest heaving, dark curls a mess like he'd been running. "Not happening."

"I don't need any help, Matteo. Especially not from *you*," I shouted, louder than I meant to, voice cracking like I was about to cry, which I *wasn't*.

"You're so damn stubborn," he muttered, closing the distance. "Do you even hear yourself?"

I shoved him. Hard.

He stumbled a little—more from surprise than force—but then he steadied himself.

Just in time to catch *me* as I nearly tripped over my own feet.

His arms came around me automatically, and I hated how safe I felt in them. "Careful, Princess."

"Don't call me that," I muttered, but it came out breathy.

He sighed, reaching for his phone with one hand, the other still around my waist. "I'm calling a car. You're not walking anywhere like this."

"I don't need—"

"You're drunker than I am," he said. "And more dramatic."

"Bite me."

The car pulled up not two minutes later, and Matteo ushered me in. I slumped against the window, arms folded and glaring at the blur of lights.

When we got to the hotel, he walked me in without saying a word. I swayed on my feet in front of my room, jabbing my keycard at the door but missing the slot completely.

"Stupid fucking door."

He took the card gently from my hand. "You've got the hand-eye coordination of a sleep-deprived raccoon."

"Do *not* insult raccoons," I slurred. "They're resourceful."

"Uh-huh," he said, unlocking the door and pushing it open.

I tripped over the threshold.

Matteo caught me again. "You and your heels are lethal."

"It's a gift," I said, and then I groaned, face twisting. "Oh no."

"What?"

"I'm gonna—" I didn't finish the sentence before bolting for the bathroom.

Matteo was behind me in a flash, pulling my hair back as I threw up, misery coating my tongue.

"Jesus," I muttered between heaves. "This is humiliating."

"You'll live," he said, kneeling beside me, soothing a hand down my back. "You party like a rockstar. You crash like one too."

Eventually, the nausea faded and I slumped to the tile, forehead pressed to the cool porcelain. "I hate this."

"I know."

"I hate you."

"You don't."

"Okay, fine. I hate your face."

He chuckled, and damn it, it was warm and real and kind. "You'll feel better after some sleep."

He helped me to my feet, guiding me to the bed. I kicked off my shoes with a dramatic sigh.

"You gonna tuck me in too?" I mumbled.

He didn't say anything. Just grabbed a pillow and dropped it onto the floor.

"What are you doing?"

"Sleeping here. In case you get sick again."

"That's dumb," I whispered, eyes already slipping shut. "You're dumb."

"You're welcome."

I woke up to sunlight slicing through the curtains and a *very* unsexy taste in my mouth. My head was pounding like someone was playing drums inside my skull. I sat up, groaning—and froze.

There was a body on the floor.

A familiar one.

Curly brown hair. Long limbs.

*Matteo.*

My heart slammed into my ribs like a battering ram.

"Oh my God." I gasped, clutching the blankets to my chest even though I was fully dressed. "*Did we—?*"

He stirred, eyes opening slowly. "You scream like a banshee."

"What happened last night? Did we—did I—did *you*—"

"We didn't," he said, rubbing his eyes. "You puked. I held your hair. You fell asleep. I slept on the floor to make sure you didn't choke or die or something."

I stared at him, heat flooding my face. "Oh."

He yawned. "Nice to know your first thought was *hookup panic.*"

I threw a pillow at his face.

"Next time," he muttered, catching it, "I'm letting you flirt with random people and puke in *their* lap."

"Next time," I said, my voice hoarse, "I'm wearing noise-canceling headphones and pretending you don't exist."

He smirked, standing up and stretching. "You're welcome, Princess."

He stretched like a cat—an annoyingly smug, sleep-creased cat—arms high, shirt riding up just enough to flash skin I had no business noticing.

"Stop doing that," I muttered, shielding my eyes with the blanket like a vampire seeing sunlight for the first time.

"Doing what?"

"Looking like a Calvin Klein ad after you slept on the damn floor."

He grinned. "You're checking me out, Moretti?"

"I'm checking to see if you broke something. So I can tell Lucia her brother needs a leash."

"Ooh," he said, moving toward the door. "Kinky."

"Out," I said, throwing the blanket off dramatically. "Before someone sees you sneaking out and assumes we *actually* hooked up."

He stopped at the threshold, one hand on the door, looking far too pleased with himself. "You know, if we *had* hooked up." He paused. "Again, might I add." A smirk. "I bet you'd be nicer this morning."

I grabbed another decorative pillow off the bed and hurled it at his head.

He caught it. *Of course he did.*

"You're impossible," I mumbled, dragging myself off the bed and immediately regretting it when the room tilted.

He was still grinning as I stumbled toward the bathroom. "Drink water. Brush your teeth. You smell like vodka and vengeance."

"Go away, Matteo."

"I'm leaving, I'm leaving." He opened the door and peeked into the hallway. "But for the record, you're kind of cute when you're hungover."

"I will end you."

"Adorable."

A knock hit my door sooner than I'd liked. I shuffled over—still in an oversized tee with the remnants of sleep in my eyes—and opened it with a glare. Anna stood there, smirking.

"How was your sleepover?" she asked.

I shushed her immediately, yanking her inside by the wrist before anyone in the hallway heard. "How do you know everything?"

"It's my job, babes," she said with a shrug. Her hair was pulled into a perfect slicked-back bun, makeup flawless and outfit sharp. Of course she looked like she just walked off a runway while I looked like I'd been hit by a bus named Regret.

"It was nothing," I mumbled, flopping back onto the bed. "I drank too much, and Matteo stayed to make sure I didn't choke on my tongue or whatever."

"Hm," Anna hummed, scrolling through her phone. "Well, I was going to ask if you want to fly with Alexander and Lucia tonight or with your dad? I'm organizing the group's travel and need your call."

"I'll go with Lucia and Alexander," I said. "I just need to pick up Monty from my dad's place first. He gets anxious on flights without me." I needed some down time and some girl time desperately. Debriefing on the plane and letting Gia and Monty play together felt like a good solution. I was getting used to flying with them rather than on the flights with other corporate members or my father. Lucia had once said that we kind of made our own mismatched family. I liked that idea a lot; it made my icy heart melt and all. Plus, having to mask my hangover for my father and God knows who else? No thank you.

"And you won't somehow manage to crash the plane with your least favorite DeLuca on board?" she teased, arching a brow. *Damn,* I thought. He was a side effect of wanting to spend time with Lucia, and while I'd rather not confront the way my heart fluttered at his heavy stare, I could just ignore him. It would be fine!

"I'll be on my best behavior." I shot a smile at Anna. She gave me a pointed look, not buying it in the least.

"I promise," I said, raising a hand in mock-scout's honor.

She hummed again and stared down at her screen, her brows knitting together in a way that said whatever was on it wasn't good.

"What's going on?" I asked, sitting up and patting the bed beside me. "You okay?"

"Just some family stuff," she said vaguely.

"Wanna talk about it?"

"It's...a lot."

"I've got nothing but time," I said, grabbing the hotel phone. "And I can order us room service. Have you eaten?"

She offered a sheepish grin. "Does coffee count?"

"No," I laughed, dialing. I rattled off a ridiculously large breakfast order, and just for kicks, I charged it to Matteo's room. Petty? Maybe. Satisfying? Absolutely.

Once I hung up, I turned back to her. "So. Family stuff?"

Anna exhaled, rubbing her temples. "My family...they're sort of media mogul people."

"Which means?"

"They created, own, and run the parent company that controls a good chunk of the marketing and media industry. Globally."

My eyes widened. "Oh, *damn*."

"Yeah," she said flatly.

"So...someone blackmailing you or something?"

Anna gave me a look. "Does my grandfather count?"

I blinked. "Um...the one who...?"

"Died a few months ago? Yes," she said, voice dry. "He's blackmailing me from the grave."

"That's—" I blinked again. "A lot."

She let out a short laugh. "Welcome to my life."

"So what kind of blackmail are we talking about here?"

She inhaled deeply, bracing. "If I don't get married by the end of the year, I forfeit my entire inheritance."

I nearly choked. "I'm sorry—what kind of *backwards* nonsense is that? Is that even legal?"

"It is," she said grimly. "Had my lawyer comb through everything. No loopholes."

I stared at her, heart dropping. "And the inheritance?"

"It was for my daughter," Anna said softly. "All of it. Her future. School. College. Everything."

"Oh, Anna..."

She shrugged, but her voice wavered. "So yeah. It's just been...a lot."

I reached over and grabbed her hand. "I had no idea. I'm so sorry you've been dealing with all of this."

Anna exhaled shakily and leaned into my shoulder.

"Don't worry," she muttered. "I'll come up with something. I always do."

By the time we made it to the tarmac, the sun was low on the horizon casting long golden shadows across the private runway. Alexander's jet gleamed ahead of us, sleek and impossibly cool, like it knew it was out of everyone's league. Anna strode ahead like she owned the damn plane, her heels clicking purposefully against the pavement. I lagged behind, Monty trotting beside me in his little travel vest, tail wagging like he didn't have a care in the world. Lucky bastard.

"Hold up, Princess," Matteo said behind me, drawing out the nickname just to see if he could get a rise out of me.

"Don't call me that," I muttered, not turning around.

"But it fits so well." He grinned, catching up and walking backwards in front of me. "A little dramatic, high-maintenance, thinks she's above everyone else..."

"Keep talking and I'll tell Lucia you clogged the hotel sink with your protein powder."

His mouth dropped open. "You swore you'd never speak of that."

"Then don't test me."

Monty barked like he was proud of me.

The moment we boarded the plane, chaos and comfort merged into one. Gianna squealed as she spotted me, her curls wild and a juice box already in her hand. I barely got seated before she ran over and showed me her glittery unicorn stickers. I obliged with the appropriate *ooh*s and *ahh*s while Monty nestled beside me, already curled up and half-asleep.

Lucia was settled in with a warm blanket, while Anna kicked off her heels and curled into a window seat with her phone clutched tightly in one hand. I caught the two of them whispering, their heads bent together, brows furrowed.

Matteo slid into the seat across from me. He lifted a brow, glancing between Anna and Lucia, then at me. When I avoided eye contact, he took out his phone and typed something. A second later, my phone buzzed.

**MATTEO:**

What's going on over there? Secret girl meeting?

I sighed, thumb flying over the screen.

**NICOLA:**

Anna's got family drama.

No, I'm not telling you.

**MATTEO:**

Damn. Okay.

You're very bossy when you're being protective.

It's kinda hot.

I blinked and glanced up at him. He was grinning. The worst part? He knew I read the message.

**NICOLA:**

Delete that.

Go flirt with someone else.

MATTEO:

No thanks. I like you grumpy.

Makes it fun when I make you smile.

Making you blush is my new favorite pastime.

I rolled my eyes so hard my brain rattled. Monty nudged my hand like he was telling me to stop getting flustered and get back to his ear scratches. I obliged, silently praying Matteo would find someone else to torment.

I pulled out my book and tried to let the world slip away, my trusty queen of hearts playing card acting as a bookmark for all my books. The words started to settle around me like a blanket, the stress dissolving bit by bit. I fell into the pages easily, shoulders dropping as I escaped into a world where the only thing I had to worry about was whether the heroine would stab the prince or kiss him. Monty snored beside me, and I leaned my cheek on his head. Time floated by as I got lost in my pages and I tried to ignore the burning feeling as Matteo kept looking at me.

The plane hummed beneath us, everyone settling in for the flight. Lucia had already dozed off with Gia curled against her side, and Anna had finally relaxed, one foot tapping lightly as she texted someone back. It was quiet. Peaceful. And somehow, still laced with this magnetic pull that kept dragging my attention back to the boy across from me.

My phone buzzed one more time.

MATTEO:

Admit it.

You like it when I say things that make you blush.

Or how you made those little noises when I kissed that spot behind your ear?

NICOLA:

You know there's open seats on the other side
of the plane right?

MATTEO:

Ouch.

This is flirting in your world, huh?

NICOLA:

If it was flirting, you'd be dizzy by now.

MATTEO:

So you are flirting?

I didn't respond. Not with words, anyway. I glanced up and
leveled him with a glare.

MATTEO:

You'd miss me if I wasn't on this flight.

NICOLA:

I miss the sound of my own thoughts, actually.

MATTEO:

And here I was thinking we were making
progress.

NICOLA:

We're not. You're hallucinating from too much
cologne again.

MATTEO:

Rude. It's designer.

Alexander got it for me.

NICOLA:

I hate it.

Across the aisle, he gasped and clutched his chest like I'd

physically wounded him. I snorted and returned to my book, only for my phone to buzz again.

MATTEO:

You say you hate me but you've been looking at me every 3.5 minutes.

NICOLA:

Bold of you to assume I'm not just dreaming of you disappearing.

MATTEO:

Dreaming about me already? Damn, Princess.

I shot him a look so sharp it could cut glass. He grinned wider. Of course he did.

NICOLA:

You know what's wild?

Airplanes have emergency exits.

MATTEO:

You trying to throw me out mid-air?

NICOLA:

Just saying. Hypothetically.

MATTEO:

You'd miss me.

NICOLA:

Nah, I'd be too busy toasting with the flight attendant.

MATTEO:

Savage.

You always this mean, or is it just with me?

NICOLA:

Just with you. Congrats.

MATTEO:

I'm honored. I'd like to thank the academy.

I glanced up again and caught him watching me with that cocky little half-smile that made me want to roll my eyes and—unfortunately—also kind of smile back.

NICOLA:

Leave me alone. I'm busy escaping to fantasy worlds where men don't act like 12-year-olds.

MATTEO:

Fantasy world?

Lemme guess—enemies to lovers?

NICOLA:

What?

MATTEO:

You love a guy who pisses you off and makes your heart race.

NICOLA:

Shut up.

I bit my lip, because unfortunately, the man had a point. I *did* love a good enemies-to-lovers plot. Which made the irony of this whole thing unbearable.

NICOLA:

I hope Monty farts in your direction for the rest of the flight.

MATTEO:

He would never.

I take it as a sign of loyalty.

NICOLA:

Lies.

MATTEO:

Just say you're jealous he likes me more now.

NICOLA:

Literally never.

MATTEO:

Literally always.

Monty shifted in his sleep and let out a soft snore, completely unaware that he was in the middle of a custody battle.

I sighed and closed my book just long enough to shoot off one final message.

NICOLA:

If you keep texting me, I swear to God I will ask Anna to seat you in the cargo hold.

MATTEO:

If you wanted to go somewhere just us, we can always sneak into the bathroom. Heard mile high club is pretty exclusive.

NICOLA:

I will not hesitate to strangle you.

MATTEO:

Kinky, I like it.

I glared across the row and locked my phone, but it buzzed again, making me sigh.

MATTEO:

Can you even reach my neck?

At that, I leaned forward and kicked Matteo in the shin. Lightly. Mostly. He winced with an exaggerated *"Ow"* and then grinned, trying—and failing—not to laugh.

*He deserved it.*

I normally wore heels everywhere to offset my vertically-challenged situation, but today was a travel day, which meant sneakers and leggings.

I grabbed my phone, turned it face-down, and shoved it under my thigh like it personally offended me.Opening my book again, returning to the men I preferred: tall, dark, and fictional.

A few hours passed in silence, the soft hum of the plane lulling most of the cabin to sleep. Monty was still curled against my side, and my book was just getting good when I heard a sleepy shuffle and soft voice.

"Zietta..."

Gianna quietly interrupted me clutching her bunny with her curls, a wild halo of blonde chaos.

"Can you wake up Zio?" she murmured, her voice a sleepy mix of slur and pout. I'd become fluent in Gianna-speak by now. She meant business.

"I think we should let him sleep, honey," I whispered, nodding to Matteo—currently drooling in the most undignified way across the aisle. "Wanna hang with me until he wakes up?"

"'Oh-tay," she replied, climbing onto the seat beside me. She curled into my side like a tiny, warm blanket, bunny still clutched tightly in her hand.

We sat quietly for a bit, her head resting on my arm. It was peaceful. Sweet.

Too sweet.

"Zietta?"

"Hmm?"

"Can we wake up Zio *now*?" I glanced down at her, then over at Matteo who was still snoring. Then back to her. I could see the gears turning, see the intrusive thought take form. It was the same one her uncle got before he said something deeply dumb or chaotic.

"Gia..." I warned.

*Too late.*

She launched the stuffed animal right to her Zio. It smacked Matteo square in the face.

He jolted awake with a confused grunt, looked down at the bunny in his lap, then up at me. I was already laughing so hard I could barely breathe.

"Did you *need* something, Nic?" he groaned, voice low and scratchy with sleep—and oh God, it sounded exactly like his morning voice.

Which unfortunately reminded me of that morning after the gala. Shirtless. Window light. That smirk.

Nope. Shook that image out of my brain immediately.

"Maybe don't teach my sweet niece to throw things at people's faces," Matteo said, giving me a pointed look.

I started to protest, but before I could defend myself, Gianna crossed her arms, puffed up her cheeks, and said matter-of-factly, "I did it. I wanted you to wake up."

Matteo's expression softened instantly. The man was powerless against her.

He picked up the bunny, leaned forward with mock seriousness. "Alright, next time maybe don't throw things, yeah? Just come over and tap my arm like this." He used the bunny's paw to tap her shoulder gently, and she giggled so hard she snorted.

"'Kay, Zio. I sorry I throwed bunny at you."

"That's alright, G." He opened his arms, and she launched herself at him, giggling as he lifted her effortlessly into his lap and hugged her tight. He whispered something into her hair, soft and tender, something I didn't catch—but then his gaze lifted to me, warm and amused.

"You're rubbing off on her."

I smirked. "Oh please, she's far too sweet to pick up *all* my bad habits."

"She just threw a stuffed animal at my face."

I shrugged. "In her defense, it worked."

# 8

# MATTEO

Race day mornings were almost always the same.

There was rhythm to it, like muscle memory laced with adrenaline. Wake up early. Hydrate. Light workout. Media duties. Team briefing. Suit up. Then, the shift—the one that happened when the helmet is in my hands and suddenly, nothing else matters.

Except that day, my brain was a little too busy to shut off.

The Moretti Racing garage buzzed with activity. Screens flickered with telemetry, engineers speaking in clipped, rapid tones. I nodded through it all, hyperaware of the weight in my chest that had nothing to do with the car.

Lucia was over at the Belen Racing garage today, which wasn't anything too crazy. She'd been over there since they'd struck up a fake dating scheme to help Alexander's image and secure a contract for next year. I wouldn't be losing my mind about it if it wasn't my baby sister and my best friend. The whole '*my two favorite people ever dating*' thing made my insides twist. It could be great, but it could also be horrible. I exhaled, flexing my fingers as one of the mechanics passed me my gloves.

Before we started prepping for the race, I had seen her at the

Belen Racing garage. Lucia was laughing at something one of the engineers said, holding Gia on her hip. Gia had on her little earmuffs, custom made smaller for her. She had identical Moretti red ones too.

And then, just like clockwork, Nicola appeared.

She looked extra dressed up today, and I took a moment to take it in: a matching power suit and heels that made her reach my chin today. Effortless, smug, and unreadable as ever.

"You ready to score some points today?" She smirked, arms crossed.

"Wow, so supportive. Really warms a guy's heart," I shot back, grinning.

She shrugged, strolling closer, and lowered her voice just enough for only me to hear. "My dad sent me over to talk to you about an event but I know you're about to start your prep so we can talk later." She paused. "Good luck, DeLuca."

Something soft flashed behind her eyes. It threw me for a second. I nodded, mouth suddenly dry. "Thanks."

She walked off without another word, and I didn't even pretend not to watch her go.

*Bloody hell.*

I shook my head and grabbed my helmet, heading toward my private room. On the way, I FaceTimed my parents. One of my favorite traditions.

"*Ciao, Amore!*" Mama's voice filled the screen, bright and familiar.

"Matteo!" Papà waved, already wearing his Moretti Racing cap, seated at their kitchen table back in Italy. "Focused?" Papà huffed from beside her, adjusting his glasses. "He looks nervous. Are you nervous? Drink water. And carbs! Did you eat carbs today?"

"*Ciao, ciao!*" I said, laughing. "I'm fine. I promise."

Mama leaned closer. "Is Lucia with you?"

I hesitated. "She's with Alex. At the Belen garage."

Papà frowned. "Why?" My mother raised an eyebrow and smiled.

"She...it's complicated."

They exchanged a look I knew too well. Mama softened first. "She's allowed to live her life, Matteo. And Alexander has always been good to her."

"I just don't want her to get hurt," I admitted instead.

"She's stronger than you think," Papà said. "And you don't always have to fix everything. Just race your race. Make us proud."

"Always."

We said our goodbyes and I hung up, letting the screen fade to black before slipping the phone away. I stayed there for a moment longer, phone tucked away, but my mind still lingered with my parents' voices. Their love, their pride—it settled into my chest, warm and heavy. I exhaled slowly, letting the ambient roar of engines echo through the pit lane, grounding me like a tether.

The world hummed around me. Technicians calling out times, tires screeching during last-minute checks and the smell of fuel and heat rising in the air like static. *Race day.*

I sat down against the wall of the garage helmet in my lap, and stared at it like it held all the answers I couldn't find in myself. My thumb ran over the Moretti emblem—the name, the legacy. I didn't take it lightly. Not the name. Not the team. Not the weight of everyone who counted on me.

Truth is, I was used to being the one people relied on. The guy with the jokes. The lightness. The buffer between tension and breakdown. I was the one who talked Lucia down from a panic spiral at 2:00 a.m. when she thought she was failing as a mom. The guy who kept morale up in the garage after a rough qualifying. The guy who pulled Alexander back from overthinking and reminded him to breathe.

And I liked being that guy. I liked being needed. If me being a little chaotic, a little loud, a little annoying—okay, a lot annoying —made it easier for people to breathe, then I'd do it a hundred times over. It was easy to slip into. It was safer, even, than sitting too long with the things I couldn't fix. Like the way Lucia looked at Alexander when she thought no one noticed. Or how Alexander looked back at her like she was the sun and he was starving for light.

Alexander had told me he cared for her and I wanted to trust him—I *did* trust him. But she was my little sister. The one I used to walk home from school. The one who used to curl up in my room when the world got too loud. And she'd already been hurt enough. She didn't need another man burning her to ash just because he didn't know how to hold on.

I scrubbed a hand down my face and glanced up.

Nicola was on the other side of the garage, clipboard in hand, phone pressed to her ear. She was all business and grace, her heels clicking against concrete as she multitasked like she owned the place—which, to be fair, she kind of did. She must have felt my gaze because she looked over. We locked eyes for a second before she arched a brow and mouthed, *Focus, DeLuca.*

I flipped her off subtly and she smirked like she had already won.

That was the thing about Nicola. She called me a pain in the ass, but *she* was the one who drove *me* completely insane. In those red lips and razor-sharp one-liners, there was something that made my pulse stutter.

"Alright, Teo," one of the engineers called out, snapping me back to the moment. "Time to get in."

I nodded once, shook out my hands, and pushed off the wall.

Balaclava up.

Helmet on.

All of it—worries about Lucia, whatever the hell Nicola did to me just by existing, the pressure of legacy—it faded the second I slid into the cockpit. In there, I knew who I was. The noise was different. Louder, but clearer.

I buckled in, fingers flying over the wheel. I saw the lights ahead, and pulled into position, only one spot behind my teammate, Carlos.

Adrenaline surged through my veins as I took the inside line on Turn 12, hugging it like a second skin. I was in third. Fucking *third*. The car was responding like it was born for this track—tight, aggressive, alive.

"Nice move, Teo," my engineer's voice crackled in my ear, calm but charged. "Eyes forward. Two laps to go on these tires."

*Copy.*

I barely registered the crowd, the blur of grandstands, the roar of engines around me. It was all instinct now—pressure on the brake, feather the throttle, feel the grip bite beneath me. My pulse was synced with the engine's rhythm, the world narrowing down to one singular goal:

*Podium.*

I shifted, leaning into the next turn—too fast.

The moment it happened, I felt it in my gut.

Wheels locked.

The car jerked, grip vanished, and I was spinning.

"Shit, shit, shit—"

The world blurred. My rear tires screamed against the asphalt, smoke billowing, and then gravel. The violent bounce as my car hit the run-off jolted every bone in my body. I slammed the brakes, but it was too late. I was out of control.

Metal screeched.

A loud *crack* behind me.

Then chaos.

In my mirror, I saw the debris from my car scatter across the track, another car veering to avoid me—and failing. I watched in horror as, ahead of me, the two cars made contact, and I saw the familiar pink and blue livery spinning out—

Alexander's.

His car clipped the tangle of wreckage and went airborne. Time *stopped*.

"Fuck."

The world tilted as I watched his car flip once, twice, and slam into the barriers with the kind of impact that made my soul lurch. Someone was trying to talk to me over my radio. I knew I needed to confirm I was okay, but my mind was buzzing like the static of a radio.

"Red flag, red flag—incident on Sector 3. Medical on the way."

"Matteo, status check. Are you okay?"

Smoke filled my back wing, but I was moving.

"I'm fine. I'm okay," I gasped, ripping off the steering wheel and forcing the harness release. I shoved my body out of the cockpit and jumped down, boots sinking slightly into gravel.

But I wasn't thinking about the crash anymore.

I wasn't thinking about my race.

I was *only* thinking about him.

Alexander's car had rolled, and was half-crushed against the barrier, with smoke pouring from the engine. The marshals hadn't reached him yet.

I broke into a sprint, lungs burning, legs heavy from adrenaline and panic. I heard someone yelling at me, but I didn't stop. I couldn't.

"*Alex!*"

No movement.

I was slipping on gravel, dodging bits of debris, a sick, sharp fear cutting into my chest like glass. Not him. Not now. Not when things were finally—fuck, not when he was finally *happy*. Not when Lucia was waiting in the garage. Not when Gia looked at him like he hung the damn stars.

I reached the car just as two marshals converged. One grabbed my arm to hold me back, but I wrenched free.

He was still in the car, helmet on.

"Alex," I called, voice cracking. "Come on, mate. Say something. Move. *Do something.*"

The marshal beside me radioed something I couldn't hear. Everything was muffled under the roar of fear in my head.

If he didn't move—

"Alex," I said again, voice loud, desperate. "Get up! Get up!" It felt like a thousand moments before he moved, before he responded.

"I'm okay, I'm okay." His voice was scratchy and muffled. He pushed up his visor, seeing me, and thenI finally allowed the marshals to pull me away, a medic car arriving behind us.

I climbed in behind Alexander in the medic car, just watching for any signs. Hand on his shoulder to steady him, or me, I wasn't sure. Did I know what signs to look for? No, but fuck, I just wasn't about to take my eyes off him.

"I'm okay," Alex said, turning to look at me, eyes clouded. My hand squeezed his shoulder before letting go.

"Scared the hell out of us, mate," I said on an exhale. Alex only nodded then rested his head back on the headrest.

*He was okay,* I kept repeating it to myself until we pulled up to the medic tent. I stayed with him for a bit before they dragged me away to check me too. When I was finally cleared, I walked straight to my family,half-answering and half-ignoring everyone who saw me on the way.

The moment I laid eyes on my sister, my heart broke a little. She looked so small, her eyes glassy and red. She looked scared, and I wanted to fix it. I wanted to do anything or everything to make that fear disappear.

"He's okay," I said as I approached, her mouth opened and a strangled sob came out, her knees giving out. I leaned forward, collected her into my arms, and tried to block out the world.

"It's alright, Luce. He's okay, he's okay," I said softly. She took a moment, cleared her throat and wiped her tears, standing up, shoulders back.

"He's bruised up, maybe a concussion, but the Halo did its job. He's asking for you." She scooped up Gianna from Anna's arms and looked at me with determination.

"Lead the way."

I was behind the paddock, tucked into a little alley of scaffolding and crates where the camera crews wouldn't find me—yet. I had a handful of minutes before I had to smile and say everything was fine. That I was fine. That crashing out was unfortunate, but part of the sport. *That I didn't just watch my best friend's car fold like tinfoil and think for three long seconds that he was dead.*

I scrubbed a hand down my face and tried to steady my breathing. I didn't even hear the familiar heels clicking until she spoke.

"You look like shit."

I glanced up, and there she was. Nicola. Arms crossed, hair pulled back into a ponytail that had long since given up on being polished, eyes sharp but soft at the edges.

I tried for a smirk. It didn't land. "Thanks. I really needed that boost."

She didn't fire back. Not like I expected.

Instead, she stepped closer, glancing around like she was making sure no one could see her before sitting down next to me on the low barrier., not saying anything for a beat.

That's what got me. Nicola Moretti not saying something was *worse* than any snark she could throw at me.

She nudged her knee against mine. "That was a nasty crash."

I swallowed hard. "He's okay."

"I know." Her voice dropped. "But that doesn't mean *you're* okay. Are you?"

And just like that, the tight knot in my chest nearly split open.

"No one ever asks me that," I said before I could stop myself. "Everyone assumes I'm the one who *is* okay."

She was quiet for a moment. Then she shifted, her knee brushing mine again. "Yeah, well. I don't believe everything people say about you."

My head snapped toward her, surprised. She wasn't looking at me. She was looking straight ahead, lips pressed together like she regretted saying that out loud.

And it *undid* me a little.

"I thought I was about to watch him die," I said softly. "I spun out, and he got caught in the wreck. That could've been it. And I was thinking...it was my fault. I don't know how to come back from that."

Nicola didn't say anything. Instead, she reached for my hand. *My hand.* Her fingers slid between mine and she squeezed once.

It rocked me more than I cared to admit. We sat there like that, her hand warm in mine, the muffled sounds of the race in the distance, engines still screaming as if nothing happened.

And me?

I was absolutely fucked.

Because in the middle of all that chaos and fear, it was her that grounded me. Not the race. Not the team. Not even my family.

*Her.*

The girl I'd been annoying all year. The one who rolled her eyes when I flirted and called me an idiot like it was my damn name. And yet, she was the one sitting here now. Knowing what I needed before I could ask. Comforting me without calling it out.

When she finally let go of my hand, I felt the loss like a punch.

She stood and smoothed down her trousers, all business again. "You've got interviews waiting, the team wants you to do the

Pitspark magazine one too. Better put on the charming idiot mask."

I blinked. "You calling me charming?"

"I said *mask*. Don't push it, DeLuca."

But she said it with a half-smile.

And I couldn't stop watching her as she walked away.

*God, I was so screwed.*

## 9

## MATTEO

It had been a day since the crash. I had to move, to do something, to make everyone smile again and leave the haze of the last day. So I called a meeting with a brilliant idea. We were all crammed into Alexander's hotel suite like it was a boardroom and not the nicest room on the floor. The place smelled like the fresh espresso and pastries we had delivered. Lucia and Alexander sat curled together on the couch, Gianna giggling on the floor beside them making her tiny racecars zoom along a makeshift track built from throw pillows and a room service tray. Nicola was parked against the wall, eyes glued to her phone. I clapped my hands once, all enthusiasm. "All right, I have a master plan."

Gianna didn't miss a beat—revving one of her cars and yelling, "Go go go!"

"That's what you're calling it?" Nicola said, finally glancing up with a skeptical arch of her brow.

"No one asked for your opinion, Princess," I shot back, aiming a half-hearted glare at her.

"Don't be rude," Lucia chimed in, narrowing her eyes at me.

I sighed. "Okay, okay. But seriously, I have a plan."

Alexander, scrolling his phone like he was trying to fall into it, didn't even look up. Since he was being forced to rest after the crash, he had been locked in on the gossip sites that were whirling about him being a loose cannon or hothead after he punched Lucia's ex who had been harassing her, spinning him into someone he absolutely was not. "What exactly is this so-called plan?" he asked flatly, voice edged with exhaustion. I walked over, plucked the phone from his hand, and tossed it across the room.

"Seriously, mate?" he snapped, jerking upright. "You had to bloody throw it?"

"Yes, pay attention," I said with a shrug. Lucia looked over to Alexander, the worry clear on her face. I knew that look—she was checking out and zeroing in on Alexander instead. So I focused on Nicola. "Listen, I couldn't stop thinking—about how we finally have a week off. No races. No sponsor events. No drama. Just relaxation."

"Suspicious," Nicola muttered.

"So," I continued, pacing, "Why not take advantage of it? Recharge. Eat real food. Drink a little wine. Maybe not almost-die for seven straight days. A holiday."

Gianna sat up straighter. "Holiday?" she said all the syllables smashed together.

"Yup. I planned the whole thing. Anna handled the logistics— obviously. She booked us this super fancy private villa. We're taking Alexander's jet—thanks, mate—and we're going to the seaside," I said, hands outstretched. "One week in Portofino. The views are unreal, the food is basically heaven, and the town is so quiet we might even go unrecognized—assuming Alexander wears a hoodie and sunglasses and doesn't speak. One week to ignore our phones and float in the sea."

Nicola finally glanced up. "You're bribing us with a holiday in exchange for a digital detox?"

"No," I said, pointing at her. "I'm *inviting* you to relax for the first time in your life. You're welcome."

I received a patented Nicola glare. "But picture this: wine tastings. Sunsets over the sea. Fresh pasta. Gianna eating gelato the size of her head."

Gianna stood up like a queen delivering a command. "I want pink gelato!"

"There will be so much pink gelato," I promised solemnly. "Endless pink gelato, Your Majesty."

"Yay!"

I turned back to the group, smug. "See? It's already a success. Right, so in conclusion, since you two are in love and refusing to admit it—" I gestured at Lucia and Alexander.

Lucia choked. "Wait, what?"

"—Nicola here is miserable or moody or whatever—"

"Hey!" Nicola protested genuinely offended.

"—and Gianna is clearly a Moretti fan, not a Belen fan—red is better, come on—the only solution is obvious: we should all go on vacation."

Lucia turned to Alexander, stunned. "I'm sorry—what? Did you just say we're in love? Where the hell did that come from?"

Alexander looked equally thrown. "And how does any of this even connect?"

Nicola muttered, "I am a ray of sunshine."

"Way to just jump the gun, bud," Alexander added, dry as ever.

Gianna perked up, eyes wide and curious. "Who's in love?"

"It's nothing, baby," Lucia said quickly, scooping her up and heading to the balcony, Alexander immediately following behind. My gaze caught, anxiety taking root that my words upset my sister. I loved Lucia, I loved Alexander, and they obviously loved each other, so it was about damn time they admitted it.

Nicola tilted her head. "And there's enough space at this place?"

"Plenty," I nodded. "Everyone gets their own room. Monty can come if you want. There's a private pool, beach access, and a kitchen we're absolutely not going to use."

Nicola narrowed her eyes. "What's the catch, DeLuca?"

"No catch," I grinned. "Just vibes. And wine." She stared at me too long, like she was trying not to smile. Gianna ran back inside and began twirling in her dress.

"Can we play princesses on holiday?" Gianna asked, eyes going large and bottom lip jutting out. I sighed, as if I could ever say no to this one.

"Of course!" I scooped her into my arms and spun her around. Then, I planted her right in front of me as we both stared over at the feisty brunette. I needed maximum impact here. "Nicola? You on board?"

She sighed, long and dramatic. "Fine. But if you play the *Mamma Mia!* soundtrack unironically, I'm stealing your passport."

I beamed. "So that's a yes?"

She crossed her arms. "It's a threat, DeLuca."

We sat for a while, spying on the two on the balcony before Nicola spoke up in barely a whisper, "I'm not miserable."

I raised an eyebrow. "You've been extra spiteful lately." Her gaze flickered,the tiniest crack in the wall. "Relaxation would be good for everyone," I added gently.

She exhaled like she wanted to say something else, then hesitated. "There's this event I'm trying to show that I can lead. It's important. And I—" She stopped mid-sentence, the softness disappearing as quickly as it came. Her shoulders went rigid again. "But who can say no to a free trip and the beach?" she said with a plastic smile.

Something was off—more than usual. She was hiding something.

"There will be Wi-Fi," I said, more carefully now. "I was being dramatic. I just...thought we could all use a break."

"It's a good idea, Matteo." Her voice was quiet, and for once, real. She swatted my arm and pointed out the window where my sister was kissing my best friend.

"About damn time!" Nicola shouted across the room. They turned and smiled at us, and I couldn't help my own smile grow. Mission complete.

"So I booked us all on a flight in an hour to Italy," I announced.

"Yeah, not a chance." Nicola glared. Alexander and Lucia walked back in.

"Mate, what do you mean you booked a flight?"

"I texted Anna!" I said it like it was the most obvious thing in the world.

"Hmm." Alexander picked up his phone and started typing. After a minute he looked over to Lucia. "How about tomorrow, Angel? Is that enough time?"

"That's better than in an hour," she laughed.

"Thank God." Nicola rolled her eyes.

"Maybe we can find you a hot vacation man?" Lucia whispered not at all quietly to Nicola. My blood immediately started boiling. Maybe the fuck not.

Nicola's eyes glanced at me for only a second before snapping back to Lucia.

"Sounds perfect!" Her voice was too high, too cheery. She flashed an all too-bright smile and headed for the door.

Nicola had shut down before my eyes.

I didn't like that.

I stomped out the door, right after her. I caught sight of Nicola halfway down the hallway, walking fast, her heels clicking sharply on the marble floor like warning shots.

"Nicola!" I called, jogging to catch up. She didn't slow down.

"Nicola, come on—" I reached for her arm.

She spun around so fast I almost collided with her.

"What, Matteo?" she snapped. "You got your yes. Everyone's onboard. Congrats on your team bonding vacation or whatever."

I blinked at her, thrown. "Why are you being like this? You were fine ten minutes ago."

Her laugh was hollow. "Fine? That's rich. You stormed in, tossed a phone across the room, dropped a bomb about your sister and best friend being in love like it's a game, and then roped me into a romantic seaside group trip I didn't ask for."

"It's a holiday," I said. "A break. I thought maybe you'd want that. God forbid you take one second to breathe."

"I breathe just fine, thanks," she said, her jaw tight. "And don't act like you did this for *me*."

I stepped in, too close now, deliberately so. "And what if I did?"

She flinched like I'd struck a nerve but didn't back away. "Then you're an idiot."

"Why?" I demanded, voice low. "Because I want you to stop killing yourself trying to prove something to people who already know you're good at your job? Or maybe because I'm sick of watching you act like you don't care when I know you do."

Her eyes flashed. "You don't know anything about me."

"Don't I?" I said, and that time, my voice was rough. "I know you hide behind sarcasm and late nights and that fucking phone. I know you're tired, and you won't admit it. And I know you're scared shitless to let anyone take care of you."

She stared at me, furious and breathless, and for a second, I thought she might slap me.

Instead, she hissed, "Fuck off."

I blinked. "Fine."

I started to step back but she grabbed my shirt and yanked me forward.

Our mouths crashed together like we were trying to win a fight with teeth and lips and frustration. She tasted like coffee and tension, and something sweet I couldn't name. I slid one hand into her hair, the other gripping her waist, hauling her closer as her back hit the wall with a soft thud.

She pulled away first, breathing hard, eyes wide, lips swollen. "That was a mistake."

I smirked, breathless. "Didn't feel like one."

"I'm still mad at you."

"Yeah?" I murmured, leaning in until our noses brush. "You gonna slap me or kiss me again?"

She grabbed me by the collar, yanking me back in, and this time it was deeper, messier. Her hands in my hair, my thumbs digging into her hips. I kissed her like I was starving and she was the only thing that could ever satisfy me. She moaned low in her throat, and I nearly lost it right there in the damn hallway.

When we finally broke apart, we were both gasping, chests heaving.

"Still mad?" I asked, voice wrecked.

She glared at me. "Yes."

But she didn't move away.

Neither did I.

# 10

# NICOLA

 didn't know what the hell I was doing.

One second I was storming out of that hotel suite, trying to keep it together, trying to pretend like I wasn't unraveling at the seams—and the next, Matteo was right behind me, dragging all his golden-boy sunshine and ridiculous charm into my storm.

When he called my name, I didn't stop. I couldn't. If I had turned around then, I would've shattered.

But then his hand wrapped around my arm—warm, solid, familiar—and I spun, ready to bite.

"What, Matteo?" I snapped, the words sharp and fast. Anything to keep my heart from spilling out.

And of course, he looked at me like I was a puzzle he could solve, like if he just pressed all the right buttons, I'd stop pretending I didn't feel everything.

He stepped in too close, his body heat licking up my spine, and said, "And what if I did?"

The world narrowed. Just him. His breath, his scent of spiced citrus mixed with leather and whatever shampoo he stole from luxury hotels. My pulse crashed like waves inside my ribs.

Then I said it, the only defense I had left.

"Fuck off."

He blinked, those stupidly pretty lashes fluttering over his stupidly warm eyes. "Fine."

He started to pull back—and it should have felt like relief.

It didn't.

So I grabbed his shirt—fisted it in one hand—and I *dragged* him to me since he walked off the track after the crash.

The moment our mouths collided, it was a goddamn supernova.

His lips were hot and demanding, teeth grazing mine as he kissed me like he'd wanted to for years. Like he was angry about it. Like he was starved.

And I matched him, kiss for kiss. I poured every bit of frustration and tension into it. He groaned against my mouth, deep and low and absolutely wrecked, and it did something dangerous to me.

His hands were everywhere. In my hair, gripping my waist, splaying across my spine like he needed to keep me tethered or he'd fly off the earth. He crowded me against the wall, his thigh sliding between mine, and I *felt* him—every hard, heated inch—and my hips rolled without permission.

I gasped into his mouth. He swallowed it like it was a drug.

His tongue swept into my mouth and I moaned—*God*, I moaned—and I should have been embarrassed but I was too far gone.

I kissed him harder.

We were breathless, devouring. Every graze of his lips, every pull of his fingers in my hair, every grind of our bodies. It was molten. Raw. Unforgiving.

He bit my bottom lip and I gasped again, arching into him.

His mouth found the underside of my jaw and the curve of my throat. I swore I forgot what year it was. My head fell back against the wall with a soft thud, eyes fluttering shut as he trailed kisses up to the shell of my ear.

"Still mad?" he murmured, voice dark and wrecked, breath hot against my skin.

My eyes flashed open. "Yes."

But my fingers were still in his hair, and I was still pulling him back down to me, and we were kissing again like the world was ending.

Because maybe it was.

And maybe I didn't care, as long as I could burn with him.

I broke away just enough to breathe, just enough to grab his wrist and pull.

"Room. Now."

I fumbled with the key card, breath heaving, heart hammering like I'd ran miles. His fingers ghosted over my hips as I swiped it, and the lock clicked. Then we were inside.

And the door slammed shut.

We collided.

There was nothing gentle about the way we kissed. There was no patience, no hesitation, just this frantic ache that had been building for far too long. Every brush of his lips was a question I was too tired to keep dodging. Every press of his body said what neither of us had dared to speak out loud.

It was all hands and mouths and moans. He backed me against the wall again, our bodies crashing like waves. His hands gripped my thighs like he was memorizing the shape of me. I hitched one leg around his waist, dragging him closer, and the groan he let out was *filthy*.

"Christ, Nicola—" he growled, mouth hot at my neck, biting just enough to make me gasp.

"You talk too much," I breathed, yanking his shirt up, desperate to feel skin. My nails dragged over his abs, and he shuddered.

He grabbed my jaw and kissed me like he wanted to *own* my mouth. His tongue tangled with mine, deep and slick and desperate, like we were trying to crawl inside each other.

We stumbled toward the bed, tearing at clothes, hands frantic. My top went first. Then his shirt. Then my bra was sliding down my arms and his mouth was *everywhere*—my collarbone, the swell of my breast, down my stomach. He was worshipping, devouring, like he'd been waiting to do this forever and now that he had me, he wouldn't waste a second.

"You're unreal," he murmured against my skin, voice hoarse and reverent. "Fucking dream girl, aren't you?"

I yanked his face back up to mine and kissed him like a woman starved.

When he finally pressed his hips into mine, when I felt the thick, heavy line of him against me, I lost every last coherent thought.

We grinded together, mouths clashing, bodies moving in sync like we'd always known how to do this. His name fell from my lips like a prayer, and he groaned like it was the first time he'd heard it.

"I want you," I whispered, raw and honest, voice trembling.

He stilled, his forehead pressed to mine. "You have me."

And then he kissed me again, slow this time, deep, a promise in every movement.

His hands slid down, gripping the back of my thighs, dragging me flush against him. The friction was brutal and *perfect*, sparks licking up my spine, my fingers digging into his back as I arched into him.

This wasn't careful.

This was wildfire.

His touch felt like it too, memorizing me, pinning my hands against the wall when I tried to take control, making heat spread throughout me.

*I hate him.*

*I hate him.*

*I hate him.*

I hated the way he looked at me like he knew exactly what I

was thinking. The way he smirked when I got flustered. The way his voice dipped when he used my name like it was a sin.

And right now, I hated the way I couldn't stop staring at his mouth.

"You done glaring at me like you want to kill me," Matteo asked, stepping in closer, "or are you still convincing yourself you don't want to fuck me?"

My laugh came out sharp, mocking. "You think you're irresistible, don't you?"

He tilted his head, the corner of his mouth lifting like he already knew the answer. "Not irresistible. Just inevitable."

His hold on my hands loosened, giving me the option to leave, to end it here. I should've backed up, put space, told him this was a bad idea and we shouldn't do this again. But I *did* want to do this again. Again and again. I ignored that small part of me, the voice in the back of my head screaming at me, knowing I would get hurt just like every time before.

Instead, I shoved him.

He didn't budge. His chest was firm beneath my hands, hot. I could feel his breath on my cheek, ragged like mine.

"You drive me insane," I hissed.

"Likewise," he muttered—and then he kissed me.

Hard.

His mouth was on mine before I could take another breath, and it was everything I didn't know I'd been craving. Rough. Desperate. A collision more than a kiss. My fingers clawed at his shoulders as his hands slid under my breast, a teasing sweep. His palms felt like fire with every brush against my skin.

I gasped into his mouth and he took advantage, deepening the kiss, tongue sliding against mine with a hunger that sent sparks down my spine.

"Fuck," he growled against my lips. "You like this." Another kiss. "And you're all mine."

I bit down on his lower lip in answer, hard enough to make

him groan, and pulled him with me as I stumbled backward, toward the bed, the wall—I didn't care where, just somewhere I could feel all of him. I felt drunk on his words. Parts of my brain were firing off warnings at him using the term '*mine*,' but somehow it was also the hottest thing I had ever heard. It seemed like something to analyze later, so I kept getting lost in his kisses, letting myself get drunk on them.

We crashed into the wall.

He pressed me against it, his thigh between mine, his hands mapping every inch of skin he could find. I was burning, unraveling, desperate and wild and—

"You're such an asshole," I whispered as he trailed kisses down my neck.

"You say that," he murmured, mouth brushing the swell of my breast, "but you're not telling me to stop."

I wasn't. I couldn't. My hands were already under his shirt, nails dragging down his spine, and the sound he made—low, guttural, wrecked—was addictive.

"Shut up and get on the bed," I snapped.

His eyes flashed, dark with something dangerous. "Bossy."

"You love it."

He didn't respond. Just lifted me, carried me like I weighed nothing, and tossed me onto the bed before crawling over me, settling between my thighs like he belonged there.

Maybe he did.

Maybe I hated how right this felt.

Maybe I didn't care anymore.

"Last chance," he murmured, his forehead pressed to mine, voice raw. "Tell me to stop."

I wrapped my legs around his waist and pulled him down, lips brushing his. "Don't you fucking dare." I watched him let go at that moment. His eyes darkened, lust clouding my own vision the same.

I didn't recognize the man above me.

Not like this.

This wasn't Matteo DeLuca—the charming, cocky flirt who grinned at press conferences and cracked jokes even under pressure. This wasn't the man who teased me mercilessly in hotel lobbies or poked fun at the way I double-checked every schedule.

This Matteo—his body heavy between my thighs, voice gravel-thick with hunger, eyes black with need—was *feral*.

He'd stripped me bare with the efficiency of someone who'd imagined this more than once. The moment his mouth hit my neck again, I arched off the bed, grasping at the sheets.

"Touch me," I whispered, breath catching as his hand slid up my thigh.

"Already am, Princess," he murmured, lips brushing my collarbone. "But if you want my fingers inside you, say it."

I blinked up at him, stunned at the shift in his voice—deeper, darker. Every trace of his usual playful sarcasm was gone, replaced with heat that made my stomach clench.

"Say it," he said again, mouth ghosting over my breast. "Use that smart mouth for something other than arguing."

My jaw tightened. Of course he'd push me, even now. But god, he was so close, and my whole body was pulsing, desperate.

"I want your fingers inside me," I said through gritted teeth.

His grin was slow, filthy. "That's my girl."

The praise landed low in my belly like lightning. Before I could react, his fingers slid through my slick folds, teasing, testing.

"Fuck," he muttered, kissing the swell of my breast. "You're soaked for me, Princess. All this from one kiss?"

I hated how smug he sounded. I hated that he was right.

He slid a finger in, then another, curling them expertly as his thumb circled my clit with maddening precision. My hips jerked.

"Stay still," he ordered, and the sharpness in his voice nearly undid me. "You wanted this. Take it."

I bit my lip so hard I tasted blood. His fingers moved faster, deeper, hitting that perfect spot with every thrust.

"Matteo—" I gasped, clawing at his back.

"What do you need?" he asked roughly. "Tell me."

"You. I need—fuck—*you*."

He withdrew his fingers suddenly, and I whimpered at the loss. But then he was undoing his belt, and my breath hitched.

"Condom?" he asked.

"Mmhm, we...uh, yeah, we should," I stuttered on the words, trying to make good decisions under this high of pleasure ripping through me. Matteo hurried himself away to get a condom, then he began ripping off the edge of the foil. I pulled the condom out, letting my eyes drop to him, watching him and his own want clear before me. I rolled the condom on with slow movements, letting my eyes drift back up toward him. He let out a strangled groan.

Once the condom was on, he didn't tease, didn't stall. He dragged my legs apart and slid into me in one slow, devastating thrust.

My back arched off the bed. "Holy shit—"

He began to move—deep, punishing thrusts that left me gasping. Every stroke was precise, relentless. His mouth was on my jaw, my throat, murmuring filth into my skin like prayer.

"You love it when I take control, don't you?" he growled.

"God—" I choked out, nails digging into his shoulders. "You're such an asshole."

He just smirked. "And you're dripping for me. You gonna come on my cock like this?"

I was close—too close. He could tell.

He reached down, thumb circling my clit again, merciless.

"That's it," he whispered. "Come for me, baby. Be my good girl."

And I did.

My orgasm slammed into me like a wave, sharp and shattering. I cried out his name, legs trembling, every nerve on fire.

He kept moving, chasing his own release, and with a ragged groan, he buried his face in my neck as he came.

For a moment, we just breathed.

Sweaty. Shaking. Tangled in each other like something inevitable.

He kissed my jaw, gentler now, like he hadn't just ruined me. "You okay?"

I nodded, dazed. "You're not nearly as annoying when you're shutting me up with orgasms."

He laughed, boyish and breathless. "Don't tempt me to make it a habit."

I rolled my eyes, already sore and already wanting more.

***

I should've known better.

We were supposed to be *cleaning up*. Just rinsing off the sweat, the sex, the mistake. But then Matteo pressed me against the cold tile wall with that now-familiar glint in his eyes—hungry and dangerous and way too pleased with himself—and I knew we were fucked.

Again.

"Just once more," he said, voice a low rasp in my ear. "Just to get it out of our system."

I was already breathless, already arching into him.

"This is a terrible idea," I muttered, palms flattening against the slick tile as the hot water poured over both of us. My skin was flushed, oversensitive, my thighs still trembling from before.

"Yup." He kissed my neck, then bit gently. "So don't think."

His hands were on my waist before I could reply, dragging me back against him. I felt how hard he was again—already. The bastard had stamina like a fucking god. He pressed himself between my thighs, one hand sliding down my front with an obscene kind of confidence.

I hissed, hips bucking back against him.

"I've been dreaming of this since that night after the gala," he said, like we hadn't just been tangled up ten minutes ago. "This perfect, bossy mouth. These fucking hips." His fingers slid lower. "This wet pussy."

"Matteo—"

"It's all I see when I close my eyes." His hand clamped over my hip. "Every fucking night, then you wear those damn heels and walk around the paddock like you own the place. So fucking sexy, baby."

And then he was sliding inside me, slow and deep, like he had all the time in the world to drive me completely insane.

I gasped, forehead hitting the tile.

"Fuck," I whispered, voice breaking. "You feel—God—even better than before."

"You feel so good," he growled, thrusting hard enough to make me cry out. "Like your body *knows* who you belong to now."

I would've argued if I could form a single coherent thought.

But all I could do was *feel*. Him. The water. The slippery, filthy sound of our bodies meeting again and again as he fucked me into the wall like he was trying to erase the space between us.

"You keep clenching around me, baby," he murmured into my ear. "You close like that again, I won't last."

"Then don't—don't hold back—"

He didn't.

His rhythm changed, rougher now, each thrust slamming me against the cold tile with a slap. His hand slipped between my legs, fingers finding my clit again and circling in a tortuous pace.

"Come again," he ordered. "I want to feel you fall apart."

My knees nearly gave out.

"Say it," he growled. "Tell me who's fucking you."

"You—*you are*—" I gasped, crying out as the heat coiled in my stomach snapped.

I shattered around him, sobbing his name, and that was all it took. Matteo groaned deep in his throat, slamming into me once, twice more before he spilled inside me with a ragged curse. He collapsed forward, both of us barely staying upright under the stream of water. For a long, breathless second, we didn't move.

Then he laughed softly, brushing my wet hair from my face.

"Feel better?" he asked, voice smug.

"I hate you."

"Debatable."

"Shut up."

He kissed my temple.

# 11

# MATTEO

*I* slipped out of Nicola's room in the afternoon. Her sheets still smelled like us—salted skin and sweat, and her perfume that I was starting to associate with sin. With addiction.

I left her sleeping, tangled up and flushed, like something I didn't deserve to touch in the daylight.

The hallway was quiet, and I moved like a thief. Because that's what this was, wasn't it? Stealing moments. Stealing touches. Kisses. Time. The day passed like that: a workout did nothing to clear my head, I ate dinner alone in my room, too stuck in my head about wanting to walk across the hall to Nicola's room. By the time the moon was high in the sky, I stared blankly at the ceiling, sleep evading me.

I should've started packing, done anything productive at all, but I just sat there in a trance. We had a flight to Portofino in four hours. But instead, I stared at my suitcase like it might bite me and tried to pack avoiding the thudding in my chest.

Every time I looked at my hands, I could still see them on her —bruising her hips, threading through her hair, holding her down while she screamed my name. She was fire and ice, and every single thing I wasn't supposed to want.

But fuck, I *wanted* her.

I threw off the covers, giving up on sleep and began packing up my things around the room. I was halfway through folding a shirt I definitely wasn't going to wear when the knock came.

Three soft taps.

Not urgent. Not impatient. But deliberate.

Nicola stood in the hallway in nothing but a coat—open at the front, revealing midnight-blue lace and sheer panels that made my throat go dry. Her hair was tousled. Lips swollen. Her expression? Dangerous.

"Nic—" My voice caught. I swallowed it down. "What're you doing?"

She tilted her head, eyes raking over me like she owned every inch. "I couldn't sleep."

My hand gripped the doorknob like it might anchor me.

She stepped inside without waiting for permission, brushing past me, and dropped the coat.

I nearly dropped to my knees.

"Thought you said last time was the last time," I managed, voice rough.

She turned, that defiant tilt to her chin softening just a little. "Well," she said, walking toward me with slow, sinful steps, "What's *one more*?"

I didn't move. I didn't breathe.

"In the morning," she added, right in front of me now, "It never happened."

That wrecked me.

Because I wanted it to count. I wanted *her* to count.

But I also wanted her so fucking badly it made my teeth ache.

So I nodded once. Shoved it all down—every stupid feeling, every flash of hope—and buried it under the heat rising between us again.

"You're playing a dangerous game," I whispered, gripping her hips.

She leaned up, brushing her lips over mine, featherlight. "Then play with me, DeLuca."

The morning sun felt like judgment.

Nicola was already halfway dressed when I woke up. Her back was to me, one hand braced against the dresser like she needed it to breathe.

I didn't say anything, just watched her. I knew the exact moment she put the walls back up. I could feel it—like the air in the room changed temperature. She didn't look at me when she said it.

"This can't happen again."

Four words. Soft but lethal.

I sat up slowly, the sheet pooling around my waist. "Right," I said, forcing my voice to sound casual, light. Like I hadn't just memorized the sound of her moans or kissed her like I'd die without her.

"I didn't mean to sleep over. This isn't anything, just sex, but that was the last time."

My jaw clenched. "Funny, you didn't seem too regretful when you were coming on my—"

"Don't," her voice cracked like a whip.

She turned then, and yeah, her face was composed—but her eyes weren't. They flickered like candlelight about to go out.

"I mean it, Matteo."

I nodded. What else could I do? Beg?

"Cool. All good," I said, throwing on a smirk like it was armor as she gathered her things. Nicola harshly pulled on her shirt that laid across a chair and her coat. A shirt that happened to be mine, making my smirk grow. "See you on the plane."

"Yeah." She hesitated for half a breath too long. "See you."

And then she left.

And I sat there like an idiot in a bed that still smelled like her, smiling to myself because she stole my shirt.

The ride to the airport was a blur. Lucia talked, Gianna played with her toys, someone spilled coffee, and the sky looked like it might rain. I smiled and joked like I always did. Laughed at my own dumb stories, kept the mood up.

Because if I didn't, I might've broken.

Nicola didn't ride with us, instead meeting us at the tarmac in her own private car.

When we boarded the plane, I let Alex drag me into the back half of the cabin. I didn't ask where she was sitting. I already knew —front row, next to my sister.

Far away. Where it was safe.

Where she didn't have to look at me and remember what she'd said. What I still *felt*.

I pressed my forehead to the window, watching the tarmac blur, pretending the ache in my chest was from lack of sleep.

Alex nudged me halfway through takeoff. "You good, mate?"

"Peachy," I said with a grin so wide it hurt. "Just pumped for Portofino. Sun, sea, sin—what more could a man want?"

He gave me a look. One of those, *'I know you're full of shit'* looks. But thankfully, he didn't push.

And I didn't crack.

Not until I caught sight of her—Nicola, leaning her head

against the window a few rows ahead, sunglasses on even though we were inside, pretending to nap.

She looked untouchable. She *was* untouchable.

I forced my eyes away, leaned back, and threw on a pair of headphones. I tried to drown out the memory of her skin under my hands by blasting music. Her voice gasping out my name. Her walking away.

# 12

# NICOLA

*I*t was just sex.

Just *really* good sex.

The kind that made you forget your own name and see constellations behind your eyelids. The kind that made your legs tremble for hours and your throat sore from all the filthy things you moaned without meaning to.

But still. Sex.

I repeated the word like a prayer.

Because it *couldn't* be more. Not with Matteo. Not with the man who made it his life's mission to charm everyone he met and who flashed smiles like currency and never took anything seriously —except maybe racing. And certainly not with someone like *me*. Someone who had everything planned. And that plan did not include a relationship. Dating casually? Good sex? Sure. But a serious relationship? No, thank you.

It was already a mistake. A few mistakes, actually. If I let it become more, I knew it wouldn't stop there.

So I pushed it down. I packed my suitcase, my self-respect, and my emotional whiplash. Then zipped it all up and got on the damn plane.

Portofino was sun-soaked and beautiful. It would've been perfect if everything hadn't immediately started falling apart.

"Where the hell is the car service?" I asked, glaring at my phone like it might suddenly decide to be useful.

Matteo wandered up beside me, wearing a backwards hat, sunglasses, and that dumb, lazy grin that should've been illegal on a man that attractive.

"Maybe they heard you were coming and fled the scene?" he offered with a wink.

I didn't dignify him with a response. Not with the memory of his mouth *still* lingering in too many places on my body.

"We'll rent something," Lucia said, ever the peacemaker. "We'll figure it out."

And we did.

Sort of.

We ended up in a compact rental that looked like it had been born in 2003 and hadn't been cleaned since. Five of us. Luggage piled like a Jenga tower between seats. Elbows in ribs. Knees jammed against dashboards.

And of course, Matteo ended up next to *me*.

Because the universe *loved* a good joke.

I turned sharply when his thigh brushed mine. "Can you not?"

"What?" he said, way too innocent. "My leg's just existing. You're the one taking up all the space with your overpacking."

"Why don't you crawl into the glove compartment then?"

He grinned, infuriatingly unbothered.

Lucia choked on her water. Alexander laughed like it was the funniest thing he'd ever heard.

I shot Matteo a look that could curdle milk. He just smiled wider, resting his arm behind me like he owned the air I breathed.

By the time we got to the hotel I was ready to throw myself into the sea. Lucia and Alexander, however, seemed blitzed out. Maybe if my thoughts would be quiet, I would feel the same.

"Ah, Mr. Wright," the front desk receptionist smiled

apologetically. "We've had a slight issue with the room allocations. Unfortunately, only the Lemoné Villa is available, which is a two bedroom villa. Each room has just one king-sized bed."

"That's fine, we'll make it work," Alexander smiled graciously while alarm bells began going off in my head. Sharing a room with Matteo? Sharing a bed with Matteo? *Fuck me.*

"Excuse me?" I snapped, voice too sharp, too mean. I immediately felt guilty knowing it wasn't the poor receptionist's fault.

Matteo whistled under his breath. "Guess we're bunking together, Nic."

When I heard him call me Nic, shot ice straight through veins. "Don't call me that, and no, we're not sharing a bed," I seethed.

"Well, there's always the floor," Matteo shrugged, "But I'd hate for you to hurt your back."

"Here is the second room key..." the receptionist cleared her throat.

I forced a smile to the woman, then leaned into Matteo. "You are being an unbearable idiot."

"She's with me," Matteo announced and slings an arm around my shoulders. I tensed like he'd poured ice water down my spine.

"I am *not* with you," I hissed.

"Technically," he whispered, mouth way too close to my ear, "You were with me. Multiple times."

My entire body flushed.

Lucia coughed behind us. "We'll, uh, see you two later."

I sent her a '*What the hell*' look and she just shrugged with a soft smile and sent me a thumbs up. I clenched my fists and followed Matteo to the elevator, praying I wouldn't strangle him before the trip was over.

Or worse—let him kiss me again. Because deep down, under all the snark and fury, my body still ached for him. And no matter how hard I tried, I couldn't forget how good it felt to let him ruin me.

"Are you done being moody?" Matteo asked in a surprisingly soft voice.

"And what of it?" I snapped at him, staring at my phone to ignore him and scrolling through work emails with the charity team.

"Hey," his voice was low and soft; it was enough to make me turn and look at him. I wasn't wearing heels, so my head barely reached his chest. His finger hooked my chin and he ever so softly pushed with the pad of his finger to get me to look up at him. I was met with his eyes, all soft and concerned. I hated how my belly flipped at the sight. How he could see past my normal jabs and annoyance.

"What's going on?" His thumb brushed my cheek. I couldn't help but pull away as I felt the hurt radiate off him. We were not in public, we were in a damn elevator, and sometime during the last few weeks, private spaces became where we gravitated toward each other, not away. I didn't have time for feelings or being distracted, not when I was just finding my place in this cutthroat world. Planning a huge fundraising campaign and gala had taken up most of my mental space. And I needed to ask Matteo about doing some promos and if he'd be willing to help out with the media. No driver wanted to do more media, but somewhere deep down I knew if I asked, he would say yes. And yet my anxiety bloomed just thinking about asking.

We walked in silence to the villa. When he unlocked the door and held it open, I was hit with the reality of the one bed conundrum. There it was in all its glory: soft white sheets, a fluffy duvet, and giant pillows. I felt my anger bubble to the surface as I tossed my bag onto the floor and spun to face him. "I'll take the couch."

Matteo raised a brow, leaning against the doorframe like he owned the damn place. "Nic, the couch is a glorified ottoman. We'll share the bed or we'll both wake up with spinal injuries."

"Sounds preferable," I snapped and jabbed a finger at his chest. "If you so much as snore, I'm smothering you with a pillow."

He smirked and leaned in so only I could hear. "If you want to try new things in bed, all you have to do is ask." His hands pulled up as if in defense, one dimple starting to show as he smirked. Then, voice louder, "But don't worry—you'll be too busy dreaming about me to notice.

"Shut up or people will hear you!"

He walked farther into the room, brushing past me on the way to the window. "You know, for someone who says it didn't mean anything, you're really going out of your way to prove it."

My spine straightened. "Don't."

"Don't what?" he asked, not even turning around. "Don't point out that every time I get close, you run? Or that you kiss me like I'm oxygen but look at me like I'm a mistake the second it's over?"

"Because it *was* a mistake!" I snapped, my voice cracking under the weight of my own lie.

Matteo finally turned, his expression softer than I expected. "Nicola."

I closed my eyes, because I hated how my name sounded in his voice.

"I don't do relationships," I said, the words low and brittle. "I don't do real. Real gets messy. Real ends. I've spent too long proving I can hold my own, and I won't blow it all."

He blinked. "So...you *do* have feelings."

"I didn't say that."

"But you didn't *not* say it."

I stared at him, exasperated. "You're impossible."

"And you're scared," he said simply, walking closer. "And that's okay."

My breath hitched. His nearness was dangerous. Warm and grounding and far too tempting.

"I'm not asking you to fall in love with me," he said, voice softer now, more careful. "Just...don't shut the door before we even open it. Let's take this week and forget the rules. No pressure. No expectations. Just...you and me. Vacation time. Exploring time."

I arched my brow. "Exploring time?"

He shrugged with a smirk. "Sunsets. Gelato. Occasional heavy petting. We'll call it research."

A reluctant laugh broke out of me. "You're an idiot."

"But I can be your idiot. At least for the next seven days."

I hesitated. "And then what?"

"We get on the plane, and if you want to pretend none of it happened, I'll let you."

Something tightened in my chest. It wasn't fair how easy he made it sound—how gently he held the very thing I was afraid to name.

Matteo stepped back, like he was giving me space to choose. "But for now," he said, "We're in Portofino. It doesn't count."

I stared at him for a long moment, then slowly exhaled.

"Fine. One week."

A grin spread across his face, all dimples and triumph. "Best non-relationship of your life, I swear."

"Shut up," I muttered, but I was smiling despite myself.

Matteo was still grinning when I walked to my bag and started organizing my clothes into the dresser, pretending to look for something to wear.

"So," he said casually, flopping back onto the bed like he didn't just emotionally unzip me, "What do you think about cliffs?"

I turned slowly. "Cliffs?"

"Yeah," he propped himself up on his elbows. "Rocky things. High up. Over water. Very scenic. Very '*take a picture and make it your phone background*' vibes."

"I thought this week was about relaxing."

He sat up now, eyes sparkling with a boyish enthusiasm I pretended not to find devastatingly charming. "Exactly! What's more relaxing than driving down the coast with the windows down, your hair blowing in the wind, me singing obnoxiously to ABBA—"

"Oh my God."

"—followed by a top-secret lookout point over the cliffs, and then—wait for it—dinner at this tiny family-run trattoria I found online last night?"

"Did Anna find it?" I asked, narrowing my eyes.

"She's the one who found the cliff thing," he conceded. "But *I* picked the restaurant. It's got five stars and exactly twelve tables. Romantic without being too obvious. Rustic charm. You'll pretend not to love it."

I paused, pretending to be unimpressed. "Sounds like a date."

"Wrong," he said, hopping off the bed and heading to the door like a man on a mission. "It's an outing."

"Oh?"

"Yup. Purely platonic, non-committal, cliff-adjacent...outing."

"You're unbelievable."

"Thanks," he said, flashing me a grin that should honestly be illegal. "I'll meet you downstairs in fifteen. Wear something... flowy."

I arched my brow. "Flowy?"

"For the photos, obviously."

"You're assuming I'm coming."

He was already out the door when he called back, "You hate missing out, Moretti. You'll come."

And God help me—I did.

Fifteen minutes later, I found him in the lobby leaning against the rental car, sunglasses on, wind already ruffling his dark hair. He opened the passenger door with a dramatic bow.

"Your chariot awaits, Princess."

I rolled my eyes, but I got in anyway.

Because this was Matteo DeLuca, and he'd crawled under my skin like a disease, and I couldn't seem to say no to him.

The drive wound up the edge of the coastline, sharp turns carved through wildflower-covered hills, the sea glittering below like spilled sapphire. It was all postcard-worthy—annoyingly beautiful, just like everything else in this country.

And then there was Matteo, who was tapping the steering wheel to the beat of a 2000s playlist and belting out lyrics like he was headlining a stadium tour.

"You know," I said dryly, "if this whole Formula One thing falls through, you could always audition for *The Voice*. In another country."

He gasped. "Harsh, Moretti."

"You're off-key."

"I'm emotive," he corrected, flashing me a grin. "That's the difference between karaoke and a performance."

I didn't respond. Mostly because I was distracted by the way the wind tossed his hair, the crinkle of sun in the corners of his eyes, the tanned skin of his forearm resting casually on the wheel.

No. We were *not* going there again.

This wasn't real. It was vacation energy. Temporary. But he was so golden. One night was not enough to get him out of my system, but hey, maybe a week would do the trick.

"You okay over there?" he asked, glancing at me briefly.

"Just wondering when we're supposed to start cliff diving."

"No diving," he promised. "Just views."

A few more turns later, we parked at a small, dusty pull-off. There was nothing around except nature and the occasional hand-painted wooden sign in Italian.

"Are you taking me somewhere to murder me?" I asked, squinting at the path that snaked into a patch of cypress and wild thyme.

"Wouldn't dream of it," he replied, grabbing his backpack and coming around to open my door. "You'd haunt me. Very aggressively."

"You're not wrong."

The trail was narrow and a little steep, the smell of the sea mingling with the warm dust of the hillside. I focused on the uneven ground, not the way Matteo's hand kept brushing mine, not how aware I was of every step that brought us closer to the edge of something bigger.

Finally, the path opened.

And the view *actually* stole my breath.

Cliffs stretched in both directions, plunging into turquoise water. Gulls dipped and cried over waves that crashed in rhythmic power. The sun was low now, spilling molten light across the water. Everything smelled like salt and rosemary and the sea.

"Oh," I whispered, before I could help myself.

"See?" Matteo said softly behind me. "Worth it."

I nodded, barely hearing him over the roar of my own thoughts.

He didn't move closer. But I felt him, a step away. His silence was strange—for him. I snuck a glance at his profile. His jaw was tight. Eyes distant.

"Why did you really bring me here?" I asked, voice quieter than I meant it to be.

He shrugged. "You needed it."

I swallowed. "Needed what?"

"This," his voice dipped. "A moment. A breath. Something just for you."

Something about the way he said it—soft and certain—made something crack in my chest. I exhaled hard, like I was trying to let it out. Whatever *it* was. Whatever it *always* was with him.

"Matteo…"

He finally looked at me, and God, I wished he hadn't. His eyes were so open, too honest. It was the look he gave before saying something that might split me open.

"I know," he said gently. "You don't do feelings. You don't do this."

I stiffened, ready to retreat, to joke, to *cut*.

But he didn't let me.

"But maybe," he continued, voice low and almost tender. "For once, just let yourself enjoy. Let me spoil you."

I blinked at him.

He smiled crookedly. "Vacation, remember?"

"And when it gets messy?"

"Say it was just the heat. Too much sun. One too many glasses of wine. Whatever helps you sleep at night, Moretti."

I didn't answer right away.

Because I was staring at his mouth, at the curve of it when he smiled like that—mischievous and maddening and beautiful. I was realizing I wanted to kiss him, which seemed to be some sort of addiction at this point.

"I'm not climbing into bed with you again just because you start showing me sunsets and plying me with food," I blatantly lied.

He stepped just a fraction closer, his voice nearly a whisper. "I never said anything about a bed, but good to know where your mind is."

The air between us hummed. We stayed like that until the sun dipped beneath the horizon, pretending we were not aching, pretending we weren't dissenting into dangerous territory. And yet I felt my heart relax, in this fantasy bubble. Maybe I could just lean into it.

"I wanted to ask you something," I said after a while, wrapping my arms around myself to calm the nerves.

"Anything," Matteo replied seriously.

"I've been working on this charity campaign for the Foundation," I started. I felt his eyes on me, and the attention made goosebumps riddle my arms. "I think it would help to have some specific promo with the drivers. I was wondering if you'd be willing to tack on some with your other media days when we're back. The admins can film behind the scenes and maybe ask some questions in more of a vlog setup so it feels more personal. I'm trying to team up with local charities along each race stop till the end of the season. I know it's a lot to ask, but..."

"Of course I will." There it was, the way I knew he would agree immediately in his casual shrug kind of way. Matteo lived and breathed Moretti Racing. The camera loved him, the fans loved him. He did more media than most of the drivers by far, so asking to add on another felt selfish. But I found myself feeling relieved that he agreed so fast. "Send me the details and I'll make it work. Maybe we can visit one of the charities in person too."

I stared at him in awe. "Um, yeah, wow that would be amazing. Are you sure?"

"Absolutely."

We talked about the charities I was focusing on, how I wanted to donate to local food banks, shelters for women and children, and a few animal rescues. Matteo listened diligently, asking follow-up questions and even offering some ideas like a recorded Q&A while he was at the shelter with the puppies or kittens that the fans would no doubt share far and wide. It was a great idea, so great that I was typing furiously on my phone, noting it all down.

Matteo nudged my shoulder, pulling me from my notes app. "Hungry?"

"Famished."

The trattoria was tucked into the side of a hill, with stone walls that glowed gold in the early evening light and faded blue shutters that looked like they'd survived a hundred summers. The kind of place that smelled like garlic, grilled fish, and magic.

"I can't believe this place is real," I murmured, half to myself as we climbed the crooked stone steps.

Matteo grinned beside me. "You're welcome."

The hostess greeted us in rapid Italian, and of course, Matteo charmed her in three sentences and a crooked smile. Suddenly, we were led to a candlelit table on a tiny terrace that overlooked the sea. The tablecloth fluttered in the breeze, a tiny vase of wildflowers in the center. The only table on the secluded terrace. It was all very *romantic.*

Which was not helping.

At all.

"Seriously?" I hissed as we sat down. "You brought me to an actual date location."

"This isn't a date," he shrugged, handing me a menu, "It's vacation."

"That's your answer to everything now?"

He leaned back in his chair, lazy and golden in the light. "You like the view, admit it."

I pretended to be staring at the menu. "It's fine."

"I saw your face. You were about to cry when that lady offered you focaccia and wine"

"Focaccia and wine is really all I need to survive actually."

He tipped his head with a dimpled smile. "Noted."

We ordered grilled calamari, truffle pasta, and wine. By the time the food arrived, the sun had fully set, replaced by the soft hum of string lights above our heads and distant waves below.

Matteo forked a piece of his pasta and reached across the table. "Try this."

"I have my own food."

"It's better."

"DeLuca—"

"Say *ah*, Moretti."

He was smirking. Teasing. And for some reason, I let him feed me. Because I was fucking weak. And the pasta melted on my tongue, rich and earthy and unfairly good.

"Well?"

I rolled my eyes. "Fine. You win. It's amazing."

"I always win," he said, eyes darkening slightly as he watched me chew.

That look sent heat pooling low in my stomach. I took a long sip of wine.

The breeze picked up again, tugging at a loose strand of hair, and he reached out before I could stop him, brushing it back behind my ear. His fingers trailed for a second too long across my cheek.

I cleared my throat and looked away. "You said something about no pressure."

He leaned in, voice low and smooth. "No pressure at all, Princess. I'm just sitting here. Existing."

"You exist very annoyingly."

He grinned. "And yet you're still here."

I was halfway through pretending I was unaffected when music drifted from inside the restaurant—a slow, lilting tune played by a small trio in the corner courtyard.

Matteo stood and held out his hand.

"No," I said immediately.

"Come on. Just one dance."

"I don't dance."

"You danced at the gala."

"That was different. There was tequila involved."

He wiggled his fingers. "I'll buy you tequila after."

I didn't know why I took his hand. Maybe it was the wine. Or the wind. Or the fact that I was so tired of fighting whatever this was.

He pulled me into the courtyard, just one of a handful of couples slow-dancing under the stars. The music was soft, dreamy. Matteo moved easily, one hand at my waist, the other holding mine.

"You're terrible at letting go," he murmured.

"I'm dancing with you, aren't I?"

"You're *enduring* dancing with me. It's different."

"You're so full of yourself."

"I'm full of wine and calamari and the sight of you in that sundress, actually."

"Don't push your luck, DeLuca."

He laughed, low and warm, and I hated how much I loved the sound.

We swayed like that for a long time, the stars twinkling above us under the dim light of the terrace. I wanted to stay in the moment, wrap myself up in it. When he pulled me just a little closer, I rested my cheek against his shoulder and let myself imagine: what would it be like if this *was* real?

If it wasn't just vacation.

But the song ended. And I stepped back before he could say anything.

"Come on," I said, smoothing my dress, trying to find my footing again. "You promised me tequila."

He watched me like he saw *everything*. Then smiled.

"Let's go find you a bottle."

# MATTEO

urned out, tequila was not so easy to come by in a sleepy coastal town well past midnight.

"I told you it was a long shot," Nicola muttered as we wandered down a cobbled side street, lit by string lights and the occasional flickering lantern. She kicked a pebble and sighed dramatically. "No tequila. What a tragedy."

"You doubt my resourcefulness," I shook my head in a low laugh.

"I doubt your sanity."

"Same thing," I grinned, then pointed toward a small shop window glowing in the distance.

"Look. Open late."

She gave me a skeptical look, but followed.

Fifteen minutes later, we were walking out with two bottles of wine, a sleeve of biscotti, and a bag of the kind of overpriced chips that only taste good at 2:00 a.m. on vacation.

"No tequila," she said smugly.

"Shut up and open the wine."

We wandered until we found a hidden hilltop overlook, a crumbling stone wall, and a view that could make a poet out of a cynic. Below us, the sea glowed dark blue and endless, the stars bright enough to see your whole past and maybe your future too. Nicola hopped up on the low wall and sat cross-legged, her sundress fluttering in the breeze.

We drank straight from the bottle, passing it back and forth between bites of cookies and chips, our knees bumping, shoulders brushing, everything soft and *close*.

I glanced at her, lit in moonlight, wild hair and sharp tongue, and the kind of eyes that look like they *dared* you to get too close. Rather than her usual pin straight hair and red lips, she was devoid of bright lipstick tonight, and her hair was down and curly, falling off her shoulders in the light breeze. It was so easy to get lost in trying to memorize every inch of Nicola. I could spend a lifetime doing it, and it would be a worthwhile life. But the crashing waves made me turn back to the sea.

"Look," I said, pointing, "There. See that stone archway down there?"

She squinted. "Near the tree?"

"There's a stairwell. It goes all the way down to the beach."

She followed my line of sight, catching on fast.

I let the grin spread, slow and dangerous. "Wanna go swimming?"

"At"—she checked her phone—"two forty-two in the morning?"

"It's technically tomorrow now. A brand-new day. Anything's possible."

"That sounds like something you read off a Pinterest quote board."

"Don't knock my Pinterest boards" I nudged her foot with mine. "Come on. Skinny dip. It'll be fun."

"Have you met me?"

"Mmhm, becoming rather a big fan."

She rolled her eyes, but I saw the way her lips twitched,

betraying the smile she didn't want to give me. I hopped off the wall and offered her my hand.

"This is such a bad idea," she muttered, but she took it anyway.

We tiptoed down the steps, trying not to spill the wine or wake up any sleeping Portofinese residents. The stairwell was narrow and steep, carved into the side of the cliff, and by the time we reached the bottom, the soft rush of the water surrounded us.

It was quiet. Just the stars above, the sea stretching endlessly, and us.

Nicola toed off her sandals and hesitated.

"What?" I asked, already tugging off my shirt, "You scared?"

"No," she scoffed, peeling off her dress and folding it neatly over a rock, "I just don't trust you not to drown and make me drag your dumb body back to shore."

"I'm a great swimmer for your information, Moretti."

"I bet you dog paddle."

She turned her back to me and walked into the waves in just her black lace underwear, moonlight catching the water clinging to her skin. I swore I forgot how to breathe.

I stripped and followed her in, the water frigid and biting until we were both waist-deep, then chest-deep, floating side by side.

"This was a good idea," she admitted, her voice softer now, almost reluctant.

"Told you."

The silence stretched comfortably between us, punctuated only by the gentle lapping of waves.

"When did you get your tattoo?" she asked. I had a pair of swallows on my thigh, usually under clothing and unseen, but Nicola picked up on most things. I was slowly realizing she was rather perceptive.

"Few years ago now. There's this old church a town over from the vineyard. My parents got married there, same as my grandparents and great grandparents. Swallows were around almost every time we visited. My grandfather didn't like them much, but my grandmother did. She said life should be lived loudly and that she liked that they found homes where they could. They were resilient. I always wanted a tattoo too, so figured it should be the first." I was staring at the stars as I talked, floating on my back.

"I like it," she said quietly. I felt like I could fucking soar at the casual compliment. She looked so damn beautiful under the moonlight it was almost painful. Her cheeks were red from the chill. I looked at the mole on her left temple. I remembered reading once that moles and freckles were reminiscent of long-lost loves, of a spot where they were kissed over and over again and that after however many lives were lived, it left a permanent reminder. I liked that theory. I wanted to kiss her temple, wanted to kiss her forehead, and her nose and her lips. It took up most of my thoughts these days.

Then she bumped her shoulder into mine. "You're staring."

"You're stunning," I admitted in a breathy whisper, unable to cover it with a line or make it less serious. Because she was the most stunning woman here in the sea under the moonlight.

She turned toward me slowly. "You're drunk."

"I'm not. Not on wine, anyway." She burst out laughing first and I was quick to follow. She splashed water at me before I pulled her close to me. Her arms wrapped around my neck as if in response. Her eyes darkened, pupils wide in the moonlight, and I felt the shift in the air. Like everything was tipping.

"Matteo—"

"I know. But it's just vacation; it doesn't count," I reassured her with the words I knew she wanted to hear.

"It doesn't," she whispered, even as she floated closer.

I let my fingers brush her waist, slowly trailing up to her bra line, teasing along the wire.

She breathed in sharply but didn't pull away.

Our lips met, and it was familiar and warm against the cool water around us. The kiss was slow at first—wet, soft, teasing—

until she grabbed my jaw with both hands and pulled me deeper. And I went willingly, hungrily.

Her body pressed against mine, slick from the water, our mouths moving like a storm building at sea, dangerous and inevitable.

I pushed her gently against a flat rock, kissing down her neck, tasting salt and her skin and the wine we shared like a secret.

She gasped as I whispered against her mouth, "Vacation, right?"

She kissed me back hard enough to bruise, and I felt myself fall even more.

I woke up slow, tangled in hotel sheets that still smelled like her.

The morning sun bled through the sheer curtains and casted pale golden light across the bed. Nicola was still asleep beside me, half on her stomach, one leg stretched out over the cool linen. Her hair was a mess across the pillow, and her lips were parted just enough to make my chest twist.

She looked soft like this. Peaceful, even.

Like the warzone we usually were in didn't exist between us. Like we hadn't spent the last year arguing across race paddocks and pretending we didn't watch each other when the other wasn't looking. *God, I could wake up like this for the rest of my life.*

I let myself imagine it—for one selfish minute.

That she was mine.

That this was real.

But then she shifted in her sleep, murmured something unintelligible, and the spell snapped. I was reminded exactly where we were. *Portofino.* The rulebook echoing in my head: *It doesn't count.* That's what we agreed on. This vacation was a bubble, a break, not real life.

I slipped out of bed carefully, grabbed my hoodie and wallet, and left the room as quietly as I could and headed toward the main part of the hotel past the private villas. The hotel hallways were quiet, the early morning light pouring through the tall arched windows. I followed the scent of fresh coffee down to the ground floor lounge, where a few early risers were grabbing breakfast from the café bar.

And of course, Alexander was already there.

"Morning," he said, calm and polished even in a T-shirt and linen shorts. He was fixing up two coffees on a tray. "You're up early."

"Could say the same to you," I replied, heading straight to the espresso machine. "Let me guess—coffee delivery for Lucia?"

He didn't answer right away, just added a spoon of sugar to one of the cups like he knew exactly how she took it.

I smirked. "Boyfriend of the year. Bold strategy."

"She deserves it," he said simply.

Something about the way he said it—steady, no hesitation— made my chest ache a little. He meant it. Lucia had grounded him in a way I never expected to see. He looked *happy.*

"I've never seen her like this," I admitted. "She used to be... always on edge. Distrusting."

"She still doesn't trust half the people around her," Alex said, finally looking at me, "But she trusts me. And I don't take that for granted."

I nodded slowly. "You make her better."

"She makes me better."

And damn, if that didn't hit harder than I expected it to.

Before I could say anything else, he slid a juice box onto the tray and raised an eyebrow at me. "Gianna wants a pool day. Said to meet her down there or she'll start without us."

I laughed. "She's not even three and already planning social events?"

"She demanded snacks and floaties," he deadpanned, "I'm just the delivery guy."

"She gets it from *you*, I'm sure. I'll see you down there," I said, grabbing a coffee to-go. "Tell my girl her favorite person is on the way."

"She said Monty's her favorite," Alexander called as I walked off.

"Rude."

I headed back to the elevators, taking the long way through the lobby, trying to shake the image of Nicola asleep in that bed,the mess of us from last night still clung to my skin.

# NICOLA

The next morning arrived in slivers of gold through gauzy white curtains. The scent of salt and citrus drifted in from the open balcony doors, the sound of distant waves lapping the shore. I stretched out in bed, my limbs heavy with that soft, glowy exhaustion only wine, sea air, and kissing someone you're definitely not supposed to be kissing could cause.

Matteo wasn't there.

I told myself that was a good thing.

Still, the imprint of him was everywhere. His laugh echoed faintly in my head. My skin still tingled from the memory of his hands on me, the way he looked at me like I was something wild and sacred and entirely his.

I brushed it off, grabbed a towel, and made my way downstairs sporting a loose dress over a bikini after Lucia texted me that it was a designated pool day.

By the pool, it was already a picture of calm chaos. Gianna's squeals echoed as she splashed in the shallow end, bright pink floaties on her arms and curls flying everywhere. Lucia sat perched on a lounger in oversized sunglasses and a floppy sunhat, flipping through a book while keeping one eye on her daughter. Alexander was sitting on the ledge of the pool with Gianna, smiling at her.

"Nicola!" Gianna shrieked when she saw me, paddling over like a tiny hurricane. "Come swim!"

I smiled. "Only if you promise not to splash me."

"Nope," she said, then walked up the steps only to immediately jump in, with a splash to my legs.

Lucia snorted behind her book. "You walked into that one."

I shrugged and peeled off my robe, slipping into a lounge chair beside her. "I was hoping to ease into the day, not get attacked by a mermaid." I stuck out my tongue to Gianna who giggled and dipped back under the water.

"You look suspiciously happy," she said, peering at me over her sunglasses, eyebrows high.

I made a noncommittal noise. "Wine and sea air. Works wonders."

I glanced across the pool just as Matteo appeared, hair damp, T-shirt clinging to him, sunglasses pushed up into his curls. He was carrying a tray of fresh juices and pastries from the kitchen, whistling softly like it was the most natural thing in the world to be that annoyingly attractive and cheerful in the morning.

He met my eyes, giving me a lopsided grin.

I looked away, heart thudding like a traitor.

"Breakfast delivery," he announced, setting the tray down between the chairs. "One orange juice, one mystery smoothie, and about fourteen pastries."

Alexander eyed the tray. "Thanks, Mate!"

Gianna climbed out of the pool, soaking wet, and beelined straight for Matteo, who caught her without flinching.

"I swam like a fish," she announced proudly.

"You did," he agreed. "Like a very loud, splashy fish."

He wrapped a towel around her and ruffled her hair, and something in my chest squeezed.

Matteo lifted his head, brows raising, perceptive eyes meeting mine. "You okay, Moretti?"

"I'm good," I said quickly, my heart rate picking up. It was like he could sense something was off even while immersed in Gianna Land. I pushed out a smile, trying to brush it off. I could feel his gaze on me as I pulled out a book and leaned back on the chaise lounge.

Alexander and Matteo were poolside with Gianna who was showing them her pool tricks which consisted of spinning in her floaties. I smiled to myself watching them adore Gianna.

Lucia pushed up her sunglasses, peering over at me. "You alright?" she asked casually, flipping a page in her book.

"Mm," I sipped. "Jet lag."

Lucia snorted. "We've been in Italy for over a day."

"Emotional jet lag."

She side-eyed me. "Right."

A deep laugh grabbed my attention, shifting my eyes under my oversized sunglasses to Matteo. Like there was some sort of gravitational pull there. His hair was a mess, getting curly with its length, chest bare, sunglasses perched on his nose. He had Gia in one arm and a juice box in the other, doing a dramatic reenactment of her flying around. She was giggling so hard she nearly fell over.

My heart did that annoying little skip thing again, and I already knew Lucia had caught me staring.

"So," Lucia said slowly, "What's going on with you and my brother?"

I nearly choked on my drink. But I really shouldn't have been surprised at my friend's bluntness.

"What?" I replied, trying not to sound guilty immediately.

She shrugged. "You've been weird. He's been weird. I'm not blind."

"I'm not weird."

"You *just* said you had emotional jet lag."

"Which is a real thing," I argued. "Look it up."

Lucia just lifted her brow and waited.

"I know what you probably think..." I said finally, careful not to look over at Matteo. "But nothing real is going on. Your brother is—" I paused, searching.

"Infuriating?" she offered helpfully.

"Yes. Exactly."

Lucia took a long sip of her drink, watching me over the rim. "You two bicker like an old married couple."

"Gross," I muttered. "Don't you start romanticizing. We're just fundamentally incompatible."

"Sure."

"And he's your brother."

"And?"

"And I'm not looking for anything."

Lucia turned her attention back to her book, but there was a smirk tugging at the corner of her mouth that made me want to dunk her in the pool.

"He makes you laugh," she said, not looking up.

"That's just his whole thing. He jokes. He flirts. It's harmless."

Lucia hummed. "Nothing about the way he looks at you seems harmless."

I went still, heartbeat stuttering, and tried to let out a fake laugh. "You're imagining things."

"Hmm," she hummed to herself with a smirk.

I took another long sip of my drink, willing the bubbles to settle the war going on inside me. This thing with Matteo—it was nothing. Temporary. *'Burn it out of our systems'* kind of thing.

But the way my body reacted when I saw him? The way he looked at me when no one else was paying attention? The way I *felt* when I was around him?

Not. Nothing.

Lucia finally looked over, sunglasses sliding down her nose. "Just...be careful, okay?"

I offered her a dry smile. "When am I *not* careful?"

Lucia laughed, tipping her glass toward me in a silent toast. Before I could sip again, a splash of water slapped against our loungers, soaking the bottom half of my dress.

I jolted upright. "What the—?"

That was no tiny splash from Gianna.

I glanced toward the pool just as water settled from a large cannonball. My swim cover dress clung to my thighs, soaked and wrinkled. With a resigned sigh, I stood and pulled the damp fabric over my head, revealing the swimsuit beneath.

I felt it before I saw it—heat on the back of my neck. A weighty stare that dripped down my spine like honey.

I lifted my gaze slowly.

Matteo was in the pool, water lapping at his waist, skin glistening in the sun. His curls were slicked back, droplets tracing the lines of his abs. A hand pushing into his hair, smoothing back the wet strands in what felt like slow motion. But it was his eyes that hit me hardest.

Locked on me.

My pulse skipped. I forced myself to roll my eyes and turned back toward Lucia like his gaze didn't just ignite a full-body flush.

"Your brother is a menace," I muttered.

Lucia hummed knowingly into her straw. "Tell me something I don't know."

# 15

## MATTEO

$\mathcal{N}$icola Moretti was a knockout.

Not that it was new information, actually something that played over and over again in my head every time I saw her. And yet, it still hit me like a punch every damn time, made my world spin.

One second, I was horsing around with Gia in the shallow end, trying to convince her to let go of the pool noodle and race me to the edge. I had jumped into the pool to earn another giggle, and it worked. The next, I looked up and she was there—standing at the edge of the chaise lounge chair, peeling off that soaked little cover-up.

And *fuck*. It took everything in me not to drop my jaw like a cartoon character. Her bikini was a shade of blue that made me wonder how I could convince her to wear that color every damn day. Made me think blue was my new favorite color. Every inch of her was golden and glowing in the late morning sun, legs endless, curves carved like art, eyes hidden behind those oversized sunglasses that did absolutely nothing to hide her attitude. Or the flush crawling up her neck.

She knew I was watching.

She always knew.

And instead of pretending not to notice like a normal person, I just stood there in the pool like an idiot, water swirling around my waist, staring like I'd never seen a woman in a swimsuit before. She finally turned her head toward me, giving me a perfectly unimpressed look. One brow arched above her sunglasses. My brain short-circuited.

I smirked, mostly to cover how wrecked I already felt. "You trying to kill someone, Moretti?"

She rolled her eyes, like I was being dramatic. "It's a bikini, Matteo. Grow up."

Yeah, sure. Just a bikini.

And I was just a guy slowly drowning in the deep end of *'she's not yours, idiot.'*

I leaned back against the pool edge, stretching my arms out along the warm tile, keeping my gaze shamelessly fixed on her as she dropped back into her lounger like she didn't just set my bloodstream on fire.

"Tell your brother to keep his eyes to himself," she muttered to Lucia loud enough for me to hear, not bothering to glance my way again.

Lucia just snorted. "He was born incapable of that."

The rest of the afternoon at the pool was *trouble*. And by trouble, I meant Nicola Moretti reclining across from me in that blue bikini, hair now curly from the water and piled on top of her head in one of those scrunchies my sister always had on hand, sunglasses shielding her eyes so I couldn't tell if she was looking at me, but I felt it. Every damn time.

She played it cool. Acted like I wasn't even on her radar as she lounged with Lucia, sipping her drink like she wasn't the most distracting person within a five-kilometer radius. I overheard them talking about work and latest paddock gossip. Lucia even tried to get her to open up about her ideal wedding venue, to which Nicola snorted and said, "No thank you, I'm single-rich-aunt material."

I barked a laugh from where I was floating with Gia, who immediately splashed me in retaliation. "More swimming, Zio!"

"Yes, boss," I saluted her and dove under.

Still, between games of mermaid tag and poolside snacks, my eyes always found Nicola. Her skin glowed under the Italian sun with her legs stretched out. Her real laugh was rare, but when she let it slip? It echoed in my chest for longer than it should.

I made a mental note: *Make her laugh more.*

By the time late afternoon rolled around, Gia was dozing on a lounger, sun hat drooping over one eye, and Alex and Lucia were swimming, in their own private world.

I grabbed a towel, dried off, and sauntered over to Nicola. She was sitting at the edge of her chair, flipping through something on her phone, legs crossed. I tapped her foot with mine.

She looked up, one brow arched. "What?"

"You think you can spare an hour with just my wonderful company?"

She blinked at me.

I grinned sheepishly and pushed a hand through my hair. "There's something I wanna show you."

"Is it edible?"

"It's beautiful."

She eyed me skeptically. "You already used that line for the cliffs. You planning to drag me up another mountain?"

"No cliffs," I said, backing away and jerking my thumb over my shoulder. "A boat. Private. I asked the concierge to hook it up earlier. We'll be back before sunset. I already promised Alex we'd watch Gia tonight so he can take Lucia out."

Her expression softened just a fraction.

"And," I added, "I made sure they stocked snacks and drinks this time. No tequila, but two bottles of wine. Your pick."

"Color me intrigued."

The sun was low by the time we were skimming across the water. The boat was sleek, white and gleaming, quiet except for the soft churn of waves beneath us. I made sure that some of the snacks I saw her gravitate to were stocked. Nicola leaned on the railing at the bow, hair tangled from the breeze, loose white shirt fluttering over her swimsuit. I was starting to get genuine laughs from her, and I stored each of those moments away like treasures. The boat pulled to a stop once we were out at sea.

"This doesn't count," she said over her shoulder as if it needed to be said, *again*.

I poured her a glass of wine and walked it over. "As?"

"A date."

"Of course not," I said, standing behind her. "It's a not-date. Two colleagues enjoying a scenic view."

She laughed again, soft and low. "You're such a problem."

I stepped closer. "You keep saying that like it's a bad thing."

I looked over to the stairwell at the stern. Knowing it led to a little private platform just above the waterline. I motioned toward it. "Come with me."

She eyed me. "Why?"

"I want you to see the best view."

She hesitated for a second, then followed silently.

When she turned to say something, I stepped in close, watching the shift in her eyes when she realized how little space was between us.

"I suddenly have this dream I can't shake," I announced, and she raised a brow as if to say '*Go on*'. "Kissing you on a boat." She rolled her eyes. "Care to help me achieve it?"

I was smirking because even though she found me annoying,

her eyes dipping down to my lips gave her away. She wanted to kiss me. But I waited. I was a patient man after all.

"Well?" She crossed her arms.

"Well what?"

"You going to kiss me, DeLuca?" A playful taunt in her gaze. I moved forward, taking her face in both my palms and pressing my lips to hers. Her mouth opened under mine like she'd been waiting, like we had both been waiting too long. My hands slid to her waist, and hers fisted in my shirt, yanking me closer. I spun her around against the side of the ship pressed up against her back, far out of view from the captain of the boat we were on. Boat was probably a conservative term—I had spent much too long picking it out and the deluxe yacht just felt right. Her chest pressed to mine, and I groaned into her mouth. She tasted like a mix of wine and something I couldn't get enough of. I kissed down her throat, biting softly at her jaw, licking the dip of her collarbone. Her breath caught, and I felt it all the way to my spine.

"You want to stop me, Moretti," I murmured against her skin, "Now's the time."

She tilted her head, her voice wrecked. "Don't you fucking dare."

I grinned against her neck, then slid one hand down then up, dragging it under the hem of her shirt, fingers brushing the edge of her bikini bottoms. Her hips jolted forward, needing friction.

"Matteo—" she said my name on a gasp, making any semblance of self-control snap. I let her take what she needed, my leg between her as she rolled into me. And it hit me that seeing Nicola like this, the undone, mess of a woman was a goddamn honor. My other hand slipped under her shirt, her warm skin greeting me with goosebumps as I went. I pushed aside the top of her bikini top, let her pretty pink nipple come out as I rubbed a thumb over it in a teasing motion. She let out another whimper and I knew she needed more.

"Shh," I whispered, curling my fingers into the fabric of her swimsuit and slipping between her thighs. "Let me take care of you."

She gasped, one hand gripping the rail behind her, the other twisting in my shirt as my fingers found her and slid slow. Her body arched, jaw clenched, eyes fluttering shut.

She was wet. Soaked. For me.

I kissed her again, harder this time, as my hand moved in tight, practiced circles. Her breath stuttered against my mouth, her thighs trembling. I didn't stop, even when she moaned into my neck, biting down on my shoulder like it would keep her grounded.

It didn't.

She came undone quietly, shaking against me, her hips grinding into my hand as I kept kissing her, kissing her like I needed her to remember exactly how it felt. When it was over she clung to me for a moment, head buried in my chest.

I held her. Let her catch her breath. Let myself *feel* her without pushing, without demanding anything more than this.

Eventually, she lifted her head. Her eyes were glassy, lips swollen, cheeks flushed.

"Starting to like this whole vacation thing," I smirked and kissed her temple.

"Big fan," she smiled, drunk off pleasure.

"Want to cool off?" I asked, nodding at the water.

"You trying to get me naked, DeLuca?"

"Nah, but enjoy the view," I winked, pulling my shirt over my head, tossing it to the side and jumping off the side of the boat.

I broke the surface with a splash and pushed my hair out of my eyes, blinking up at the boat. The water was cold but refreshing, and the sun was dipping low enough to throw gold across the waves.

"Come on," I called up, grinning, "Don't leave me out here alone."

Nicola leaned over the edge, arms folded across the railing. Her hair was a mess, and she was still catching her breath. She had never looked more beautiful. Smug, glowing, dangerous.

"Not my fault you threw yourself into the sea," she said lazily. "Bit dramatic, don't you think?"

"Please," I teased. "That was graceful as hell."

"You cannonballed."

I splashed water in her direction. "You're just mad you didn't jump first."

She disappeared from view for a beat, and I was about to call something smug when I heard her voice again.

"Catch me, DeLuca."

I barely had time to react before she was flying over the edge, limbs tucked, squealing as she hit the water with a laugh that shot straight through my chest.

She popped up beside me, shaking water from her face and grinning like she forgot to hate me for five whole seconds.

"That was reckless," I said, treading water closer to her. "Kind of proud of you."

"That was fun."

I drifted toward her slowly, letting the current pull us together. She was wearing the same blue bikini that made me want to buy her everything in that damn color. Her legs brushed mine. Her hands floated up to my shoulders. We were quiet for a moment, letting the sea hold us, our bodies close but not quite touching. The air between us sizzled anyway.

"I could get used to this," I said softly, studying her face—the way her wet lashes clumped together, the way her lips curved up like she was trying not to smile. I leaned in and brushed my lips to hers, a teasing brush. Egging her on. '*Kiss me back,*' it said. Her fingers slid up my neck into my hair, and she tugged me into her, her legs wrapping around me as she deepened the kiss.

"Used to what?" she asked after she was breathless.

"This. You. Being less terrifying."

She laughed and dunked me under.

I came up sputtering, reaching for her with both hands. "Okay. That's it."

She shrieked and tried to swim away, but I caught her around the waist and pulled her back against me. She was slippery and squirming, laughing too hard to break free.

I held her there in the middle of the water, both of us breathless, and she finally settled, her back against my chest, her head resting on my shoulder.

"You know," she said, barely audible, "It's fun to be reckless."

She turned, and I wrapped my arms around her more securely. "Good to let go once in a while."

She snorted. "Maybe."

"You look good like this," I pointed out, water dripping down my nose as it almost touched her. I was holding her up, her legs wrapping around my core as if in reflex.

"Like what?"

"Free."

I expected her to answer, make it a joke, or roll her eyes.

Instead, she closed them and tilted her head back, and I swore I felt her heart start to match mine, one quiet beat at a time. I wanted to stay here, floating in this moment. I liked all versions of Nicola, the scary fierce one, the sassy comeback one, and the slightly mean but flirty one. But this version, the quiet one, the soft one—I felt like it was a version of her she didn't share easily. One she didn't show the world. But she was starting to show me. I wanted to do whatever I could to make her feel like she could be this version with me, that she was safe to be herself.

Later, the boat swayed gently as it cut through the water, the golden afternoon sun wrapping us in warmth. Nicola and I were stretched out across the sun-warmed cushions at the bow, our legs tangled lazily, a breeze whispering over the waves as we began the slow trek back to the dock.

"Ready to babysit the cutest kid in the world?" I asked, glancing over at her, shielding my eyes from the glare. She didn't answer right away. Her head was tipped back, resting on her hands behind her head, her eyes closed as the light brushed across her face. It wasn't like her to be this still, this quiet.

When she spoke, her voice was softer than I expected. "You know...I'd never really been around kids before Gianna. I always thought they were loud and sticky and exhausting."

I huffed a laugh. "Not wrong."

She cracked the smallest smile but went on. "But she's different. I didn't expect that. I didn't expect to love her like this." Her throat bobbed on a swallow. "Like...I'd burn the world down to keep her safe. She smiles at me, and I feel like my heart wasn't even mine before."

That cracked something open in me. I turned my head, watching her, letting the weight of her words settle between us.

"I didn't know I could love like that," she added quietly. "Not until her."

I felt my chest pull tight. I knew exactly what she meant. Being Gia's uncle had reshaped my entire world. The first time she called me Zio, I'd nearly burst into tears like some kind of sap.

"I get it," I said after a beat. "When she runs up to me yelling my name or throws her arms around me just because...that's it. That's my whole universe right there."

Nicola turned her head to meet my gaze. Her expression was open in a way I rarely saw, stripped of all her usual bite and fire. "Did you always want kids?"

I shook my head, thinking. "Not always. But I do now. After Gia, it's...yeah. I want that. A family. Messy breakfasts. Chaos. Little shoes everywhere."

She smiled, small and wistful. "You probably want a whole football team."

"At least," I said, smirking.

"You'd be an insufferably good dad." Her voice was quieter, like she hadn't meant to say it out loud. My heart squeezed. I turned my face back to the sun, trying to play it cool, but the words hit somewhere deeper than I expected.

"I hope so," I murmured. "That's the dream, anyway."

She was quiet for a moment, then asked, "What about after racing? Where do you see yourself?"

The image came easily, painted in the back of my mind like a permanent daydream. "Back in the countryside. Taking over the vineyard from my parents. Building a house on the edge of the property. Waking up with the sun, walking barefoot through the vines, drinking wine before lunch."

She let out a breath that sounded almost like a laugh, but not quite. "That sounds peaceful."

"Yeah," I said, glancing at her again. "I think I'm chasing that kind of peace. That's the end game for me."

"Sounds rather nice," she said thoughtfully.

"What about you? Ten years from now, where will Nicola Moretti be?" She laughed lightly, again she seemed free and light, I cherished it, like soaking in her sunlight.

"I started this year trying to find a spot for myself within Moretti Racing. I think my father has spent so long trying to get my brother, Michael, to get serious and involved in the family business that he just assumed I wasn't interested. I mean, I didn't really ever say anything. I finished university and worked a few different jobs, but nothing really stuck. I just didn't have that spark about any of it. My dad, my grandfather, they've all had that racing spark. I've grown up in the sport, going to races, growing up around racers themselves. I was never super into racing; did a few karting runs with my brother when we were young, but that was about it. I really like the charity side though. Doing the gala was the first time I felt that spark. I think maybe I'd like to take up that end of the business. I've been working on new ideas and presentations, had a few calls with the chairwoman, Henrietta."

"That's really amazing, finding your spot in motorsport," I said, reaching out and going to intertwine our fingers. It was a reach; she wasn't always a huge physical touch person except in heated moments. She kept these walls up so high, not letting people in. But I understood it, I had friends and teammates who grew up in motorsport with stupid amounts of old money, families that were riddled with legends. They had a different level of expectation: always on, always perfect, always prepared.

Her fingers curled around mine, squeezing once. My heart squeezed right along with it.

"You know there's really this whole other person under carefree, happy-go-lucky Matteo DeLuca, huh?" she said to the sky.

"I am basically an onion," I replied, and Nicola burst out in laughter.

"Why is *that* what you picked as your metaphorical food?" she asked between fits of laughter.

"I have layers, baby," I said, winking.

# 16

# NICOLA

"**Y**ou're a literal angel on this earth. I'm endlessly grateful for you!" Lucia said, blowing me a kiss and running out the door with a wave. "Have fun! Don't kill each other, bye!"

"God, they're so disgustingly in love," I said to Matteo once the door shut. I had curled Lucia's hair and let her borrow my classic red lipstick for her night out with Alexander. She looked amazing, and her sunshine was damn near contagious. Or it was spending the day with Matteo, the way he pulled me close after we jumped into the water or talked while we lay in the sun. Matteo was so easy to talk to. I had never had that. Those damn DeLuca siblings were making me soft.

"Zietta?" Gianna spoke up. I turned, crouching down to her level, Matteo catching my eye as I did.

"Yeah babe?"

"Can we watch a princess movie?" she asked. And who was I to tell her no? She looked up to me with identical green eyes to her mother, little blonde ringlets in pigtails, and she was clutching her bunny stuffie as usual.

"Of course, *Principessa*," Matteo spoke up, scooping her into his arms as she giggled.

"Put me down!" she laughed and laughed.

"Oh, you didn't want to fly?" Matteo asked as he started moving around the room and holding her like she was flying.

She put an arm out and started chanting, "Faster!"

Watching Matteo with her was basically the cutest thing to exist. It made my heart soften even more. We played princesses—Matteo and I in crowns while Gianna held her 'royal court'—before we put on one of her favorite princess movies on the living space television. Not even thirty minutes into the movie, Gianna was asleep leaning against me. Matteo pulled up a blanket around her, smiling softly.

"For knowing literally no kids other than G, you're damn good at this Moretti," he whispered.

"You're not so bad yourself," I whispered back. "She adores you."

"Please, I didn't miss how she's been calling you Zietta lately, that's a huge honor."

"I almost cried the first time," I admitted.

"Didn't know you were capable." He smirked. I smacked his arm in mock annoyance. It seemed to all be mock annoyance lately. Because Matteo DeLuca was growing on me, was making me blush, and was making my stomach fill with butterflies. I shook my head, trying to shove down the feelings. Not safe feelings. Feelings led to hurt. Nope this was just vacation, a truce was made. It would go back to normal next week.

We watched the rest of the movie in silence, Gianna fast asleep. Then Matteo flipped the channel, scrolling through other movies to rent.

"I feel like you hate romcoms?" he joked.

"Excuse you, I love them!"

"Careful Moretti, your icy heart is melting! Don't tell the others!"

"Shut up," I rolled my eyes.

"*You've Got Mail* or *10 Things I Hate About You*?" he asked.

"Have you seen both?"

"A requirement when you have Lucia as a sister," he rolled his eyes.

"Hmmm," I tapped my chin trying to decide. "*10 Things I Hate About You*," I finally replied, and he started the movie.

I must have fallen asleep at some point during the movie, because I woke to end credits,missing a Gianna-shaped human curled into my side.

"Sorry I didn't mean to fall asleep," I said, yawning.

"That's okay, you're cute when you snore."

"I do not snore!" I threw back.

"You one hundred percent snore, Moretti."

"Oh my God, that is so embarrassing!" I said, covering my face.

"Oh, she's blushing!" he said, leaning over and poking my side.

"I will slap you," I swatted away his hand. He raised an eyebrow and got up on his knees on the couch. And he fucking crawled to me. I swore time had stalled.

"You keep being mean to me and I'm gonna fall in love with you," he smirked, getting closer. I pushed myself back and held out a foot to his chest.

"Fuck right off, DeLuca," I said, trying to hold back a laugh.

"If there wasn't a child sleeping in the next room, I'd do just that," he smirked. I pushed him back with my foot and he let himself fall back, now on the opposite side of the couch. "Your loss."

"You are so fucking annoying," I rolled my eyes again.

"Hmm, that doesn't sound so convincing anymore," he teased. I opened my mouth to reply, but we heard footsteps and the key card beeped at the front door to the villa. Alexander and Lucia entered, Alexander holding Lucia's heels as she walked in barefoot and smiling.

"Hey!" she greeted us, "How'd she do?"

"Perfect as always," Matteo replied easily, getting up and greeting them both.

"And you two behaved?" she asked, raising an eyebrow to me. I mocked a gasp.

"We can be civil adults," I said.

"One of us can be," Matteo added, crossing his arms.

"Shut up."

"Thank you for watching Gia," Alexander added and smiled down at Lucia, leaning in and kissing her head. "We had a lovely night."

"Gross," Matteo gagged and I smirked at my friend. We said our goodbyes, and I whispered to Lucia that she owed me an update. We walked down the hall to our own shared suite.

"I think Alex really loves her," Matteo said as we reached our door.

"I think she really loves him too," I replied.

"I was worried for so long she wouldn't let herself be loved again, after everything she went through with Gianna's dad," Matteo said quietly. I took in the confession. It was so obvious how protective Matteo was of his sister and Gianna. How much he just wanted them to be happy, how he wanted to give them the whole world.

"It's hard to accept love after loss," I said into the dark room as we walked in. Like a confession into the night.

"You say it like you know that feeling," he said without turning on any lights.

"Something like that," I replied.

We got ready for bed, and I sat in my thoughts as I showered off the day. Slipping into a satin pajama set, I was feeling rather cute. Anticipating how Matteo would react to the outfit gave me an onslaught of butterflies. But when I left the bathroom, I spotted Matteo knocked out on the bed. And while I had other plans in mind, I couldn't help but smile at it. I slipped under the covers after flipping off the bedside lamp. As soon as my head hit the pillow, Matteo shifted, his arm wrapping around my stomach and pulling me into him. Stupid butterflies erupted in my stomach as a result. His cheek was smashed against the top of my head, and he let out a sigh.

"You faking being asleep right now?" I asked, not even really caring.

"No," he replied too clearly to be asleep.

"Liar," I silently laughed, "I hope I snore extra loud and you don't sleep."

He only squeezed his arm around me once and muttered, "You don't actually snore."

"What?" I gasped and flipped around, facing him. His eyes were sleepy but open and I swore there was a twinkle under the moonlight coming through the window.

"It's just so easy."

"What is?"

"Annoying you."

"You infuriate me, DeLuca."

"Keep telling yourself that, Moretti," he whispered back leaning forward, brushing his lips to my forehead and leaving a light kiss. Then he pulled me into his chest. "Go to sleep, trouble."

I went to argue—I really, truly meant to argue—but it was so warm and comfortable there and only a grumbled response came out of me, because I was fast asleep before I could make out the words he said next.

Waking up next to Matteo was quickly becoming addicting. Today, however, he woke up first and started bugging me. I sleepily swatted away his hand that poked my cheek.

"Wake up, Princess."

"No," I mumbled, pulling my pillow closer.

"Can you use a pillow so I can get up then? I assume you don't want to get up before the sunrise to go on a run?" he asked, and my eyes flew open. Because I didn't have my hand on the sheets but his shirt, and the pillow was in fact not soft at all, and it smelled fucking divine.

"Oh."

"Who knew you were such a cuddler?" he smirked down at me. I smacked his chest.

"Fuck off."

"You could ask nicely, ya know."

"Have fun with your torture!" I flipped around, trying to readjust. Getting up before daylight should be a cardinal sin. Getting up before the sun to go for his runs, just plain psychotic. Matteo laughed and I felt the bed dip as he stood.

"Be back soon," I heard him say as I drifted back off to sleep.

The next time I woke up, it was to the smell of coffee and an empty room. There was a coffee cup on the bedside table, a note with messy handwriting under it.

'*Enjoy your coffee, Princess.*' I caught myself smiling at the stupid piece of paper before pushing it away and flopping back on my pillow.

Then I pulled out my phone and typed out just about ten different versions of messages before landing on:

NICOLA:

A pastry would go really nice with this coffee

MATTEO:

...

Sweet or savory?

NICOLA:

Surprise me.

A knock at the door startled me, just as I caught myself smiling down at my phone like an idiot. I blinked, shook my head, and tossed it onto the bed like it betrayed me.

*Get a grip, Moretti.*

I opened the door to find Lucia on the other side, eyes wide, hair slightly windblown like she power-walked here on a mission.

"I need girl talk," she announced, already stepping in before I could say anything. She moved through the hotel suite like a mini hurricane, pacing in a tight line near the foot of my bed. I closed the door behind her, a sinking feeling already forming in my gut. I'd only recently learned how to be a decent friend, and whatever this was felt...heavy.

Then she blurted it out like it was physically painful, "I love him."

She dropped onto the edge of the bed like her knees gave out. Her eyes darted to mine, wide and terrified, like she just confessed to something shameful instead of wonderful.

I sat next to her in the chair, softer than usual. "Okay," I said gently, "That's a good thing, right?"

"I don't know!" she breathed out, her voice tight. "It started as nothing. Just fake. Just PR to help Alexander's image, and mine by default. But then he started kissing me like he meant it. And then he started *meaning* things. He says things that make me feel so... seen. And safe. And it scares the hell out of me."

I reached for her hands, taking them into mine, grounding us both. "Love is terrifying," I agreed, "But it's also rare. And it's not even a question that Alexander loves you back. The way he looks at you, Luce—like you're the sun and he's just trying to bask in the light."

Her eyes widened. "He does?"

"It's fucking precious," I muttered. "And that's coming from me. I'm basically allergic to feelings according to your brother."

That earned a small laugh from her. A win.

"About that," she said, narrowing her eyes.

I groaned and leaned back in the chair. "In my defense, I'm still new at this whole '*having girlfriends*' thing, and he *is* your brother. And we're talking about *you* right now, remember?" I tried.

"Nice try. You're avoiding, I'm deflecting. We're both disasters."

"What a pair we make, huh?" I said with a huff, smiling despite myself. She squeezed my hand this time.

"You deserve to be loved, you know. And to love again," Lucia said, squeezing my hand back.

"I think I know that," I said quietly, "Logically, I *know* it. But my head and heart feel like they're still at war."

She nodded along in agreement, "It's hard for me to trust myself too...after everything. But with Alexander, I feel...safe. It's worth it with the right person."

"That's a big deal," I murmured.

She exhaled like she'd been holding it in for weeks. "And Gianna loves him."

"Of course she does. He's been showing up for her since day one. I heard about you two *long* before I met you."

Lucia bit her lip, but her eyes glinted with something soft. "Okay, back to you. Are you sleeping with my brother?"

I groaned, dropping my face into my hands. "Jesus. You just dive right in, huh?"

"Nic," she dragged out, tilting her head. "You went from loathing him to acting almost nice. You don't even snap at him anymore."

"I *do* snap at him!" I argued.

"Not like you used to. I know you."

I lifted my hands in surrender. "Okay. Fine. He's still annoying, but yeah...we are."

Lucia gasped. "I *knew* it! Alex and I had a bet going."

"You did not," I laughed despite myself, "Who won?"

She grinned. "Me. Obviously. When did it start?"

"The gala," I admitted, tugging a pillow into my lap like it might shield me.

Lucia whistled. "That was *weeks* ago. Are you two...dating?"

I froze. The word sounded so heavy. Like a tether I wasn't sure I could hold.

"Um. No?" It came out as more of a question. "It's not like that."

Lucia's brow lifted. "You haven't dated anyone since Nathaniel."

"Exactly. After that shitshow? I swore off anything serious. Relationships aren't for me. Too messy. Too much pain. I can't do it again."

"But this *thing* with Matteo..."

"It's just fun. We've called a truce for vacation. We enjoy ourselves, then we go back to normal."

Lucia studied me, too perceptive for her own good. "And that's what you want?"

"Yes," I said quickly. Too quickly. "He's fun. It's fun. It doesn't mean anything."

But the words felt sour in my mouth. Because it didn't feel meaningless. It felt warm. Safe. Easy and impossible all at once.

It felt like *more*.

And that terrified me most of all.

The suite was quiet, save for the hum of the sea breeze whispering through the cracked balcony doors. I sat at the little bistro table on the balcony, nursing my coffee as I replayed Lucia's words over and over again in my head.

*You deserve to be loved too.*

I stirred my spoon in slow circles, watching the cream swirl until it disappeared.

I didn't know what to do with that kind of statement. What did "deserving love" even mean? It wasn't like you won a reward for surviving enough heartbreaks. If it were, maybe I'd believe I'd earned it.

So, here I was— trying not to think about how good it felt to fall asleep with Matteo this whole vacation.

The front door creaked open. Footsteps echoed through the airy villa, light and familiar.

"Back from your daily punishment ritual?" I called, glancing up as Matteo walked in. His T-shirt clung to his abs in a way that should be illegal, and he had two paper bags balanced in one arm like some kind of smug, sexy delivery boy.

"You say 'punishment,' I say 'endorphin high,'" he smirked, kicking the door shut behind him. "Brought you something."

He sat the bags on the counter and pulled out two croissants— one chocolate, one almond—and a flaky sfogliatella, my favorite. My stomach growled like a traitor.

"About time," I said, pretending not to be touched.

Matteo only grinned. "You're welcome."

He leaned in close, brushing a kiss across my forehead before I could react.

*My breath caught.*

And just like that, he was gone—sauntering down the hallway toward the bathroom, whistling under his breath, towel draped over his shoulder.

I sat frozen, croissant halfway to my mouth.

The kiss shouldn't have meant anything. It was just a forehead. Harmless. Friendly. Soft.

But somehow, that made it worse.

Because there was something so tender about it—the easy way he did it, like it was a reflex. Like I was his to kiss.

My usual reaction to that kind of intimacy was to bolt—to tear it all down before it could unravel me. But instead...I felt warm.

Like maybe I *didn't* hate it.

Like maybe I wanted it again.

*God,* I groaned and shoved half the croissant in my mouth. I needed to clear my head.

I came into this vacation to unwind, and we made a deal. A truce. It was just fun. No feelings. It wasn't my fault he was being soft and golden and deliciously Matteo.

He wasn't my forever. That's not who I was.

I didn't *do* forever.

So I would stick to the original agreement. Keep it light, no feelings.

I took another bite of pastry and tried to convince myself that I believed it. Then I stood and walked with determination to the bathroom, where the shower was running.

Time to enjoy my damn vacation.

I knocked once, more for drama than necessity, and pushed the door open.

Matteo's head whipped around from behind the glass shower door. Water glided down the line of his back, glistening against golden skin and defined muscle. His eyes went wide when he saw me, like I was the last thing he expected and the only thing he wanted.

I leaned against the frame, arms crossed, and pretended my heart wasn't hammering against my ribs.

I reached for the hem of my tank top, dragging it up over my head, slow enough to catch the way his gaze sharpened. Like he was watching something sacred. Or sinful. Or both.

The tank top fell to the floor with a soft whisper. I shimmied out of my sleep shorts next, standing there in nothing but lace and a rising pulse.

Matteo said nothing, but his breathing changed—deeper now. Hungrier.

I hooked my thumbs under the waistband of my panties, holding his gaze as I slid them down.

His jaw ticked. His hand curled slightly against the fogged glass door like he was physically restraining himself from opening it and pulling me in.

The tension coiled between us like a living thing.

I crossed the rest of the space without breaking eye contact and opened the door, stepping into the warm cascade of water and right into the gravity of his body.

My skin sparked as the steam surrounded us, his chest rising and falling, eyes locked on mine like I was both a threat and a promise.

"Good morning," I murmured, lips curving.

Matteo grinned. "Best damn morning of my life."

# 17

# MATTEO

Nicola stepped into the shower like she owned it—like she owned me.

Steam curled around her, gliding over bare skin and damp hair, water beading along her collarbone. And I swore I forgot every coherent thought I'd ever had.

"Good morning," she said, eyes dark and glittering with mischief.

My heart stuttered. "Best damn morning of my life."

She moved closer, not touching—just letting the air between us buzz. Her hands trailed lightly down my chest, fingers brushing through the droplets of water collecting along my ribs. My stomach tensed under her touch.

"You know," she hummed, circling me slowly, deliberately, "You talk a big game for someone who didn't even invite me in."

Her voice was low, playful. Dangerous. She trailed her fingertips along my shoulder blades and down my spine, then back around my front until she was facing me again. She looked up at me through thick lashes, her lips slightly parted, and the urge to kiss her warred with the desire to let her do whatever she was planning.

I reached for her waist, but she stepped back just out of reach. Teasing.

"Oh no," she grinned, "You just stand there and look pretty."

"I think I'm being seduced," I murmured, my voice hoarse.

"You absolutely are," she tilted her head and pressed a kiss to my chest. "And the best part?" Another kiss, lower. "You're going to let me."

She sank to her knees, slowly, deliberately, water cascading over her like something out of a dream. Her hands trailed down my thighs, and every muscle in my body locked with tension and want.

My hand found the back of her head, fingers threading into her wet hair as she looked up at me with that knowing smirk—like she was about to ruin me and enjoy every second of it.

And I'd let her. Again and again.

Because it was her.

Nicola Moretti: the girl I shouldn't want, the girl who drove me insane, and the only one who made me feel like the whole world could catch fire and I wouldn't care—as long as she was the one holding the match.

My voice dropped, rough and reverent. "You're going to be the death of me."

She grinned. "Then die happy, DeLuca."

# 18

# MATTEO

*V*acation was over.

Alexander looked relaxed, refreshed even, like the weight of the last race and that awful crash had finally lifted off his shoulders. Lucia was lighter somehow, her laughter easier and brighter than it had been in months. And Gianna—well, Gianna was just pure sunshine, bouncing around with that endless energy only a kid can have.

Overall, the trip was a success. A much-needed win for all of us.

Except for one thing.

The fragile truce between Nicola and me? It was over now. Our carefully crafted excuse for late-night talks, sharing a bed without strings, those 'non-dates' she let me take her on—none of it was real anymore. I tried to shake it off, tried to reset my mind, put myself back where I needed to be. Free Practice was two days away, and with it came training, interviews, team meetings—the grind that kept me sharp on the track. We were in Vegas, and the amount of media days and content the teams were all pushing out was next level. I tried to focus on the poor admins who were walking us through the content. I tried to focus on the interviews with some other drivers. Carlos bumped my shoulder when I didn't manage to answer the interviewer. I snapped out of my daze and looked around to the other drivers.

Theo Bauer, sat across from me, shooting daggers at everyone, looking like he would rather be anywhere else. He had that cocky asshole thing down, so honestly it wasn't surprising, but when I looked back at the interviewer, I immediately felt guilty for not being the easiest to interview either right now. The poor red-headed woman interviewing us looked young, maybe even her first interview and here I was fucking it up. She was asking good questions too, technical things, strategic comments like she knew the game well. I had turned on the charm after that, determined to not let my stupid heart affect someone else's career.

But no matter how hard I pushed, my thoughts kept slipping. They kept winding back to a certain brunette. Those damn cherry red lips and heels she wore around the track. It was a power moveshe needed to assert herself in this chaotic world, and it fucking worked. I caught glimpses of her throughout the first few days but not a single word was exchanged. Which only drove me to the brink of insanity.

After we wrapped on interviews, we were free to get back to training. When I finally made it to the empty team gym, I felt the stress start to fall, my shoulders softening. I pulled on my training gear, the fabric snug against my muscles, trying to get back in the race weekend headspace. I paced the gym, doing laps around the weights to warm up while listening to loud music, trying to drown out the constant replay of her smile in my mind, the way her eyes sparkled when she caught me looking.

The woman had waltzed into my life this year and flipped my world upside down with that perfect blend of fire and ice. She was snark and sarcasm and challenge—and something softer, something I didn't have the right to want. Sure, I had dated here and there, had one-night stands that never turned to anything more, but it was all dull and boring. Nicola was something else entirely.

The worst part? I wasn't just wanting her in bed. I wanted the moments in between: the mornings when she'd let her guard down, the laughs she thought I didn't see. The damn way she made me feel like I could actually stop running, settle down even. She saw me in a way others didn't. I didn't need to pretend, didn't need to be anyone other than my actual self.

But I knew better. She didn't do relationships, and it wasn't like I hadn't seen this coming. It was my own damn idea to just let vacation be vacation. Because she was always honest and upfront with me, and I knew that was all that she could give. Her heart couldn't take any more risks, not after that idiot cheated on her. And I understood it. But I still spun the lie to myself that we were just getting it out of our systems. Now there was a glaring red sign that read '*you're fucked!*' in some overly cheery font in the mental picture. I did this to myself. Dug myself into this hole.

I shoved a dumbbell aside and clenched my fists, sweat dripping. I reached back and pulled my shirt over my head in one movement, tossing it to the ground.

"Hey DeLuca," Carlos greeted as he entered the team gym.

"Hey," I greeted half-heartedly.

"You ready for more media?" he sighed. I rolled my eyes. We all hated media days but usually I was the upbeat one, the one that told the guys it was just a part of the job.

"I guess." I shrugged.

"Damn, what's got you down?" Carlos looked shocked at my unusual non-chipper attitude. I just didn't have it in me. I couldn't pull the mask back up, couldn't be the happy one, the positive one. My mind was too full, too busy. I couldn't separate it all into their boxes, couldn't push aside all the thoughts and be *the* Matteo DeLuca. Always happy, always positive.

I glanced at my phone. No new messages. She was probably doing the same, trying to convince herself this was just fun. Just a vacation fling. Or she wasn't thinking about it at all. That thought stung.

I fucking hated it.

"Nah, I'm good, man. Just pushed myself on the last rep." I brushed aside his look and took a long sip of water before waving goodbye to my teammate. He nodded, laughing at something on his phone. I peered over, curiosity winning out, his phone tipped toward me, and I saw a picture of a familiar brunette.

My blood boiled.

"What's that?" I asked as calmly as I could. Was it any of my business? Probably not, but fuck that. It was *my* name she was screaming a few nights ago, *my* bed she slept in.

"Just Nic being an idiot," Carlos laughed. I glared.

"Don't fucking call her that."

"Mate, relax," he said, looking taken aback.

"The fuck I will," I seethed.

"Okay, what the hell is going on?" Carlos said, crossing his arms, looking unbothered at my rather territorial reaction. I knew in my head that I needed to fucking relax. But I couldn't. Why was she sending him pictures? And they were flirting at that gala. Now that I thought about it, they were together a lot, always finding each other at events throughout the year, laughing together.

I was an idiot.

How could I be this damn blind?

"Nothing," I snapped and stormed out of the room. I didn't get far, Carlos following after me as I was talking myself into a mental spiral.

"Matteo!"

"What!" I yelled at him, spinning around. "What could you possibly want from me?"

"Is this about the picture?" Carlos asked.

"Sure, yeah. And that I'm blind and stupid, and that obviously you have something with her, I don't know how I didn't notice it before. Haven't you two known each other since you were little?

Friends to lovers or whatever. I've seen that movie. You win in the end."

"Woah, woah woah," Carlos held up his hands. "First of all, this is the picture." He turned his phone to me. Nicola's selfie showed her with red lipstick smeared across her cheek, lipstick tube in hand and a glare on her face, Gianna giggling to the side.

"Second of all, yeah, we've known each other forever, she's basically an extra sister, mate. It's not like that."

"Sure," I scoffed.

"No, it's really not like that," Carlos insisted.

"Whatever, man. She's all yours." I started to walk away again.

"You fucking blind idiot, we are not interested in each other, not like *that*."

I stared at my teammate blankly.

"I'm not interested in her," he said, brushing a hand over his face. "Or anyone that is a *her*." He waved his hand like I should understand what he was saying.

"I'm gay, you dumb blind idiot," Carlos rolled his eyes at me.

"Oh," was all I could form. A whole damn word, my brain restarted at the comment. "Oh!"

"Yeah, oh," Carlos rolled his eyes. "It's not like public knowledge, but Nicola is my friend, that's it. She knows. God, she was with me when we went out and found me drunkenly kissing a boy when we were teenagers and made sure no one saw us and distracted the rest of our friends."

I smiled, because of course she did, that was so Nicola.

"That—um. Congrats?" I stumbled.

"Don't make it fucking weird." Carlos rolled his eyes. "Literally nothing has changed, except now you know I'm gay, and I know you're down bad for the boss's daughter."

"Um—"

"Mmhm."

"Well...I—Uh, sorry that wasn't cool of me to react like that.

And I'm happy for you man. That's great, really. Nicola just makes me lose my mind sometimes."

"She has that effect on men in general, actually," Carlos smirked.

"Don't I know it," I sighed, "Seriously man, sorry for my reaction. And I won't tell anyone. It's yours to share when you feel it's best, but I've got your back and if anyone gives you any trouble. I'll punch them straight in the jaw." I nodded seriously.

"Okay, now you sound like Nic is rubbing off on you. That's terrifying. But thank you, I appreciate it."

"I mean it."

"I know," he smiled. We parted ways, and I headed to a meeting with my engineers to finish out the day. Qualifying tomorrow loomed. We needed to place high to get as many points as possible for the end of the season. The higher we placed, the more sponsors, the more money, the more upgrades to be able to have a shot at the Constructors' Championship next year. The itch beneath my skin to get back behind the wheel, the taste of the track, the roar of the engine, it fueled me. I'd missed it more than I had allowed myself to admit. This was what I was made for. Racing was what made sense, my lifelong dream, and here I was racing for my favorite team. I couldn't let my distractions bleed onto the track. So I focused on that, on my parents watching the race from their living room, my dad wearing his old Moretti cap as he did every race.

Race weekends were sort of a circus. Drivers and teams arrived like a swarm, unpacking their setups and rebuilding the motorsport world in this new location. Seventy-two hours passed in a blur of training and meetings. Free Practice came and went, then qualifying. If you weren't wholly focused, and everything didn't go as planned, the outcome was brutal.

Carlos found that out the hard way. He crashed during the second round of qualifying. The impact was more than just physical; it echoed through the team. His car was mangled, forcing him to start near the back tomorrow since they couldn't fix the car in time for Q3. It was a gut punch for all of us. Every point mattered. Now the team had to focus on getting his car repaired before race day. Vital parts of the car being crushed never had good timing.

That left me with the heavy burden of carrying the team on my shoulders and clawing back the ground Carlos couldn't. The weight was not lost on me. I felt it during the last round of qualifying.

As I stretched my fingers and flexed my hands, I could almost feel the mental checklist ticking in my head: check the brakes, feel the grip, visualize the perfect lap. I qualified in 5th place for race day. It was a good start, but I still found myself itching for more, wanting to do better.

Tomorrow's race was not just another weekend. It was a test, a chance to prove I was the driver this team needed. To earn the points that could keep us in contention. To remind everyone, especially myself, that I belonged here. Carlos was the more seasoned driver, but we ranked closely. I wanted to prove my worth to the team and ultimately to myself.

When I finally got back to the hotel after the chaos of qualifying, sleep didn't come easy. My bed felt empty after a week spent sharing a room with Nicola. She wasn't even staying at this hotel. We had all grown accustomed to being at the same hotel, even the same hall. Rallying around my sister and making sure she had support for her and G, Nicola had become a part of our group easily. But now, being back in the thick of the racing world, I was reminded that Nicola, while part of our group, was also the daughter of my team's owner. She grew up around this circuit. It was her damn palace.

The next morning started with a knock on my hotel door. Some small part of me—okay, maybe a not-so-small part—wished it was Nicola. But before I even reached the handle, I knew better. The familiar sound of giggles gave it away.

I opened the door to find Lucia juggling a tray of coffee cups and a paper bag of pastries, with Gianna peeking out from behind her leg like a tiny blonde tornado.

"Morning!" Lucia greeted, brightly, "We brought reinforcements."

"Hey Luce, Gia! Wow, thanks!" I ruffled Gianna's hair and grabbed the tray from my sister's hands. Two large cups and a smaller one, which I assumed was a hot chocolate for the sugar monster herself.

"*Grazie*, Zio!" Gianna chirped before darting past me and making herself comfortable on the couch.

"Sorry for the early invasion," Lucia said, brushing windblown strands out of her face, "She refused to let me do her hair until she saw you, so I figured I'd bring apology goodies."

"You never need to apologize for more Gia time" I grinned and rubbed the back of my neck. "Pretty sure she's my good luck charm. And I could use it today."

"Are you nervous?" Lucia asked, her voice soft in that way she had when she knew I wasn't going to admit it on my own.

"A little," I admitted, "It's a lot of pressure. But the car felt good yesterday."

"That's something, right?" she smiled.

Gianna appeared next to my knee, peering up at me with those big curious eyes. "Zio? Are you going to win today?"

"I'm going to do my very best," I smiled at her.

She reached into her tiny sweatshirt pocket and pulled out a beaded bracelet in Moretti red, white, and black. In the center, two white beads spelled out my racing number: 22.

"I made you this!" she beamed, holding it up like it was the crown jewels.

My heart clenched. "Wow, thanks, little G. I love it." Gianna was the best thing that ever happened to me. Alexander said that's why I didn't go as party crazy as he did in the beginning. Truth was, becoming an uncle kept me grounded when I first stepped into the madness of Formula One. I still loved a party, sure, but if I had to choose between a night out and flying home for family dinner, I was on the next flight.

"Matching ones were a must," Lucia said, holding up her wrist to show me hers.

"She's getting so grown up," I muttered, marveling at the bracelet. "I know she's still little, but come on. This is next level."

"Well, I made the bracelets. She dictated. Still a bit early for fine motor skills," Lucia laughed. "We had a girls' night last night. Nicola brought a bracelet-making kit, and Anna showed up with sugary snacks."

"You've got your own crew now, huh?"

"Kind of surreal. This time last year, I had zero friends. Look at me now."

"You had me and Alex."

"Yeah, but you guys have to love me."

"Pretty sure that's debatable," I teased, bumping her shoulder gently.

She blushed. "I'm glad I came. And that I fake dated your best mate. Which is not so fake anymore."

"You guys are sickening," I rolled my eyes.

"It's...yeah," she blushed.

"That man adores you, and Gia. Honestly, I couldn't have picked someone better to be by your side. After everything with your ex, after the dark days...you deserve to be happy."

She looked at me with watery eyes, the kind of look that sucker-punches your chest.

"You know you're the same, right?" she asked softly. "Maybe it's how Mom and Dad raised us, but you put everyone else first, too. With your jokes, your whole happy-go-lucky act. But underneath that...you deserve to be truly happy. Not just the people-pleasing kind. The real kind."

I looked down at my coffee and sighed. "Damn, I wasn't ready to be called out like that at six in the morning."

She smirked. "Sorry. Occupational hazard of being your sister. So, go get your girl or whatever."

I blinked at her. "Excuse me?"

"You and Nicola." She sipped her coffee, as if that clarified everything.

"Fuck. How do you know about that?" I whispered, glancing over at Gianna. She was trying to wear one of my race-day shirts, the bright red fabric nearly swallowing her whole.

"I know everything. Obviously."

"You sound like Nic."

"Oooh, Nic, huh?"

"Shut up."

"Nope."

"Zio, look! I'm ready!" Gianna waddled over, half-tripping over the shirt. I laughed, genuinely and fully, and pulled out my phone to snap a picture. It went straight to the family group chat, no questions asked. Lucia pulled Gianna into her arms and pressed a kiss to my cheek. "Good luck today. We'll see you in the paddock."

Gianna mimicked her mom with a kiss of her own, and then they were gone.

I flopped down on the couch and ripped into the pastry bag.

I needed a fucking sweet treat.

# 19

# NICOLA

I shifted the strap of my tote bag higher on my shoulder as I walked briskly through the team's hospitality suite, the click of my heels softened by the plush carpet underfoot. The hum of conversation, the clinking of espresso cups, and the occasional burst of laughter echoed through the space. The weekend might have just begun, but I was already deep in logistics mode.

Back to business. Back to normal.

The screen of my tablet lit up as I scanned over the updated run-of-show for our next charity event post season in Rome. A high profile black tie gala. The whole thing had to be seamless. I needed it to be perfect, which meant having every driver in attendance, a variety of sponsor donations, and a few big celebrities in attendance. Henrietta had become a bit of a mentor: we'd shared calls to go over details, she'd shown me how to run an event, forwarded contacts she suggested. I'd already met with two brand liaisons this morning and had another call scheduled in an hour.I was prepping for the whole pitch to the board of Moretti Racing to sign off on Monday. And seven days felt like it would barrel past me in no time. Everything moved faster during the season.

No more boats. No more cliffside views or kisses that made my knees weak.

I passed a group of interns setting up sponsor signage and offered them a tight smile before turning into the team's private suite. My father stood tall in a navy suit with a subtle Moretti lapel while speaking with one of our long-time engineers, but looked up when I entered.

"Nicola," he said with a nod, his voice warm but clipped in the way it always was when people were around. "How are preparations for Rome coming?"

"On schedule," I replied, offering him a quick kiss on the cheek, "Just finalizing the catering proposals. I'll have a brief ready for you and the board by Monday."

"Good," he nodded, "I'd like it if you spoke with the Stratos team before the end of the day. They're considering doubling their donation this year. Make sure they feel taken care of."

"Already on my list." I turned as a familiar bark echoed through the suite.

Monty trotted over like he owned the place, his paws surprisingly quiet. His tail wagged once, then he sat right in front of me like the judgmental little prince he was.

"Hey there, handsome." I crouched and gave him a scratch behind the ears. "You miss me, or just the air conditioning?"

Monty huffed dramatically and leaned into my hand. Typical.

"Nice to see you, too," I muttered under my breath, then stood, smoothed my dress, and waved goodbye to my father, taking off in search of coffee and maybe a moment to breathe.

I turned the corner toward catering and nearly collided with Anna, who was balancing her phone, a clipboard, and a half-full cup of iced espresso.

"Oh!" she laughed, steadying both our drinks like a professional, "Nic, hi."

"Hi yourself. How's it going?" I stepped back, taking her in. Sleek ponytail, no-nonsense expression. Same Anna, always three steps ahead. She was sort of my role model at this point. Everyone in the circuit respected her, she represented two drivers, surely more soon, and she was my go-to for any help. She somehow could fix any problem at all.

She gave a long-suffering sigh. "We're already down one intern to some flu that is going around, the sponsors are being dramatic about changing the champagne in the cool down room, and Alexander can't decide if he wants to wear the navy or the black suit for the press event tomorrow."

"Tell him to wear the navy," I said instantly, "The black makes him look too polished. The navy softens him. People like approachable."

"I knew you'd know," she grinned, "How are you holding up? You look...glowy."

I blinked. "Good, now that the marketing posters for the Foundation are finally up, and um glowy?"

She raised an eyebrow.

"It's just uh—sunscreen," I deflected.

"Mmhm. Okay. Glowy sunscreen." She sipped her espresso and bumped her shoulder into mine. "Look, you don't have to say anything, but if you ever want to talk about it—whatever *it* is—you know where to find me."

I opened my mouth, then closed it. I wasn't ready to say anything out loud, especially not about the way Matteo made something ache deep in my chest. Or the way waking up without him beside me felt colder than it should've.

Instead, I said, "Thank you."

She smiled again, a knowing one this time, and then her phone rang. "Duty calls. See you around!"

Anna disappeared down the hall in a blur of calm chaos, and I was left alone again, staring at the half-full espresso bar and wondering how the hell I was supposed to focus on event logistics when Matteo DeLuca existed in the same radius and his picture was splashed on every wall in the Moretti paddock.

I pulled in a breath, rolled my shoulders back, and reminded myself: this was just a job. Just another race weekend.

Whatever had happened in Portofino didn't matter. It was just vacation, just to get it out of our systems.

I repeated it silently a few times, hoping it would stick.

*It didn't matter.*

The sun had barely crested over the grandstands when I crossed into the Moretti paddock on race day, my badge swinging around my neck and my phone already buzzing with three new messages from catering. I sent a one-word reply before tucking it into the pocket of my tailored blazer. The familiar hum of activity in the garage filled the air.

Organized chaos, my favorite symphony.

"Hey," Lucia's voice pulled me from my inbox. She looked calm in a breezy linen dress, hair pulled back in a low bun, Gianna perched on her hip with a tiny pair of headphones already around her neck. She beamed with pride.

"Hi, you two," I smiled at the pair, "I see Gia's already ready for the chaos."

"She insisted," Lucia laughed, "She said she wanted to prepare to be just like the drivers."

"She's halfway there. Might need to grow a little to reach the pedals though."

Lucia leaned in, her voice quieter, "I just wanted to say thank you again. For everything. The calm room has been a total game changer."

I waved her off, but warmth bloomed in my chest anyway.

When Lucia and Gianna first joined us on track I had decided to use my pull as the owner's daughter to make a designated room for them. We called it the calm room—it was cozy and private and a place to escape all the noise when it got to be too much. "It was nothing. You and Gia deserve space that feels safe."

She smiled, and I gestured for her to follow me. "Come on. Let me show you what I added."

We walked through the paddock and toward the tucked-away side room I'd designed a few months ago. This weekend was a little different but still cozy. It had low lights, beanbags, blankets, noise-canceling headphones, and a small monitor streaming the race feed. A haven, just for them. I unlocked the door and let them in.

Gianna immediately wiggled out of her mother's arms and bee-lined for the pink beanbag.

"Oh, hang on G," I said, tapping my fingers, "We're missing someone."

I ducked into the hallway and gave a small whistle. Monty padded over, leash dragging behind him.

"Special guest for Gianna," I said as I let him in.

Gianna squealed and immediately launched into a full-on puppy snuggle.

Lucia laughed softly. "You're seriously the best."

"Stop saying nice things about me. I might start getting a reputation," I smiled.

"You're a nice person, Moretti!" she shouted as I walked to the door. I blew them each a kiss.

"I prefer to be scary!" Then I pulled the door closed behind me, slipping right back into the rush of the garage.

My phone was already in my hand as I typed out a note about signage placement. I didn't even realize someone was watching me until I felt it—heat, attention, and something dangerously familiar.

I looked up.

*Matteo.*

He was leaning lazily against one of the garage partitions, still half in his Moretti track suit, curls messy and a half-grin on his face like he'd just won something.

He didn't say anything at first, just let his gaze slide over me in a way that made me feel too seen.

"What?" I asked, arching a brow and praying my voice came out steady.

"You look hot being bossy."

I blinked. "Excuse me? Would you shut up? We're in a public hallway, idiot."

He pushed off the wall, coming closer with a swagger that didn't belong this early in the morning. "Bossy. Focused. All fire. Kind of a thing for me."

I scoffed, but the way heat shot straight down my spine betrayed me. "I'm busy, and you're annoying."

"And yet," he smirked, "You're still talking to me."

"I'm only talking to you because I haven't had enough coffee to make better choices."

He leaned closer, voice dropping. "I can make a very compelling case for being your worst choice."

I should have rolled my eyes, even tried to throw a snarky comment. Shoved him toward a debrief. But instead, my mouth curled in a traitorous smile, and I stepped just close enough for him to notice.

"You think you're *so* charming."

He grinned. "I *am*."

I turned away before I could do something foolish like kiss him in the middle of the paddock. "Go do your job, DeLuca."

"You got it, boss," his voice was teasing.

I didn't look back.

Didn't have to.

I could feel the grin on my face long after he was gone.

It was nice to be back on the circuit. While vacations were nice and all, especially the one that came back to me every time I closed my eyes, I loved working in Formula One. I loved making a name for myself other than being a Moretti. People assumed I had just been given a job without any effort because of my family. I wanted to prove that, while I was a Moretti, I loved this world, and I wanted to use my name to make a difference. I was slowly being given more responsibility in terms of planning for the Moretti Foundation. I hadn't felt this motivated in a long time, felt this passionate about something. This was it; this was my spot in the empire my grandfather built. And I would make damn sure no one doubted my ability to thrive in it.

This weekend, I had three major to-do items on my list: general marketing for the Moretti Foundation, fundraising for the local children's hospital, and perfecting my pitch to the board of the Foundation. Both needed precision, and both needed me. It was also one of the largest, most marketable weekends in Formula One: the Las Vegas Grand Prix.

By 10:00 a.m., I had already dealt with a catering truck arriving at the wrong gate, three sponsorship reps trying to weasel into VIP access they didn't pay for, and someone from the hospitality team using the wrong branded champagne for the winner's podium mock-up.

I took a sip from my second coffee of the morning and clipped my headset back in place as I moved down the paddock. My heels clicked against the pavement, a soothing melody. My ever-growing heels collection and the bright red lipstick I wore on track started as my shields, but I came to love them just for me, letting that false bravado turn to actual confidence. Fake it till you make it and all that. My phone rang with some admin team members reporting that our marketing graphics were on track for this race. It was an initiative that I proposed to the team then presented to my father and Moretti board members, to reserve marketing space for this race dedicated to the Moretti Foundation, which was fundraising for the local children's hospital while we were here. When I had been researching our upcoming locations and any local charities we could potentially partner up with, The Children's Hospital of Las Vegas was immediately the top contender—something I personally took on with the approval of Henrietta. Adding that on top of prepping to pitch the end-of-season gala was a little bit overwhelming, but honestly, I kind of loved it.

"Copy that. Let's re-route the guest list and make sure Moretti Foundation banners are up around the General Access Gates," I said, adjusting the tablet in my arm. "And tell Anna I owe her a drink if she pulls that merch restock off," I relayed to the group call in my headphones.

"Nicola!"

The sound of my name in *that* voice froze me mid-step.

I turned around, and sure enough, there he stood: *Nathaniel*. Someone who I didn't have the energy to deal with today. I hadn't known he would be present at this race, but it was honestly unsurprising, especially at the Vegas Grand Prix. This would be the one he showed up at—the man loved a good show and a spotlight.

He wore a smug grin like he'd just walked out of a men's cologne ad, hands tucked into his slim-cut blazer, hair too perfectly styled. Still working for one of the luxury sponsors, still slithering around the paddock like he deserved to be there.

"Nathaniel," I said flatly.

He leaned in for a kiss on the cheek. I offered him a step back and a polite, clipped smile instead. No way in hell.

"You look good," he said, eyeing me in a way that made my skin crawl, "I heard you've been working with the charity wing now. Making your daddy proud, huh?"

There it was. That familiar little dig. Masked as a compliment, barbed like a hook.

"I make *myself* proud," I replied, feeling the anger boiling up, "The name might've opened the door, but I'm doing something good, something important."

He raised a brow, amused like he always got when I bit back. "Feisty as ever."

I resisted the urge to roll my eyes. "Some of us have things to do, Nathaniel. Was there a point to this little reunion?"

He chuckled like I was a joke. "Relax, I just wanted to say hi. How's it being DeLuca's leg up in racing? Sleeping to the top sure is an interesting move."

My stomach tightened, anger felt like it was boiling to the service at his insinuation. "Excuse me?"

He shrugged. "People talk. Didn't take you for someone to be played like that. All that effort to be taken seriously, and now you're what? Playing house with the grid's favorite golden boy? The guy who takes nothing seriously? Who's employed by your *father*? Just trying to look out for you, Nicky."

That hit me square in the ribs. And he knew it.

"Don't call me that; you lost any right to familiarity long ago. You're just jealous that you've lost what you clearly don't deserve. Matteo is the best damn driver, he's dedicated on track and to the team and you know what—" I was out of breath from my rant, my heart rate skyrocketing with the adrenaline of saying what I always wanted to tell him: that he wasn't shit. So I added the last blow with a shining smile. "His dick is huge." Then I turned on my heels and left him standing there in the middle of the paddock, probably rehearsing what clever thing he should have said, hopefully feeling inadequate.

My phone buzzed again with a reminder alert: media tent, 11:00 a.m.

*Right.*

Back to business.

But as I stalked away, my pulse still buzzing in my throat, I couldn't help but think about what Nathaniel said about Matteo. I'd worked so hard to build my reputation. To be taken seriously. To be more than just a Moretti with a pretty face. But I also found myself protective of him. He wasn't some guy who didn't take things seriously, fuck that.

But there at the back of my mind was the little voice. '*You won't be taken seriously.*' So I did something I never would have done six months ago: I ignored the voice and texted my best friend.

NICOLA:

Ran into Nathaniel.

LUCIA:

Ew why is he here?

NICOLA:

Who knows.

LUCIA:

You okay?

I sighed, staring at my phone. A question I would usually brush off, ignore and throw my mask back on with a simple, '*Yeah I'm good*'. I was trying to learn the whole '*having a close friend*' thing, but doing the healthy version of reactions was fucking hard. So I typed out my response, closed my eyes and hit send.

NICOLA:

I don't know…no?

Sitting down on a wooden bench with a red Moretti Racing sign behind me, I heard a door open and close, then a presence next to me and a soft voice.

"Hey."

"I'm really not good at this whole feelings thing," I said looking at my hands.

"You had them all along, you're just actually letting yourself feel." Lucia nudged my shoulder. "What happened with Nathaniel?"

"He was just being a dick, but then he said Matteo was using me and some other things, and I just wanted to throw up immediately."

"Seriously fuck that guy," Lucia grumbled. I looked at her in shock, sweet little Lucia out here cursing out people she didn't even know personally. I felt proud.

"You didn't want anyone to find out about you and Matteo?" she asked gently.

"It was just vacation, but now..." I trailed off, "I know he's your brother so you're team Matteo but I need you to be team me right now."

"Of course." She squeezed my hand. "Tell me what's going on."

"We were just messing around, you know, *for fun*. But it turns out I like hearing him talk. His voice, how he tells stories. He could recite a recipe to me and I would probably enjoy it."

Lucia giggled.

"It's just—I don't do the feelings thing. I swore that off after my years-long relationship ended when I found out he was cheating on me for most of it. But then I backslid again and again and sleeping with the asshole was just...convenient maybe. That sounds so awful, but it chipped away at me, how he spoke to me, talked down to me. So I swore off dating, cause who needs it anyway—" I paused. "Sorry, is this weird?"

"I'm pretending this isn't about my brother, go on."

"Well your brother is annoying, sorry." I cringed and she smiled. "But he was always showing up, flirting with me and being a goddamn menace to society, and then he kept being there during all these moments. Being helpful and sweet; it was annoying. And then it just kinda worked, and then I couldn't get him out of my head because well—things I'm not saying to you—but *damn*."

"Ew."

"And then vacation we said was just vacation, it didn't count, basically a free pass, but now we're here back in the real world and I don't know, I don't know, I don't know."

Lucia patted my hand, holding herself back from full on hugging me because she knew me and knew I didn't like physical touch. "I will repeat what I told my brother yesterday, and what

I've said before in general." She paused for effect, making me send her a half-hearted glare.

"You deserve to be loved as you are. You deserve to be happy as you are. And if someone out in this universe meets you where you're at and loves you as you are, then hold on to that with everything you have."

"How very prophetic of you."

"I do my best."

# 20

# MATTEO

*V*egas was madness. The media circus leading up to the Grand Prix had been next-level—cameras in your face, microphones shoved at your mouth, fans screaming your name from behind velvet ropes. They paraded us around like prize ponies. Eighty percent racing, twenty percent doing whatever contractual nonsense they threw our way.

Didn't mean I hated it.

I actually kind of liked it—the roar of the crowd, the buzz in the air like static before a storm. I fed off it. That electric anticipation, the way fans lit up just seeing us—it reminded me why I loved this sport in the first place.

Carlos was grinning ear to ear beside me as we stepped onto the outdoor stage. We fielded a few half-serious questions, goofed off in the bedazzled suit jackets someone from PR thought would be funny. We played along. That was part of the job too—making it look effortless.

Behind us, the Kaz Energy team waited their turn—Theo Bauer stood stiffly next to his new teammate, Austin Rhodes. British and American. Fire and water. Austin was still green, but friendly as hell. Theo, on the other hand, had the charm of a wet towel and a large ego. While the guy was known as a bit of a total douchebag, no one could deny he was a damn good racer.

"This is so fucking stupid," Theo muttered under his breath as we passed each other on the stairs.

Carlos chuckled, "He's a joy, isn't he?"

The crowd roared louder when Kaz Energy took the stage. No surprise. They were the team to beat, neck and neck with Belen Racing in the Constructors' Championship, the final scoring for team points. Moretti Racing was clawing its way back to relevance —year after year, a noncompetitive car had left the team languishing near the bottom of the top ten. Still point-scoring, sure. But not enough. It wasn't until my rookie year that we started scoring some fighting points, but the team still had work to do. Carlos and I had scored some big points this year—it was only a matter of time till we were competing with the top two. Every race, every sprint, every single point counted. High scores meant bigger sponsorships and more opportunities for the team in the coming years.

That's where I came in. Today, it was up to me to put numbers on the board. Big ones.

Carlos bumped my shoulder. "You good?"

"Yeah," I said, "I'm good, man."

He gave me a look—like he half believed me—and then we split off to join our respective crews. Vegas was a night race, which just added to the thrill. The city was already wild on a normal night, but on race weekend? It was a live wire. Every inch of the Strip pulsed with energy, adrenaline, and the scent of gasoline.

After a string of quick meetings, a strategy debrief, and a brutal cooldown session in what could only be described as the ice bath from hell, I was toweling off in the training room when Anna walked in.

"Hey," she said, tablet in hand, always too composed, "There are a couple social matters I wanted to run by you."

I straightened, heart ticking up a beat. Anna didn't interrupt pre-race prep unless she had to. My last manager would've dumped the whole media pile on me mid-warmup just to cover his own ass or be a petty asshole. But Anna? She *knew* timing.

"I know how important this race is," she continued, "So I wanted to give you the option—either we debrief after the race, or I can give you the gist now."

My chest tightened. That itch of curiosity scraped at the back of my neck—but not enough to risk shaking my focus.

I dragged a hand through my damp hair. "If it can wait, tell me after."

Anna hesitated. Just a flicker of it. "It can wait," she said, though not without effort, "I'll handle everything until then. You focus. I just didn't want to take the choice away from you."

My shoulders eased, a small pang in my chest at her words. "I appreciate that."

And I did. It was why we worked so well together. She respected that I needed control where I could get it. This sport—this season—was chaotic. But in our partnership, there was trust. Especially today. The points were on me. Carlos had qualified farther back meaning if he managed to score points, they would be miniscule. It was up to me to keep us in the fight. And with the pressure of the team, the championship battle, and a certain sharp-tongued brunette haunting the corners of my mind—I couldn't afford any more distractions.

Besides, if I didn't bring home some major points tonight?

All five feet and one inch of Nicola Moretti would have *plenty* to say about it.

I wasn't sure if that was more terrifying...or motivating.

By the time we lined up on the grid, my world had gone still.

Engines were ready and waiting. Mechanics moved in a choreographed blur around the cars, holding tire covers and doing all the things they needed to do before they pulled away and left it to us. Everything else—media noise, social obligations, even Anna's maybe-worrying news—faded into background static.

Helmet on. Gloves tight. Harness strapped.

I was dialed in.

Night hung heavy over the Strip, but the lights were blinding —spotlights, strobes, billboards towering over the barriers like electric gods. But the moment I slid into the cockpit, it all melted away. The chaos, the glitz, the spectacle that was Vegas—it couldn't touch me in here.

This was mine. This car. This track. These next two hours.

"Alright, Matteo," came the voice of my race engineer in my ear, crisp and cool as ever. "Standard start today. Long stint. Let the chaos play out up front."

"Copy," I replied, steady.

And then the lights came on.

Five red.

My fingers twitched on the paddle. Heart rate even. Every nerve on high alert, every sense tuned like a violin string. No thoughts now—just instincts. Muscle memory. A lifetime of racing wired into every reaction.

Slowly the lights blinked out one by one. Five lights, then the racing began.

I launched clean. The car in front did not. Sluggish off the line, a fraction too slow, and that was all I needed. I darted left, threading the needle between him and the wall, knowing exactly how much space I had down to the millimeter. Years of karting taught me the lines. Years of F2 taught me the grit. And now? Now I was a damn predator.

By Turn 1, I was already up a position.

By Turn 3, I was side by side with P3.

*Breathe. Brake late. Trust the grip.*

We danced through the corners, neither of us blinking. But this was where I thrived—wheel to wheel, that razor-thin line between brilliance and disaster. I nudged the car just wide enough to own the corner, and the other driver blinked first. He lifted.

I didn't.

Coming out of Sector 1, I had secured third.

"Beautiful move," my engineer said, voice laced with calm satisfaction. "You've got clean air ahead."

I could see it—Theo Bauer up front in his smug Kaz Energy rocket ship, already thinking he had the win in the bag. But the race was long. And Vegas...Vegas had a funny way of shaking things up. Alexander had qualified mid-field in twelfth, but I knew he would claw his way back up. So I locked in and focused all my energy on the road ahead and the bright blue car ahead of me.

Still, I didn't rush it.

I stayed within DRS range, conserving tires, managing fuel, letting the laps roll down like seconds on a stopwatch. It was only lap nine. No one won a race in lap nine—there was plenty of fight left—but holding onto P3 seemed unreal, let alone scoring a podium.

Theo made a mistake on lap eleven. Tiny. Barely noticeable. A lock-up going into the tight left-hander near the Sphere. But I saw it. Felt it in the timing delta. I closed the gap, waited two more laps, then made my move down the straight. He defended the inside—I went wide, holding it around the outside with barely enough grip to stick.

We were inches apart at 180 miles per hour.

But I didn't flinch.

I took the lead on lap thirteen, fighting with all I had.

Vegas blurred past me in streaks of light and shadow, the whole city screaming with sound. My world narrowed to corners and apexes and tire temps. Then someone was on my ass in the final laps. I clicked to speak to my engineer through our radio.

"Is that a Belen on me?"

"Yeah mate, Wright is coming for the front." The radio crackled through my headphones with the response. I grinned wide. A Moretti car was no match for a Belen this year. His tires were fresh, and he easily outpaced me with the next lap, but I made him work for it.

"Stay focused, DeLuca. Hold down third."

And I did just that, crossing the finish line in third place. On the cool down lap, I thumped my fist into the air.

"Good job, DeLuca," the radio crackled.

"Fucking brilliant, Matteo!" The team principal's voice crackled through the radio. It filled me with pride; it was rare he got on the radio, but Moretti was on the up and up. And it had been too far between podium finishes lately. But here I was clawing our way back. Securing fifteen points toward the championship final. Moretti was looking like it just might sit in third for the Constructor's Championship after all, which felt like a huge win.

The moment I pulled in behind the P3 marker, I punched the air, helmet still on, adrenaline surging like wildfire through my veins. The team was screaming in my ears, my engineer half-laughing, half-cheering.

I shut my eyes for half a second, just breathing it in.

*Third place.* After the season we'd had—after everything—this wasn't just a trophy. It was proof. That the car was back. That I was back. That we could still fight.

I killed the engine, unclipped my belts, and climbed out of the cockpit to a sea of noise—cheering, roaring, music already pumping from the speakers around the finish line. The Vegas lights painted the tarmac in gold and neon, making everything look surreal.

"Matteo!"

I turned just in time to catch Alexander as he barreled toward me, still in his race suit, grinning like a maniac.

He pulled me into a hug so tight I nearly dropped my helmet.

"Fucking proud of you," he said, voice rough in my ear. "That was a masterclass."

I laughed, clapping him on the back. "You didn't think I could do it, huh?"

"I *always* thought you could," he said, pulling back to squeeze my shoulders. "You just needed the right moment."

This was it. This *was* the moment.

The Moretti crew had pushed up to the barriers, red flooding the fence line—mechanics, engineers, pit wall, all cheering their hearts out. I jogged over and threw myself into their arms. Arms slung around me. Someone handed me a team flag. There were shouts of *"Matteo! Matteo!"*

I looked up at the crowd, eyes scanning for my familiar faces. My sister, Gianna, and Nicola.

Alexander had slipped away from the celebration—just for a second—but it was enough. He was walking over to my sister.

She was cheering and smiling brightly. Her eyes bright and wide as she watched him come toward her like nothing else existed.

He didn't hesitate.

He cupped her face in both hands and kissed her like the whole damn world had gone quiet.

The crowd around them cheered even louder—Belen crew who had put the pieces together, fans who lived for that kind of *'love story in real time'* moment. But all I saw was the way her hands found his jacket, tugging him closer like she couldn't help it.

My chest squeezed. I was so fucking happy for them. For the way Alexander looked at her like she was gravity itself. For the way she softened around him, like he'd carved out a space in her armor only he could reach.

*I wanted that.*

# NICOLA

$\mathcal{M}$usic thudded from the speakers. Red, white, and gold confetti rained down and clung to the pavement like glittering footprints of victory.I stood toward the back of the crowd, watching the team's celebration from a modest distance. My father was at the front near the mechanics, laughing and clapping Matteo on the back with pride. Gianna was perched on Lucia's hip, bouncing with excitement, her tiny hands mimicking the waving flags around her.

The awards ceremony came after. Alexander stood tall on the top step, beaming as the anthem played.

And just to his left—Matteo.

Third place. A stunning drive. The kind of race that had everyone on the edge of their seats until the checkered flag dropped.

Across the crowd, over the heads and cheers and roaring team pride—he found me.

Our eyes locked.

And then he winked.

God, that wink. All heat and trouble and history, like it carried every whispered word and bruised-lipped kiss we'd shared during that stolen week in Portofino.

I barely registered the world around me. The podium celebration became a blur. I celebrated with the crew members around me, my father coming over beaming.

"That DeLuca boy, he has something," he said over the roar of the cheers. I smiled. He sure did. The trophies were handed out, Matteo holding up the track-shaped award with the biggest smile I had ever seen. I couldn't help it; the burst of sunshine that radiated off him was contagious. I was smiling right along, circling my hands around my mouth and cheering with everyone around me. His eyes caught mine again. I was in front with my father at this point below the podium stage. Being short had its perks, one of them being I was usually shuffled to the front since I couldn't see but also wouldn't block anyone. Champagne mist filled the air, fireworks went off behind the stage. It was pure magic.

After the champagne showers, the boys were pulled into interviews, and I walked back with the crew. Walking the track after the race was a different type of magic, but a night race under the Vegas lights was extra special. I took a bit of the long way, soaking it all in. I was so glad I joined this season on track, that I took the chance to do something more, to be something more. Finding a space in Moretti Racing that felt right was not something I had really expected. I was never the anticipated heir, but getting the Foundation more traction, wanting to grow that side, to make a difference in the world? It felt good.

I was smiling to myself by the time I walked into the Moretti trailers, all stupid and happy. The DeLucas were clearly rubbing off on me. I tried to fix my face as I walked in, but everyone was smiling and cheering each other on, and it was infectious. I rounded the corner near the back of the Moretti hospitality suite and a hand caught my wrist and spun me into a hidden alcove between two transport crates.

Warm.

Fast.

*Him.*

Still flushed from the excitement of the night, fire in his eyes, sweat slicking the curls at his temples. His racing suit was unzipped halfway, clinging to his waist, chest rising and falling fast from the adrenaline still pouring through him.

"Matteo—"

But then his hand was on my waist, the other cradling my jaw, thumb brushing my cheek like he couldn't believe I was real. His forehead rested briefly against mine, grounding. Intimate.

"I know we said vacation was over," he breathed, voice low and wrecked, "But I can't do this anymore. I can't pretend you didn't ruin me that week. I can't sleep. I hate when you're not around. The last few days have felt like an eternity. I need you around, I need these lips, your snark, your fucking temper." His thumb brushed over my bottom lip, pulling it down slightly. "I'm addicted, Nicola."

I swallowed hard, the back of my shoulders hitting the crate behind me.

"Matteo..."

"I see you," he said, lips ghosting over mine. "In the crowd. In my thoughts. When I'm racing. When I'm trying not to care. You're in every corner of me now. You burrowed into my bones."

The kiss that followed was devastating.

Not soft. Not careful.

It was the kind of kiss that made the stars reel and the ground vanish. That stole breath and time and reason. That said things he hadn't said out loud yet, things I wasn't sure I was ready to hear.

But I kissed him back anyway. Like maybe I could memorize the shape of his mouth, like maybe I could stop my heart from turning inside out every time he touched me.

His hands tightened at my hips. Mine slid up his damp chest, greedy, breathless, still tasting the champagne on his lips.

Then he pulled back just enough to whisper, "Fuck vacation."

My chest ached, torn between wanting to run and wanting to fall.

He smiled then, his thumb brushing over the corner of my lip.

"Tell me to stop," he said. "Tell me you don't want this, and I'll leave, I'll never bring it up again Nic, but if there's anything, anything at all, let's try."

I didn't tell him to stop, his words sinking into me, drifting into my heart, the same heart that beat fast when I saw him, when I thought of him. So, I shook my head, as if to say *'I can't tell you to stop, I don't want you to stop.'* Matteo tilted his head, dimples showing, making me melt.

"I need your words, Princess." Matteo was still too close, too flushed, too unfairly beautiful. His eyes searched mine, wild and soft all at once, like he'd just handed me his heart without even asking if I wanted it.

"Don't you dare stop," I gritted out, and his lips crashed back into mine. It was the kind of kiss that left you spun inside out and breathless. He grinned, cocky and unbothered, dimples in full effect. I hated how much I wanted to kiss him again, which I fully intended on doing until a third voice broke the spell.

"Oh good," Anna said, appearing with the timing of a tactically deployed grenade. "I was hoping to find both of you."

I jumped back like I'd been caught doing something I shouldn't be. Which was sort of ridiculous since Anna knew what was going on. Matteo scrubbed a hand through his hair, wiping the lipstick smudge from his jaw like a guilty teenager. Anna's brows lifted slightly, but she didn't comment.

"Walk with me?" she asked, already turning toward the Moretti hospitality suite with the air of someone who didn't need you to agree. We followed. Matteo beside me, casual as ever, like he hadn't just whispered life-altering things against my mouth in a racing trailer alcove. Inside, she led us to the back lounge—quiet, far from the noise and celebration. She waited until the door clicked shut, then turned, tablet tucked under one arm.

"I wanted to flag something before the press beats us to it," she said evenly. "There are whispers going around the circuit. People talking. About...the two of you."

I blinked. "Us?"

"Yes. You were seen in Portofino. There's speculation. And a lot of very interested gossip accounts who think it's more than just friendly team relations. A claimed insider confirming you're together. Which is fine. *If* you want to go public. But if you don't, we need to get ahead of it before someone else controls the narrative."

Matteo leaned back against the wall like she'd just asked him about tire strategy. Cool. Collected.

I, meanwhile, felt like someone had cracked my chest open and set my heart under a magnifying glass.

Because I didn't know.

I didn't know what I wanted.

I'd sworn this off. All of it. Relationships. Complications. People knowing too much about my life. I'd watched my last relationship unravel in the spotlight. And even if Matteo wasn't him—even if he was kind and careful and maddening in a completely different way—it didn't erase the part of me that flinched at the idea of everyone knowing.

Of everyone commenting.

And yet.

I couldn't deny the pull.

The way he saw me. The way I came undone in his arms. The way my name sounded in his voice when he said it like a promise.

I dragged a hand through my hair. "What...exactly are they saying?"

Anna gave a tight smile. "The usual. A few videos trying to match timelines. A blurry photo here and there. A Reddit thread that's weirdly invested. It's not a scandal, but it's gaining traction. And the longer we don't address it, the more room we give them to make it messy."

Matteo glanced at me. I didn't look back. My throat was tight. I didn't want this to be some public spectacle. I also didn't want to pretend it was nothing anymore. But time wasn't exactly a luxury we could afford as people in a spotlight-driven career.

Anna waited patiently. She knew how to navigate fires. But this? This wasn't fire yet. It was smoke. Rising slowly. Giving us a chance to decide which way we wanted the wind to blow.

"Let's not comment," he said gently, eyes still on me. "Let's take a few days. Let it cool down. If we decide to say something, we'll do it together."

That last word lingered.

Together.

He didn't say *If we're together*. He just said *Together*.

I exhaled, relief and confusion tangled inside me. Anna nodded. "That works—for now. But if the media gets aggressive, we'll need a new plan." She sent a smile our way before tapping away on her tablet and saying she'd be right back. The door closed behind her, leaving just the two of us again.

I didn't look at him right away. Because if I did, I might've told him I wanted to kiss him again. Or that I wasn't ready for any of this. Or that I was. Or that I'd already fallen so hard it scared me. And I didn't know which truth would come out first.

The silence still clung to the air after Anna left. I hadn't moved. Matteo hadn't either. There was too much unsaid between us, and too many cameras waiting outside to say any of it.

The door creaked open again—just as I took a breath to speak —and in walked Lucia, cheeks flushed, bright eyes sparkling under the overhead lights. Alexander followed right behind her with Gianna tucked in his arms, small and soft and fast asleep. All golden curls and pink cheeks, her tiny head rested on his shoulder. Lucia grinned as she caught sight of us. "There you are. We've been looking all over."

Alexander smirked, shifting the little girl in his arms with the careful ease of someone who'd clearly done this a hundred times.

"Gianna couldn't hang," he said softly, eyes shining with something more than podium joy. "Out cold."

Matteo chuckled, stepping forward to gently brush a hand over her head. "She lasted longer than I thought, honestly. Big day and night."

"She waved the flag for at least fifteen minutes," Lucia said proudly then her focus shifted to us, a glint in her eye. "Are we going out tonight or what?"

Matteo raised his brows, Alexander's grin turned dangerous, and I blinked in slow realization.

"Out?" I repeated.

"It's Vegas," Lucia said with a shrug. "You both podiumed; we must celebrate! That calls for a fun drink and some dancing."

Alexander shifted Gianna again. "We were thinking about that rooftop club Kaz Energy booked out. Racers, team crew, sponsors, that kind of scene. Probably half the grid will be there, but there's a bunch of parties going on so we can scope out whatever works."

Lucia glanced down at Gianna, her expression soft. "I just need to ask if—"

"I can take her," came Anna's voice from the doorway.

We all turned.

She stood with her arms crossed, but there was something unusually warm in her face—a softness that rarely slipped through the cracks of her always-composed exterior.

"I was *hoping* someone would suggest it," she added, stepping inside. "I'd rather not spend my night in some overcrowded rooftop bar with strobe lights and overpriced tequila. That sounds like an actual punishment."

Lucia blinked. "Are you sure?"

Anna nodded. "Absolutely. I'll take her back to the suite, put on a movie, maybe even relax for the first time today. Honestly? Living the dream. But I *will* be stealing your hotel robe."

Alexander chuckled as he gently passed over Gianna, still fast asleep, her cheek pressed against his shoulder until Anna took her with practiced ease.

"Thank you," Lucia said quietly, brushing a tender hand along her daughter's back. "Seriously."

Anna just waved it off like it was nothing. "Go enjoy yourselves. You all earned it tonight."

Lucia turned to me, one brow arched, all wicked grin. "Come on. Don't overthink it. Put on something slutty and sparkly."

I laughed—caught off guard by how natural it felt, like the tension in my chest hadn't just been wound tight ten minutes ago.

Matteo glanced over with an exaggerated look of offense. "What? The paddock princess doesn't want to go out on the town?"

I hesitated.

Not because I didn't want to—I did. But part of me was still stuck on the kiss, on the way Matteo had looked at me in the hallway. And another part of me was remembering how this used to feel—nights out, bright lights, dancing until our feet ached, the chaos of it all. Before everything got complicated.

Alexander tilted his head, studying me. "You good, Moretti? You've quite literally never turned down a night out."

I bit back my smile, letting the edge of it slip through. "Okay, okay. Obviously I want to go out with you idiots."

"*Rude*," Matteo said, fake-scandalized. "I took honors classes, thank you very much."

Lucia rolled her eyes. "Alright, enough. Boys—go change. Nic, let's raid your room. I'm stealing a dress. And maybe those gold heels."

Now *that* was something I could get on board with.

I grinned. "Only if I get to do your makeup."

"I wouldn't dream of going out without the Nicola Moretti touch."

We slipped out together, already trading outfit ideas and gossip, leaving the boys to their own chaos. The hallway buzzed with energy, and I realized this was easy and fun. I just needed to get out of my head.

"So..." I dragged the word out like a ribbon as I leaned against the dresser, watching Lucia rifle through my shoe lineup. "How're you and Alexander after making it official?"

Her cheeks went pink immediately, like I'd flipped a switch. She looked up with that soft, melty expression I rarely saw on her—like she'd just remembered a secret kiss in the rain or some equally nauseating moment.

"It's good, really good," she said shyly.

I smiled before I could stop myself. "I'm really happy for you, Luce."

She turned toward me, blinking like she hadn't expected that. Her eyes went all gushy, like she was two seconds from tackling me in a hug.

I straightened my shoulders like a soldier. "Please don't," I said preemptively.

She just sighed dreamily and flopped onto the bed instead, head in her hands. "He's so dreamy. I swear to God, it's like he walked off the pages of a romance novel."

I snorted. "He's obsessed with you. As he should be."

"Mmhm," she hummed, tying the straps on the golden heels she'd chosen. Then she looked at me over her shoulder, all sly and smug. "Speaking of obsessed..."

I paused, dabbing the red lipstick against my bottom lip. "What?"

"How's post-vacation going?" she asked, like she wasn't about to ruin my whole night with that one question.

My shoulders sagged. I turned from the mirror, lipstick still uncapped in my hand. "It sucks. Like, *actually* sucks. I thought I was fine, but—God, it seriously, absolutely sucks."

Lucia sat up straighter, concerned but also very ready for the tea. "What happened?"

"He found me after the race," I started, heart already picking up speed, "And basically said he wanted us to be a thing. Not just Portofino. Not just a vacation. *Us*. It was just so—"

"Romantic?" Lucia supplied, grinning like the menace she was.

I rolled my eyes so hard I saw the inside of my brain. "No. Yes. Whatever. It was very *something*."

"But I thought you swore off men?" she teased, raising a brow.

"I did! And serious things! I had a whole speech about it. Men suck."

"Totally," she said, struggling not to laugh.

"But then he goes and says stuff like '*you burrowed into my bones*' and *means it* with those big brown eyes and his stupid, stupid dimples." I snapped the lipstick cap back on and groaned into my hands, "I'm doomed."

Lucia grinned. "Okay, okay. But what if you told him you need to take it slow? Maybe your emotionally unavailable coding gets tricked into letting yourself be happy."

I tossed a towel at her face. "Shut up."

She caught it and laughed. "I'm serious, Nic. He's annoyingly good at communicating. But you have to open up. Tell him where you're at. What you're thinking."

"That's the problem," I muttered. "I don't *know* what I'm thinking."

Lucia's expression softened. "Okay. Then let's scale it down."

She tapped her chin dramatically. "Do you want a relationship?"

I recoiled. "Too big a question."

"Got it. Smaller." She leaned in. "Do you think about him when we're not on track?"

I shot her a death glare.

"I'll take that as a yes," she chirped, smug as ever. "Do you see stupid things and want to tell him about them?"

I nodded. Quietly. Pathetically.

"Do you want to date someone else?"

"God, no."

She smiled. "Hmm. Seems like you like him."

"*Obviously*. But what the hell do I do about that?"

Lucia gave a helpless shrug. "Tell him? That's usually step one."

I sighed dramatically and flopped onto the bed next to her, our knees bumping. "Can we start with just looking incredibly hot for tonight?"

"Now *that* I can do," she said, already reaching for my makeup bag like it was a mission.

We grinned at each other, that comfortable kind of best-friend quiet.

# 22

# MATTEO

My sister walked down first, doing a little spin before Alexander literally clapped and pulled her in for a kiss while she swatted him away because of her lip gloss or whatever. I was about to ask where Nicola was when I swore the room stilled and went silent, lights glowing only for her.

I was in so much trouble.

She stunned in a bright red dress that hugged her curves and silver heels. Her signature red lip was in place as usual, and her hair was down, making her look like a literal goddess.

*Fuck me.*

How was I supposed to be normal around her? Not act like a drooling dog following her around all night? There was no hope. I was in free fall for this woman, just waiting for her to jump. So I turned on the charm, the one she loved to hate.

"Hey gorgeous," I greeted.

"Hey yourself." She gave me a very unbelievable glare, but she took the arm I held out, wrapping her perfectly manicured nails around my bicep. She squeezed, and it sent a chill through me. I wanted those nails on me more, wanted them scraping down my back and that dress on the floor.

I cleared my throat trying to get a hold of myself.

"Maybe we'll get lucky and Theo bailed on his team's party," Alexander grumbled.

"He's such a tool," Nicola agreed. I tensed. Had he said something to her? Did one of his barbs get thrown her way? Did he hit on her?

"Relax, caveman," she leaned in, whispering. I tried to. But seriously, Theo was an asshole. Especially to women. He was a playboy of the worst kind: didn't give a single fuck about anything but winning. And unfortunately, he was a damn good driver.

My mind went back to being obsessed with the touch of the woman next to me in the car. Her legs pushed up against mine. There was plenty of room, but she was sitting next to me, leaving the gap to her left side. She was *choosing* to be this close. When the car lurched into a break for some crazy Vegas traffic, her hand reached out and gripped my thigh, making blood rush straight through me.

"Sorry," she mumbled, pulling her hand back. I grabbed it and put it back with a little force. I saw her eyes heat. Then she bit her lip, making me want to pull over and call a cab right back to the hotel. Going out was overrated. Who needed to celebrate anyway?

"We're here!" Lucia announced, opening the door, the lights and noise of the Strip invading our quiet space. "Let's go!" She reached out, tugging Nicola with her. They linked arms and walked a pace ahead of us. Cameras flashed everywhere. Paparazzi shouted.

"Matteo! Alex!"

"Matteo, go get your girlfriend! We want a picture!"

The crowd grew rowdy, people pushing, a barrier falling and crashing to the ground. The small walkway was flooded. A security guard came out and led us through the sea. Inside the lobby door stood Nicola and Lucia, looking a little overwhelmed.

"Um...that was extra crazy," Lucia commented as Alexander came up and tugged her into his arms.

"Sorry, Angel. I'm glad you stayed ahead with Nicola though." He kissed her forehead and took her hand in his. Nicola fell into step beside me, brushing her shoulder against mine.

"You okay?" she asked, voice low, nudging me gently.

My head was spinning from what the crowd outside had shouted. I'd learned to tune them out over the years—to block out the camera flashes and the chaos. But one line had slipped through the cracks like a needle to the ribs.

"*Are you sleeping with Nicola to get ahead?*"

What the actual fuck?

I shook my head, trying to clear the noise. "Yeah. Yeah, I'm good," I lied, flashing her a smile that didn't quite reach her eyes. "Just—the paps were saying weird shit."

Her brows pinched together, concern coloring her features. "Do you think it's what Anna was talking about? The rumors?" Her phone buzzed in her tiny glittering purse, and the moment she pulled it out, I knew. The name glowing on the screen made my blood run cold.

*Nathaniel.*

Nicola's mouth flattened. "What the hell does he want?"

She unlocked her phone with a sharp swipe. One message. One fucking sentence.

> NATE:
>
> Told you. Even the media thinks he's using you.

Below that, a link. I already knew I wouldn't like it. But Nicola tapped it anyway, thumb tight on the screen. The tabloid site loaded in seconds. Bold font screamed back at us.

*Exclusive: Inner Source Confirms Relationship Between Moretti F1 Driver Matteo DeLuca and Moretti Heiress Nicola Moretti*

But what stole my attention was the photo. A selfie.

*Our* selfie.

From Portofino. On the lounge chair outside the villa. She was wrapped in a robe, tongue sticking out at the camera like she was trying to make me laugh. I was grinning. God, I looked happy. I'd taken that picture on my phone. *Only* on my phone.

Nicola's breath hitched.

Her eyes snapped to mine, wide, hurt, betrayed.

"Matteo?" she said, her voice small. Cracked at the edges.

And fuck, that broke me.

"I didn't," I said instantly, heart slamming against my ribs. "I *swear*, Nic. I would never—I didn't give that photo to anyone. I swear to God."

I reached for her, desperate to close the space between us, but she flinched away like I'd burned her. My hand dropped uselessly at my side.

"What's going on?" Lucia paused in front of us, noticing we weren't following. We were in a hallway now, past the lobby, no one was paying attention to us. I waved her over. Nicola was frozen, phone in hand, headline displayed. Lucia walked over cautiously to her friend.

"Hey, babes. What's going on?" she asked again gently. Nicola looked to her then to the phone, in a bit of a daze.

Lucia stepped closer, eyes scanning her friend, then the phone. Her breath caught.

"Oh," she whispered.

Alexander appeared beside her, taking one look and muttering, "Shit."

"Should I call Anna?" I asked quietly.

Nicola didn't answer. She didn't even blink. Just…silent. Still. And I hated it. I craved her spark, her fire, her mouthy comebacks. Anything but this statue-like version of her.

"Where did they get this photo?" Lucia asked, sharp. Her eyes flicked to me, accusation starting to bloom there. "You took that, didn't you?"

"Yeah," I said quickly, running a hand through my hair. "But I have no fucking clue how they got it."

"Where do you store your photos?" Alexander asked, stepping in.

"My phone?" I answered dumbly. "They're backed up. You know, cloud stuff."

He gave me a grim look. "Mate...I think you've been hacked."

My stomach dropped.

"No, no—shit." I fumbled to check my phone, unlocking it, heart hammering. Sure enough, a little green checkmark sat next to the backup sync. Everything was there. All my photos, all my private shit. My digital world wide-open.

"Who's had access to your phone?" Lucia asked sharply.

"No one. Just Anna. She posts race content sometimes, but that's it." My eyes scanned the room like it could give me the answer.

Then I saw it—Alexander's face twisting. Rage flickered beneath the surface.

"Motherfucker," he muttered.

"What?" Lucia practically yelled.

We both said it at the same time: "*Matt*."

Lucia's face screwed up in confusion. "Who the hell is Matt?"

"My old manager," I muttered, jaw tight. "The one I fired before the start of the season."

"Okay..."

"He's a dick," I added, because that felt like the only way to describe him. "But the reason I dropped him was because he was leaking information. Where'd I'd be eating with friends during breaks or where I'd be between weekends. It was too frequent to make sense, but Dante did some digging and found out it was Matt who was leaking my location to tabloids and paparazzi.

. . .

"He was pissed about being dropped," I continued. "That was a huge blow to his ego."

"No way," Lucia breathed, eyes going wide. "You didn't tell me any of this. I thought you just, like...switched to Anna."

"I didn't want to stress you out," I admitted "And Anna made it easy. Seamless transition. I handled it quietly, paid him a hefty severance even. I didn't want anyone to be upset—mom, dad or you, Luce."

I raked both hands through my hair, the guilt gnawing like acid. "I never thought he'd have access to anything after. But I don't think I ever changed my passwords. He must've still had a device logged in somewhere. It's...it's classic Matt."

Lucia's jaw was tight now, fury rolling off her in waves. "So help me God, I'm going to find that piece of shit and *end* him."

That pulled Nicola back to life.

She blinked, eyes lifting to Lucia—fire returning, slow and simmering. The corner of her mouth twitched.

"Isn't the thing upstairs...Theo's party?" she asked, voice calm. Too calm.

I nodded warily. "Yeah..."

Then she turned.

And strutted down the hall toward the elevators.

"Nic!" Lucia called, hurrying after her. "Hello? Earth to Nicola? What's happening?"

We all followed, the hallway echoing with our footsteps. The silence in the elevator was sharp and tense, but Nicola? She was composed. Dangerous.

I didn't know what she was planning—but I knew that look. Her rage was back.

And I would follow her straight to hell if that's where she was headed.

The elevator dinged. The doors slid open.

Music. Lights. Bass heavy in our chests. Voices rising in laughter and celebration.

The party was already in full swing.

And Nicola Moretti was about to walk straight through it like a goddamn storm.

Nicola hadn't said a single word since deciding we were headed to the club. She didn't need to. Her posture said it all—straight spine, jaw set, heels striking against the floor like war drums. She was a goddamn storm in glitter heels and a satin dress.

Lucia looked about five seconds from panic. "Okay, listen," she started as we stepped into the club. "I fully support whatever you're about to do—but maybe, um, tell us what that is first?"

Nicola didn't even slow her stride. "I'm going inside."

"Okay..." Lucia drawled. "And to do what?"

I tried to hold in my grin. My sister looked ready to have a breakdown, and Nicola...looked mildly unhinged. Not in a bad way. More in a terrifyingly hot, goddess-of-wrath kind of way.

"Just talk," Nicola said with a wicked little smirk that lit up the adrenaline in my veins like a fuse.

I didn't even know how she knew who Matt was. I had never told her about him. But Nicola had her ear to the ground when it came to the F1 circuit. She probably knew everyone's shoe size and therapy schedule. She didn't just walk into rooms—she *owned* them. And right now, she was parting the club crowd like the damn Red Sea.

Lucia trailed close behind, shooting glances over her shoulder like we were headed into a lion's den. Alexander was a solid wall at her back, protective and silent. And me?

I followed in the rear, heart pounding. Terrified and awestruck. Ready to tear Matt's throat out and kiss Nicola senseless all in the same breath.

We spotted Matt and Theo by the bar—Matt leaning smugly against the counter, Theo looking disinterested in the way only he could, sipping his drink like the world owed him a podium.

Nicola didn't hesitate.

"Hey, shithead!" she called, striding straight up with her arms crossed.

Matt's head whipped up. Theo glanced over, looking bored.

"Excuse me?" Matt sneered, eyes narrowing.

"Yeah, *you*." She pointed.

I clenched my fists, fighting every instinct in me that screamed to shield her. She didn't need protection. Not from me. She was all fire and fury.

"And who are you?" Matt asked, voice dripping with smugness.

Her hip cocked as she stared him down. "You know *exactly* who I am."

She leaned in, voice cool and low. "I want you to know you're a pathetic little worm of a man. I want you to know I know *exactly* what you did. And if you come near me, my family, or *my* people again, you'll never work in Formula One again. I will ruin you. Burn every bridge you have left and salt the damn ashes."

A few people at the bar looked over, drivers looking impressed before going back to their conversations. Lucia blinked like she was watching a live crime drama. Alexander looked ready to put Matt through the floor, which was comforting.

Matt laughed, mean and mocking, "You gonna let your girlfriend of the month fight your battles, DeLuca?"

I didn't even get a word out before Nicola stepped in front of me.

"I'm speaking to you," she said sharply, and in a single move, swiped Matt's phone from the bar.

He lunged.

"Don't you fucking touch her," I growled, heat and fury flooding my body like wildfire.

Matt recoiled but spat back, "Give me my phone back, you stupid bitch—"

Wrong. *So wrong.*

Alexander and I moved at the same time.

"Watch your fucking mouth," Alexander snapped, pulling Lucia safely behind him.

Nicola didn't even flinch. She smiled sweetly, then lifted the phone and smashed it on the bar.

*Crack*.

"This is for being a slimy, miserable little man." *Smash*. "And this is for betraying Matteo."

She tossed the shattered remains to the floor with finality.

"And *that*," she said, standing tall, "Is for leaking that photo. For trying to spin some cheap lie like he's using me. For thinking you could touch *anything* we've built and not get burned."

Then she turned slightly and pointed back at me. "This man right here? He's earned every goddamn thing he has. So congrats—you failed."

Matt's jaw dropped.

And then she turned to Theo, who was rather calm. "And you might want to watch your back with that one," she said, nodding toward Matt.

Theo just nodded. The most serious I'd ever seen him.

And then she was marching away.

We all stood there, stunned. I glanced at Matt one last time. "Sucks about your phone, man."

Alexander snorted, "Shame."

We regrouped in a quieter private lounge, tucked into a corner of the club. Carlos waved us over, already surrounded by a few other drivers and their friends.

Nicola marched up to him, hugging him tight. "I need a drink."

Carlos pulled back, eyebrows raised. "Oh God. What did she do?"

"Matt leaked a photo," Lucia said cheerfully, because she was clearly riding the high of having a chaotic best friend. "Nic smashed his phone."

Carlos looked appropriately proud. He bumped her shoulder. "Hell yeah, you did. Let's get you that drink, Moretti."

"About damn time," she muttered, collapsing into the couch.

"You're so badass," Lucia said, flopping down beside her. "Like, terrifying, but *inspiring*. I want to be you when I grow up."

Nicola cracked a real smile then. The tension eased slightly. Carlos flagged a waitress. Drinks started flowing, and slowly, the buzz of celebration returned.

I kept watching her. Trying to read her. Trying to figure out how much of tonight had actually shaken her.

And then, about an hour in, she leaned in and whispered, "Let's go talk."

She nodded toward a hallway lit by a neon sign pointing to the restrooms. My heart stuttered. I followed her in silence.

The hallway was dim and hushed, the music just a faint thump in the walls. A few modern art pieces hung crookedly on the plaster, bathed in low light.

She stopped and turned to face me. "Hey."

My throat tightened at the softness in her voice.

"Hey, Princess," I said quietly, trying to smile. My heart was a mess—thrumming too fast, too loud. Was this it? Was she going to end it?

"I wanted to talk..." she started, voice tentative. "I'm not good with feelings. Like, *really* bad. But I need you to know it's not you. Any of this—it's not you."

I exhaled, shoulders finally dropping.

"I'm sorry about the photo," I said. And I meant it. Every syllable.

"No. Uh-uh." She held up a hand, her voice sharp, "You have *nothing* to apologize for. That piece of shit violated your privacy. You didn't do anything wrong, not a damn thing. Don't even *think* about carrying that weight."

She looked so fierce, arms crossed, eyes blazing. Tiny and terrifying. And God, I adored her.

"Still," I said, "It involved you. And that part kills me."

She stepped closer. "You know what pissed me off the most? That article didn't just leak a photo. It implied you—everything you've earned—meant nothing."

Her fingers brushed my cheek.

"That they disrespected *you*."

I blinked at her. "Not mad about the whole bombshell romance reveal?"

She shrugged. "Despite all my anti-relationship speeches...I *like* you, Matteo DeLuca. And it's driving me *insane*."

She was close now. So close I could count the gold flecks in her eyes.

"Nicola Moretti likes someone?" I teased, "Never thought I'd see the day."

She swatted my arm. "You've completely ruined my men-are-trash worldview."

"You're so very welcome."

"You're infuriating."

"But you *like* me," I teased.

She groaned. "God, I already regret telling you."

She took a breath, her gaze steady now. "But I'm serious. I'm suing that media outlet for defamation."

I grinned. "You'd sue the tabloids for me, Moretti?"

"That's exactly what I said, stupid."

And then her fingers hooked in the collar of my shirt. Tugged me down.

"Now shut up," she murmured, "And kiss me already."

I didn't have to be told twice. The second those words left her mouth, my hand was on her cheek, sliding slowly like I was trying to memorize every inch of her skin. My fingers traced the line of her cheekbone, brushing behind her ear before sinking into the soft waves of her hair.

"All you had to do was ask, Princess," I whispered, lips ghosting over hers. My voice was rougher than I meant it to be, but she made it impossible to breathe, let alone sound suave.

Then I tugged her to me, and kissed her like the world might end. The second our lips met, it was chaos and clarity all at once. It was electric when our lips collided. Kissing her was like the first sip of espresso in the morning: it shot right through me, woke me up, and invigorated my very soul. My favorite damn feeling in the world. And she kissed me back like she felt it too. Like she'd been waiting for this. Maybe not tonight. Maybe not even consciously. But deep down? She'd been craving it just as much as I had.

Her hands fisted the front of my shirt, pulling me even closer, and God help me, I groaned into her mouth. There was nothing soft or tentative about it anymore—this was messy, greedy, *real*. Every unsaid word, every lingering look from the last few weeks— it was all pouring out in the way our mouths moved together.

"You're going to be the end of me," I mumbled against her lips, kissing her again before she could answer.

Her smile broke through the kiss, lips curving right against mine. "You wish you were that lucky." She pulled back, just an inch, breath heavy, lips kiss-swollen. Her hands stayed on my chest, but her eyes searched mine like she was waiting for something.

For me to say it.

To mean it.

To prove I wasn't scared of this, even if we both kind of were.

"I rather like you too, Moretti," I murmured, brushing her hair off her face. "And I'm not saying that to complicate things. I'm saying it because it's true. And because I don't want to stop."

Her brows knitted together, but her hands tightened on my shirt like she wasn't ready to let go either.

"I don't want you to stop, DeLuca," she whispered. "And it's *very* inconvenient."

"Good," I said, kissing her again, softer this time. Slower. "Because I've got at least five more compliments and three metaphors lined up about how good you taste."

"Don't push it."

I grinned. "Too late."

She rolled her eyes, but there was a laugh tangled with it now —and I knew I'd never stop chasing that sound.

# 23

# NICOLA

"Let's leave," he whispered.

And just like that, my brain short-circuited.

His voice was low, rough from all the kissing and the yelling and probably years of ruining hearts without even trying. His thumb brushed along my jaw like he couldn't help himself. Like touching me had become a reflex.

"My room still has those chocolates you hoard," he added, voice barely audible over the thump of the club music. "I've got better ideas for us than dancing in a club."

I flushed at his words. Heated memories played in my mind like a slideshow. "Is that where the rest of your metaphors are stored? Oh God, will you start reading me poems or something?"

His grin was devastating. And my heart fluttered at the way his eyes creased. It was so easy with him, to still be silly but heated all at the same time. I watched his jaw flex as his gaze took me in under the low light of the club. I wanted to memorize the moment, this version of him, to store it away just for me. Matteo leaned in, eyes darkening, and kissed just below my ear—soft, possessive, maddening. "Sure, Princess. Among other things."

And that was it.

I grabbed his hand and muttered, "Lead the way, DeLuca. Before I start making good decisions."

We didn't even make it ten feet outside the elevator in the hotel before his hand was back on my waist, pulling me close like I was something fragile and breakable and his all at once. I had half a mind to roll my eyes at the drama of it all, but then he kissed me like he meant it again, and I forgot every smart thing I'd ever known. A blur of lips and hands and me trying to figure out when the hell I became the kind of person who felt like if I wasn't kissing this man I would simply perish.

The second the door to his hotel room clicked shut behind us, I stopped pretending I was in control.

His jacket came off first, mine shortly after. I kicked off my heels with something that was more desperation than grace and nearly tripped trying to step out of them.

"Your fault if I die," I muttered.

"I'd give you CPR," he whispered, tugging me toward him. "Very thorough CPR."

We stumbled backward toward the bed like two people who had no idea what they were doing and also knew exactly what they were doing.

My fingers found the hem of his shirt and yanked. He didn't even pause to help—just let me strip it off like I had a vendetta against fabric. Which, honestly, I might've.

Every touch. Every press of skin against skin. Every sigh. It felt like fire and clarity and danger and everything I swore I didn't want. The way my heart rattled in my chest at the way he looked at me. Wanting to touch him, to be touched by him. Having his hand on my back or secretly on my thigh under a table. I craved it now; I think I might crave it forever.

Matteo was laying on his back, one arm tucked behind his head, staring at the ceiling like it held all the answers he didn't have. His other hand was curled loosely around mine, resting between us on the sheets. Our fingers were barely touching, like even in this post-everything haze, we were still testing the weight of the moment.

I stared at the ceiling too, pretending like I wasn't turning this into a whole thing in my head.

But I was.

God, I *so* was.

I swallowed, voice low. "Can I ask you something?"

"Of course," he said, like it was the easiest thing in the world.

It wasn't.

"Do you think..." I paused, trying to untangle the mess in my chest. "Do you think we could really, actually do this? Like...a serious thing?"

Matteo turned toward me, propping himself up on one elbow. "You mean you and me?"

"No, I mean you and Carlos," I deadpanned, trying to cover the shake in my voice. "Obviously you and me."

He smiled, but it was small. Quiet. "I think about it all the time."

That undid something in me.

Because I did too.

And it scared the shit out of me.

"I don't know how to do this," I said, suddenly feeling very naked despite the sheet wrapped around me. "It's been a long time since I let someone in. I'm not exactly the poster child for trust."

Matteo didn't say anything, which only made the knot in my throat tighter. "My ex—Nate—he didn't just cheat. He made me feel crazy. Like I was overreacting. Like I wasn't enough. He lied straight to my face for months, and I still stayed. I hated who I was by the end of it."

Matteo's brow furrowed, his thumb brushing mine. "I'm sorry, Nic."

"I just...I rebuilt a whole life around not needing anyone. And then you show up, all charming and annoyingly happy, and suddenly I'm breaking every rule I made for myself."

"I'm not trying to break your rules," he said gently. "I'm just trying to be someone you can trust."

"But what if I can't?" I whispered. "What if I never fully can? What if something's just...broken in me now?"

Matteo was quiet for a long beat.

Then he said, "You're not the only one who doesn't trust people, you know."

I blinked. "You?"

He gave a hollow laugh. "Yeah. Shocking, right? Matteo DeLuca, everybody's favorite golden boy, all charm and jokes and fan selfies. You'd think I handed my trust out like paddock passes."

"You kind of do," I said, but my voice was softer now. More careful.

He looked at me then—*really* looked at me. "I let people think they know me. Everyone thinks I'm this open book. The funny guy. The '*heart on his sleeve*' type. I make them laugh, keep it light, stay in character. But honestly? I don't think most people really know *me*. Not anymore. I wear a mask I learned to wear to survive in this world."

Something in my chest cracked wide open at that. Tears pricked behind my eyes, because *damn it*, why did vulnerability have to feel like this? Like you're both falling and flying at the same time?

He sighed, "Somewhere along the way, I got so good at playing the version of myself the world wanted, I forgot what the real me even looks like. What I like. What I need. I don't even know if I know how to just...be."

I reached for his hand.

"You don't have to be anyone with me," I said, quietly but firmly. "Not the charming media-trained DeLuca. Not the grinning golden boy. Just you."

"And you don't have to pretend you're not scared," he said, gently brushing a piece of hair from my face, "Because it is scary, giving yourself to your partner, being in a relationship. That's a big deal and a level of trust I don't take lightly. So we take it slow, we listen to each other, we talk out whatever needs to be talked out. Because I don't really give a shit about labels, Nic. Call us whatever you want, whatever feels less scary, but I'm not going anywhere, and I'm not interested in ever spending my time, energy, or trust on anyone else other than *you*. You are who I want. You are who I fucking need. We take it as slow as you need."

I looked at him, my heart pounding loud in my chest. "How can you be so sure?"

"Because being with you is easy. You make life brighter and more saturated, like everything before was some sort of duller version. Because I find myself wanting to be around you more times than not. I want to watch you put on your makeup, I want to memorize the shades of red you wear. And I don't say this to overwhelm you. I just—I love being with you and around you. And frankly, I'm not interested in a life where you're not in it. So we take it slow, we do everything by your rules. I'm in this Nic. I want to be with you in whatever way you'll have me."

Matteo's voice was so soft, my insides were all knotted and messy, listening to him be so open and raw. It was one of the things I admired so much about Matteo. He was so aware of everything. Things I couldn't even fully explain. Everything about being in a relationship again made me want to run, like giant flashing lights were saying '*wrong way*'. But at the same time, I wanted to try.

"Okay," I whispered.

"Okay?"

"Yeah," I nodded. "I want to try. I mean, I'm fucking terrified, but I unfortunately also find myself wanting to be around you at most times." I shot him a smirk. "But you'll have to be patient with me...space to be messy and all that."

His smile was like the sun rising. "God, I'm gonna ruin so many press photos by staring at you now."

I laughed. Really laughed. Because somehow, even in the middle of a terrifying conversation about trust and heartbreak, *he made me feel safe.*

The morning came into the room in a burst of sunshine, the wind blowing a curtain open rhythmically. I cracked my eyes open and let myself wake up to the street noises below us. The sun cast along Matteo's back. He was waking up slowly as well, a smile taking over before he yawned. All golden and sun-kissed skin.

"Good morning, gorgeous," he said, his voice scratchy and deep from being unused. I had missed that last week. Having it back now was something I didn't want to let go of anytime soon. I would just always wake up next to him. That seemed feasible.

A text pinged on my phone, and I knew it before I even saw my father's name on my screen.

DAD:

Let's meet this morning, 9:00 a.m. Bring DeLuca.

I sighed and turned the phone to Matteo.

"I feel like a teenager about to get called into the principal's office," he said, scratching his head.

"I mean, same same but different."

"You think he'll be mad?" he asked.

"Could go either way, but he's not really the mad type. A very calm man actually. Other than if the World Cup is on."

"Makes sense," Matteo nodded.

I decided the best walk of shame would be to Lucia's instead of to my hotel that my parents were at. So I walked down the hall, counting down the numbers till I hit Room 414 and knocked. The door creaked open, a half-asleep Lucia blinked back at me.

"Hey!" she said in a voice laced with surprise. "Wait, I thought you were at a different hotel?" She rubbed her eyes and covered a yawn.

"Yeah, didn't make it back..." I trailed off feeling a blush creep up.

"Oh," she sighed, then her eyes widened. "OH."

"Yeah, so..."

"Holy shit."

"Sorry to wake you early, but I need to borrow a change of clothes because my father has requested to meet with me and Matteo and I refuse to do a walk of shame in the hotel he's staying at."

"Mmhm, yup, yup, come in" She shuffled me through the doorway. The lights were off, aside from the soft glow of the bathroom door cracked.

"Gianna still asleep?" I whispered. Lucia nodded.

"Yeah, in Alexander's arms and everything because she woke up at about 4:00 a.m. and refused to go back into her bed."

"That's fucking adorable."

"I know. Like how am I supposed to not love them?"

"Wow, the 'L' word?" I mock-gasped, but we saw it coming— literally everyone other than them knew they were destined.

"I mean, who can blame me right?" she shrugged, and walked to the little bar setup, clicking on the espresso machine. "Alright, fill me the hell in."

"The article pissed me off," I said.

"Mmhm, hell hath no fury like a pissed off Nicola," she giggled.

"They implied he was using me to get up in the racing world, like he hasn't dedicated his whole life to the sport, like he doesn't work every single day toward being a better driver, training, and working with the team. It pissed me the hell off. So you saw the anger part. But afterwards we had a rather open and honest conversation about it. And, well, I guess we're trying the whole *'together'* thing now." I shrugged, trying to appear casual as my heart thumped in my chest.

"Together!" Lucia whisper-cheered and fake-clapped. "Oh my God, this is huge! Why would you tell me this while my child is sleeping and I have to be quiet? That's so rude, I want to scream!"

"Sorry!" I smirked. "Now please, I need clothes."

"You don't want to meet your father in your club dress?"

"Christ, no."

Lucia's head fell back in a laugh. "Okay, follow me." We walked through the bedroom, trying to be as silent as possible. To my left was Alexander, absolutely knocked out with a sprawled Gianna next to him, head on his chest. It was fucking precious. My heart thudded again.

Lucia looked all gooey-eyed at them before pushing us into the walk-in closet and closing the door behind us, flipping on the light.

"Woah," I whispered. In front of me was about double the clothes I had seen before. Her wardrobe had grown significantly. It made a smile slide over my features, because Lucia was no longer making herself small, trying to not be a hassle.

She was taking up the damn space. And I was so proud of her.

"I love this for you," I smiled.

"Alexander has a sugar daddy kink," she giggled as I fake-puked. But it was in fact the cutest thing ever. He loved her so much, in their own quiet way. But it made my heart swell. Look at me, all gushy over watching people fall in love. Beginning-of-season me would have been pro *'leave him!'* but maybe this whole relationship thing wasn't the worst.

"Okay, what are we going for?" Lucia's voice pulled me back.

"Casual but put together?" I replied. Lucia nodded seriously. The girl loved fashion. She was always dressed to impress, and while I leaned more casual, she leaned more polished. She pulled out a matching denim set, with tailored shorts and a long, tailored vest. I shook my head. Not me. Next, she pulled out a cotton dress. I also shook my head. Too casual. She tapped her pointer finger on her cheek.

"Oh, I've got it." She started pulling things and putting them in my hands instead of holding them up to get my approval. She just dove in. I kind of loved it. First were cream-colored tailored pants. Next was a high neck black tank. I looked at her unsure. She held up her finger telling me to wait.

"Accessories next. It'll pull it together," she explained. "Put it on, no complaining." I held up my hands in defense and did as she said. I pulled on the outfit she'd handed me. The shirt was tight, the pants baggy and slightly long. She smiled, turned and looked through a small jewelry box, handed me a necklace, then went to her shoes all lined up on the wall. Red and white sneakers were plucked from the pile and thrown at me. I caught them with an umph before socks were thrown at my head with a laugh.

"Go on, put them on!"

"Stop throwing things at me!" I glared.

"You respond to aggression best," Lucia smirked.

"It's scary how much I've rubbed off on you," I sighed. Lucia looked proud. The final look came together, after she pulled my hair into a semi messy but somehow put-together high ponytail hairstyle and gave me earrings. We tiptoed out of the closet and into the bathroom to look in the full-length mirror. She curled some pieces of my hair, letting little pieces come out, then pushed me toward the mirror.

"See?" she raised an eyebrow. She had somehow made a base outfit that was very Lucia coded, but still felt like me. I was highly impressed.

"Okay, you're like, really good at this," I said fiddling with little things on the outfit. The sneakers made it feel more casual than my usual heels. And while I loved pairing heels with things, this was an impressive outfit. And my feet were thankful to not be in the same heels as last night. I loved those sky high, strappy little things, but they were a rare-occasion type shoe because they were rather painful.

"Rude that you doubted me," Lucia smiled.

"Honestly true, cause damn Luce. You ever thought about going into styling?"

She blushed and looked down. "Yeah, actually it was kinda my childhood dream. But I think I like dressing my friends most. Alexander loves fashion too, so going to shows and those fancy private events has been reigniting that dream. But I also love helping my parents with the business end of things for the Vineyard. Maybe one day I'll do something small, but for now, it's fun to just put together outfits!"

"I'm serious though, you're crazy good at this. This feels so me, but it's made of your own clothes. Didn't think I would feel this powerful in sneakers. Usually, my heels and a bold lip are my secret weapon."

"Now you have half a power suit and half casual. It's like '*day off*' Nicola. Still gorgeous and terrifying, maybe just a little shorter." We laughed together at the last part, slapping hands over our mouths, trying to keep in the noise.

"You still have your red lip though, right? That's a Moretti staple."

"Yeah, in my purse. She comes with me everywhere, don't worry!"

"Alright, I think you're ready. Do you think your dad will be mad?" she asked.

"Not about me and Matteo, but about finding out after it hits the tabloids, maybe," I sighed. "I feel really bad about that."

I hated disappointing my father. I wanted him to trust I could make good decisions for my future, that I could stand on my own two feet. While I had been proving that, while I had found my place in the Moretti company with the Foundation, this nagged at me. I knew he was proud of me, of everything this past season. I also knew I shouldn't have let him find out about it this way. Family being first was always a strongly-rooted motto in our household. If we got into trouble, we told our parents, and they would help us through it. Better to work as a unit than to let the press and tabloids try to blow something up.

We walked back to the front door of their suite, and I did the unexpected. I leaned in, and held out my arms for a hug. Lucia's eyes practically bulged right out of her head. She wrapped her arms around me and squeezed.

"It'll be good! This is good!" she assured me. I pulled her close, let out a breath I had maybe been holding in too long, then pulled away. We locked eyes.

"It'll be great," I replied.

"Love you, and you look great!"

"Thank you, I feel good," I replied. I wasn't great with the whole '*I love you*' thing. Maybe it was because my family also didn't say it a huge amount. But Lucia was an '*I love you*' slut. It was shocking in the beginning. I had known her less than a day before she shouted she loved me as we parted ways on the circuit. But she was persistent in the best way. Those damn DeLucas really slithered into my heart or whatever.

# 24

# MATTEO

$\mathcal{I}$ had showered and dressed by the time the click of the hotel door caught my attention. I slightly let my brain spiral into stress in the time since Nicola had left. Was I about to be cut from my dream team? Probably not, but a lecture was imminent. That alone made my anxiety spike. I'd yet to have confirmation about my contract renewal. Moretti Racing typically renewed in even years, two- or four-year contracts. The first contract was two years, but I had hoped I was proving myself, earning enough points, bringing in sponsors, and putting in the work to get a four-year contract like Carlos was on. I had a few other teams reach out, trying to vie for my attention with pretty prices and promises. But Moretti Racing was my home, my childhood dream, one that I wasn't done fulfilling. A team I wanted to take to the top, to win a championship, to get a first-place podium finish. And doing anything to piss off the boss was just straight up stupid. Yet here I was, head over feet for his own daughter.

Did I think that through?

Probably not.

But from the moment I met her, I was no better than a moth to a flame. I knew I would get burned, but I just kept flying closer.

"Hey," a soft voice jarred me out of my endless thoughts. "You look lost in your head," she noted, walking up to me, her hands finding my arm, drifting up to my cheek. "Come back out of there." She smiled. Her smiles were soft with me, unlike any I'd seen outside in the world. Like they were real and reserved for just me. It made me want to scream from the top of the rooftops like some lovesick sap that I was the luckiest bastard to exist, to have her here with me, to have her be mine.

"Hey," I replied and leaned in for a kiss. She met me halfway; her lips were soft and warm and felt like home. "Got caught in the cobwebs is all."

"Don't stay up there too long."

"You tend to pull me back."

"Really?"

"Yeah. You have quite the effect on me, Moretti," I sighed.

"You're nervous?"

"Trying not to be? But yeah, I was hoping for news of my contract renewal this year, not to be sitting down with my girlfriend's dad for the first time."

"Woah" She put up her hands at the 'G' word, playfully. "What happened to slow, DeLuca?"

"Sorry, not girlfriend," I smirked. "The woman I want to spend every day with who's also my boss's daughter. Better?" She rolled her eyes at me in response.

"Well, I wasn't expecting to have my father meet my not-boyfriend today either, but here we are."

"Not-boyfriend, huh?"

"Something like that." She kissed me. "Let's get out of here."

While walking to the car, Nicola surprised me by slipping her hand into mine before we left the lobby doors. It was such a small act, but it felt like this huge thing, like blocks placed together, perfectly matched. The flashes and shouting of paparazzi was not surprising, especially since the bombshell exclusive that dropped last night.

"Matteo! Nicola!" the crowd shouted. Nicola held her head high, shoulders back, and smiled to the crowd.

"You two made up after last night's fight?" someone shouted. I followed Nicola as she confidently walked the short way to the car, ignoring the comments and holding onto my hand tightly. I opened the door for her, letting her slide in first, before I followed suit.

"What did we fight about, you think?" she asked, cracking a smile and raising her eyebrows. I rolled my eyes.

"Who the hell knows." The media spun things however they wanted to—it was chaos transformed into catchy headlines that sold.

"Oh!" she sang, turning her phone to me. "Big fight apparently!"

*The new couple already on the fritz, Moretti Heiress and her new beau, Moretti Racing Driver, Matteo DeLuca, fighting after a podium finish!*
*Nicola won't share the spotlight with up-and-coming Formula One driver Matteo DeLuca.*

"You're such a spotlight hog," I poked at her.

"Sorry I thought we were broken up, who are you?" she threw back. I tipped her head up, hand on her chin, and then pulled her to me.

"I'm the best damn lay you've ever met," I smirked and crashed my lips to her.

"Damn right." She let her head fall back in laughter. A throat cleared from the front of the car.

"So sorry, but where are we headed this morning?" the driver asked.

"The Langlin Hotel, please," Nicola replied. He nodded then the divider began raising into place, giving us back some privacy. I did my best to keep it light in the car. Our usual jabs were softer now, more playful.

"Your sister is in love, by the way."

"Obviously," I replied.

"You knew?" she gasped.

"Yeah, I'm not blind. They were. The fake dating charade was hilarious though. Alexander's had eyes for her since the first time I brought him to the Vineyard." I shrugged.

"What?" Nicola shrieked. "How long ago was that!"

"Years ago, when she was engaged to the asshat. She came to a good amount of home races with my parents too, and back in the F2 days. I mean Alex got pulled up faster than me, but yeah, the heart eyes started early."

"That didn't bug you?"

"Nope, I just want her to be happy. She and Gianna deserve the world."

"They really do," Nicola sighed. "Their love story is kind of magical."

"Nicola Moretti believing in love?" I gasped.

"I believe in love!" she shot back, offended. "I just thought maybe I ran out of luck. I had my chances and nothing stuck. How many chances does one get at real love?"

"You deserve love, just as anyone does."

"I am loved. I have my family, my friends. I just, I don't know. Romantic love seems different, ya know? Like it's this ultra-rare thing, someone to love every part of you as you are, in all your different phases and ways. My parents love each other in this really unique way. They're totally different people but they still work. Something about that is kind of amazing. To the outside world, they don't fit. And while my dad shows maybe no love on the outside, he shows up for us in every way that counts. He's really never let me down, which is also an incredibly fortunate thing. Having parents that are still married feels insane these days. But they didn't even marry till they were in their forties, so who knows. Maybe it'll find me eventually."

"It will," I nodded, sure of it. Hopefully it would be me, but I was positive that she would find that '*sweep you off your feet*' love.

"I'm a Moretti after all—apparently even you're using me for my name." She batted her lashes at me and gave my cheek a kiss. My heart hummed at the contact.

"You being a Moretti is the least interesting thing about you."

"Um?" She shot me an unsure look.

"You're a force, don't get me wrong. But not because you're a Moretti, because you're Nicola. Because you sing when you get ready in the morning and do a little happy dance after your first bite of food, and because you care about people in a huge, life-altering way. When you put your mind to something, you dedicate everything you have to it. Like the programs you're collaborating with for the Foundation. You're scary on the outside—" She glared again. "But you've got this huge heart. The most interesting thing about you is that you are *you.*"

She stared at me, her eyes looking a little glassy before she leaned in for a soft kiss. Not rushed or heated or frantic, but slow and soft. I wanted to collect all the versions of the way she kisses. Every single damn one.

The car pulled to a stop outside the Langlin Hotel. If I thought the hotel Anna placed us at this weekend was nice, this one would blow it out of the water.

"Damn," I said looking through the window.

"Pretty right? And I get this one too."

"Excuse me?" I said looking over to Nicola.

"My family owns the Langlin Hotels," she said like it was an obvious thing.

"Holy shit, what doesn't your family do?"

"My grandfather bought a small resort in London when he was in his twenties. It was foreclosing and everything, but he turned it into what the Langlins are today. I asked him for the Vegas one, my brother will get the London one, and my father has the other four."

"I repeat: holy shit," I said, too stunned to form any other words.

"It's not that big of a deal." She gently slapped my arm. "We have access to them on our thirtieth birthdays. I'm very excited, I want them to be the premier spot for Moretti Foundation events too!"

"That's amazing Nic," I said, squeezing her hand, then cracked a smile. "What's it like being richer than me?"

She rolled her eyes. "Well, according to the tabloids, you're the one using me, remember? For all my fame and fortune."

"Do you think I can get another Moretti G8 series but in one of those custom colors?"

"Might be under the tree at Christmas," she winked. I coughed out a laugh. "Alright, let's get in there. We can't be late. Gianfranco would *not* approve."

The mere mention of Nicola's father had me adjusting my jacket like it could somehow armor me against the oncoming storm. I wasn't sure what was worse: Gianfranco Moretti being my boss and a living legend in the F1 world or him being the father of the woman I was falling for. He was the kind of man who built dynasties and dismantled egos without blinking. You didn't mess with Gianfranco. You didn't even breathe around him without double-checking your form.

I stepped out of the car and tried to mirror Nicola's calm confidence, but honestly, the nerves were tap-dancing in my stomach. My usual charm? Useless here. My smile? A minor annoyance to a man like Gianfranco. What I *did* have was a solid track record and the work ethic to back it up.

I walked around to open the door for her. Nicola stepped out, shorter than usual without her heels, but no less powerful.

"We've got this," she said as we approached the front door.

I wanted to believe her.

The door creaked open, and Nicola led us through the polished corridors of the lounge. She waved at the bartender—because of course she knew the bartender—and then we slipped behind the bar like some secret agents on a mission. The man casually pressed against a shelf of liquor, and suddenly, it swung open to reveal a hidden door.

My jaw dropped. "Respectfully? This is some mafia-type shit."

"Shut up," she muttered, rolling her eyes.

But I caught the curve of a smirk as we stepped into the dimly lit room. It looked like something out of a film: leather chairs, dark wood, floor-to-ceiling shelves lined with books that looked older than the sport itself. And at the back sat Gianfranco Moretti.

He stood the moment Nicola entered, his face softening instantly as he opened his arms. She walked into his hug without hesitation.

Then his eyes shifted to me, and the warmth vanished like it had never been there.

"DeLuca," he said, extending a hand.

I took it. Firm shake. Almost a bone-crusher. A message disguised as a greeting.

We sat. A bartender entered with three cups and a steaming kettle of chamomile tea. I blinked. Not what I expected from a man who could command a room with a single look, but then again, this was Gianfranco Moretti. He didn't need whiskey to be terrifying.

"So." He poured the tea with quiet precision. "You two are together now?"

Straight to it. *Damn.*

I glanced at Nicola, offering her the lead. It was her father. Her call.

"Yes," she said, clear and steady, and then—she reached for my hand. Interlaced our fingers. My heart did a strange little flip.

"I would have preferred to hear it from you, *Tesoro*," Gianfranco said, his voice dipping to something more personal, "not from a tabloid headline. But I understand the need for privacy. Unfortunately, this is no longer a private matter."

"I know," Nicola said. Her voice didn't waver. "We'll handle it."

He turned to me then, and I braced myself. "DeLuca, you're a valued part of this team. You've earned your place here. But this situation—it complicates things. You understand how the media spins a story. They'll say you're leveraging the relationship to your advantage."

I opened my mouth, but he held up a hand.

"If you're serious about Nicola—about *this*—then we will go public on our own terms. Make your first formal appearance at the end-of-season gala in Rome. Until then, I expect both of you to stay focused. Is that understood?"

"Yes, sir," I said immediately. I wanted to say more. I wanted to say *I would never hurt her. I would never exploit her or this team.* But I had a feeling he already knew that. He just needed to hear me agree to the plan.

Nicola straightened. "I think the gala debut makes sense. But from a PR standpoint, we should also consider announcing Matteo's contract extension early. Get ahead of the speculation."

I blinked. That...wasn't part of the plan.

But Gianfranco nodded. "I agree. And in fact, Matteo"—he turned back to me—"the board and I have already approved the extension. Should you accept, we'll move the official announcement to tomorrow."

For a second, I forgot how to breathe. The blood in my body surged all at once, pounding in my ears. *They were extending me.* They were locking me in.

"Thank you," I managed, trying not to sound too stunned, "I didn't expect to hear so soon."

"No point in delaying the inevitable," he said with a shrug, "We'll send over the documents. I trust Anna will handle the rest."

I nodded quickly. "Absolutely."

Then he turned to Nicola, and the air in the room lightened just a little.

"And how are *you*, my dear?"

Her smile was soft but proud. "Good. The Rome event is on track, and last weekend's campaign broke records for race day donations."

I watched the way his face shifted, that rare glint of fatherly pride shining through.

"I'm very proud of you," he said, "I know the gala will be a triumph. I'll see you at the board meeting for the Foundation later today. I'm excited to see what you're presenting."

She lit up under his praise, and damn it, I lit up with her.

Because this—this was the part the media didn't always see. The family behind the legacy. The heart behind the headlines.

# 25

# NICOLA

We didn't say much as we walked back to the lobby.

The kind of silence that wasn't awkward—just *full*. Like the air between us was buzzing with everything we didn't say in front of my father. I expected the same town car to be ready to pick us up, but instead there sat a red classic 60s Moretti GTO. One I knew was Matteo's from the license plate '22 Zoom.' He bought it after his first Formula One paycheck, which made quite the statement. My eyes twinkled at it, the 60s were my favorite versions of the Moretti sports cars. My grandfather had owned the same one and was rather fond of it. Matteo shot me a smile, a wicked one that said '*Surprise.*'

"Thought we could go for a drive," he said as he opened the door for me. I sat in the passenger seat, eyes out the window. The city was quiet, still too early for many to be out.

He drove with one hand on the wheel, the other resting on the center console, fingers drumming like he had too many thoughts to sit still. Which, fair. I had approximately four hundred thoughts all trying to be the loudest.

I looked at his hand.

Long fingers. Calloused in all the right places. Always warm. Always steady.

*Just hold it*, I told myself. I had done it before, and it felt grounding. I needed that.

It took a beat. Or maybe ten. But I reached over and slid my fingers through his.

Matteo stilled like I'd short-circuited his entire nervous system. Then he looked over at me—and I swore he *glowed*. Like the damn sun rose for the express purpose of lighting him up in that moment.

"You okay?" he asked, voice soft like he was afraid of breaking the spell.

"No," I said. "But also...yes?"

He squeezed my hand, letting me be unsure. God, how did he always know when I needed that?

We sat in it for a minute longer before I took a breath. Okay. Here we go. Rip off the Band-Aid.

"I'm trying to not be freaked out," I admitted, "I want to do this, to give it a real shot. But being in the spotlight, it doesn't give us the option of just existing. While I've grown up with it, I should be used to it. It still..." I paused, taking a breath, "it pisses me off."

There. Said it. Couldn't take it back. My heart was hammering in my chest, but it was the good kind of fear, I think. The kind that came right before something mattered. Because we had an on or off switch with the press. And I could ignore it, but it would always be there, dramatic headlines, *'did they or didn't they'* theories. In another world, we would just be nobodies who lived by the sea in Portofino.

Matteo didn't interrupt. Just waited, eyes on the road, thumb tracing slow circles on my knuckles.

"I built this armor around myself since I was younger, not letting it get through to me. But the press spinning shit about you makes me irrationally angry. So there's that," I sighed before bringing up yet again the fact that I was fucking terrified. I felt like a broken record, but my mind just kept circling back to it, forever overthinking.

I went on, "And then the other half is my stupid head." Matteo shot me a look like, '*Hey don't say that.*' I squeezed his hand and continued, "I know we talked about it but it's like there's this part of my mind that's screaming at me from the back, that I'm being stupid for listening to my heart. That I'm going to get hurt. But then you hit me with that stupid smile and your stupid flirting and your ability to make me laugh even when I want to strangle you..."

He snorted, glancing sideways at me, and my chest eased.

"You made me feel something I haven't felt in a really long time," I said. "Safe. *Seen*. Like I don't have to be anyone else. Just me."

I bit my lip. "And that scares the shit out of me."

He pulled the car over and turned to face me fully, like he couldn't wait another second.

"Scares the shit out of me too, Princess. But I'd rather be with you, figuring it out than anywhere else. And your head isn't stupid. You're allowed to feel it all, you *should* feel it all."

"So what do we do?" I whispered.

"What we said last night: we try," he said, "However messy or slow as you need. I'm not going anywhere, even if the tabloids try to get between us. I'll remind you every day that this is what matters, right here." He waved a finger between us. "And I know the pressure of the public eye, but this is worth it. I want to fight for this, to give us an honest-to-God chance."

I smiled, and it felt real. Like the kind that started somewhere deep in my chest and rose all the way up to my eyes.

"You know," I said, voice lighter, "this is the part of the romance novel where the heroine kisses the boy stupid."

Matteo grinned. "Yeah? What happens after that?"

"Guess we have to find out," I said, scooting closer. And when he leaned in, I met him halfway, stealing a kiss.

I stood outside the conference room at the Langlin Hotel, my red lips and heels serving as armor, a binder clutched tight against my chest. Chin high, shoulders squared.

"Good afternoon, Miss Moretti." One of the older board members—Lance, if memory served—nodded politely.

It had been years since I'd stepped into one of these meetings. As a teenager, I used to beg my father to bring me along so I could take notes and see the inner workings of his world. Now I was here on my own terms, about to present a new direction for the Moretti Foundation. Not just another fundraiser on the calendar, but a reimagined strategy. One that involved partnering with local shelters and charities at every stop instead of sprinkling in a few token events each year.

When I entered, my father sat at the head of the long oval table, tall windows spilling light across the polished surface. Familiar faces dotted the room—Lance among them—but there were new ones too. My mother sat proudly at his side, her smile radiant as our eyes met, and the knot of anxiety in my chest loosened. My parents had always been my greatest champions. Even when they weren't sure about me joining the race schedule, they could see I was thriving, and that was all that mattered.

"Good afternoon," I greeted as I slid into a seat to my father's left.

"Thank you all for coming," my father said, rising and buttoning his suit jacket. His presence commanded the room with effortless ease. "The Moretti Foundation has been expanding, and we hope to see it continue to grow. I'd like to thank Henrietta and Lance for their dedication on this past year's campaign, and also my daughter, Nicola, for leading the planning committee. Her work not only broke fundraising records here at Moretti

Incorporated, but also breathed new life into the Foundation. With her perspective, we're now ready to consider some fresh initiatives. But before we begin, Henrietta has an announcement."

All eyes shifted to Henrietta. Her silver hair was pinned neatly in a twist, her tan suit sharp as ever. She stood with a composed smile, smoothing her jacket before speaking.

"Thank you, everyone, for gathering on short notice, and Nicola, for presenting next year's plans today. I asked for this meeting because I have something important to share." Her voice was steady, but the words landed like a stone in water. "I will be stepping down as chair of the Moretti Foundation." A collective gasp rippled around the table. Henrietta had led for three decades, an institution in her own right. I tried to school my features, but the shock must have flickered across my face.

"I'm so grateful for the friendships I've made and for the Moretti family's support over the years," she continued, "It has been my greatest honor to serve as chairwoman. Today's vote will be my final business. Effective immediately, I'll be retiring."

The room buzzed to life, board members rising, shaking her hand, offering embraces and thanks. I lingered by my parents as the crowd swarmed her.

"You knew?" I murmured to my father. He gave a small, knowing smile and nodded.

"Wow," I exhaled, still reeling.

"She's been a force," my mother said warmly, "And she's been singing your praises nonstop since you got involved this year." She nudged me, and heat crept up my neck.

"I really do love this work," I admitted softly, "I want to do so much more."

"You will," she said with quiet certainty.

When the room began to settle, I made my way to Henrietta. "I'm shocked to the core," I confessed, "but so happy for you. No one will ever live up to your legacy."

Her smile turned sly as she squeezed my shoulder. "Oh, I think someone will." Her brow lifted ever so slightly, as though she knew more than she was saying. "I've had a cottage in the south of France for years with hardly any time to enjoy it. I look forward to days spent living slowly."

"That sounds magical," I said, meaning it.

"Alright everyone, if we can continue with our next order of business," my father said, his voice steady, and just like that, the room shifted back to order. Papers rustled, pens tapped. I sank into my chair, still reeling from Henrietta's announcement.

The meeting moved forward without pause, discussion swirling around new strategies and marketing initiatives. I forced myself to listen, to nod, to add a comment or two when the chance arose, but in the back of my mind all I could hear was Henrietta's calm, deliberate words. Stepping down. Effective immediately. Who would fill her shoes?

"Nicola has prepared a proposal for a new fundraising structure and update on the end-of-year event," my father announced suddenly, and all eyes turned toward me. His hand gestured with quiet pride, and I felt my nerves skitter up like static. My pulse jumped in my throat as I plugged in my computer, fingers trembling slightly on the keys.

*This was fine.* I was ready, I knew my presentation by heart.

"Hi everyone," I began, pasting on a smile as my slides lit up the screen. "This past week at the Las Vegas Grand Prix, we tripled donations in one race weekend by teaming up with local charities. With the overwhelming success and positive feedback we've received, I'm proposing we expand this model to every race on the calendar."

My words were practiced and smooth as I clicked through graphs, numbers glowing across the screen. "As you can see, marketing graphics on the track were a major investment that paid off in dividends. We also ran fan polls to vote on which local charities would be supported, which generated incredible engagement."

*Keep it steady,* I told myself, *They're nodding. They're interested. Just breathe.*

The presentation moved to the gala. My voice strengthened when I revealed, "This year, our end-of-year gala will not only celebrate the season and the teams, but will also be officially sponsored by Formula One."

Gasps rippled through the room, followed by applause. I couldn't help the rush of pride that swelled in my chest. That official seal of approval had taken weeks of negotiating, and now it was real.

When I finished, voices chimed in from every corner of the table.

"These numbers are incredible," Lance said.

"We should add more animal shelters into the mix," another suggested.

"There's a team in London that funds women's shelters, worth considering," a younger woman added. My mother smiled and seconded the idea, her eyes warm as she looked at me.

I scribbled notes, my chest buzzing with gratitude. I felt like I wasn't just filling a seat at this table—I was part of it.

And then Henrietta's voice rang out again, calm but carrying weight. "Thank you again, everyone, for your time today. I would like to end this meeting with a vote for the new Chair. I would like to formally nominate Nicola Moretti."

The air left my lungs.

My heart stopped.

*Did she just say my name?*

My pulse thundered in my ears as my father's voice followed. "Do we have any other nominations for chair?" He scanned the room. No one spoke. No one raised a hand. Heads shook.

This can't be real. Me? Chairwoman? I only just stepped into this role, and now—now they wanted me to lead it?

"Do you accept this nomination, Nicola?" My father's eyes were steady on mine.

I snapped my head toward him. My throat went dry. Chairwoman of the Moretti Foundation. The words echoed in my skull like a drumbeat. This was everything I wanted—to change lives, to build something lasting, to make an impact—but to be handed it now, so suddenly...

My legs felt unsteady under the table. My hands shook where they rested on the binder in front of me. But when I opened my mouth, my voice came out steady, clear. "Yes. I would be honored."

Henrietta gave her signature pause, her gaze sweeping the room. "If there are no other nominations...all those in favor of Nicola Moretti as chairwoman of the Moretti Foundation?"

One by one, hands lifted into the air. Every voice around me rang out, "Aye."

And I sat there, frozen, the weight of it pressing into me, trying to reconcile the girl who once begged her father to let her take notes in this room with the woman who had just been voted chair.

*Holy. Shit.*

# NICOLA

The next two weeks passed in a blur of champagne toasts, press junkets, and countless hours working on events as the new chairwoman of the Moretti Foundation. I hadn't even had time to tell Matteo about my recent huge life-altering promotion. It felt like an in-person type of announcement. However, life was a fickle bitch, and somehow our schedules doubled in size and never lined up. On top of that, it felt like once Matteo and I decided to give this thing an actual shot, we couldn't even plan our first official date, which Matteo was very insistent had not happened regardless of the number of times we'd done things together by now.

We'd landed in Abu Dhabi for the final race of the season, and it felt like I hadn't seen him in months instead of a measly fourteen days. I'd texted, called, even sent the occasional suggestive voice note, but all we'd managed were a few stolen FaceTimes and a shared craving for room-service pasta. It was infuriating. And also, maybe, kind of hot? Absence made the heart grow fonder, or whatever. But I didn't want fond. I wanted Matteo—hands-on, lips pressed to my shoulder, falling asleep mid-rant about how he missed those cheesy puffs from the first night we all went out together. That kind of presence.

So I decided to take matters into my own very capable hands. I'd flown in with my dad this time, but the second we touched down, I texted Anna.

NICOLA:

What's Matteo's room number?

ANNA:

521. You didn't get this from me.

My partner in PR crime was all too happy to participate in a little covert romance operation. Honestly, I think she'd been rooting for us since day one. That, or she just really enjoyed chaos.

Either way, I was now standing in front of Matteo's hotel room, suitcase in hand, lipstick perfect, and the full intention of staying the weekend. Not just visiting—*staying*. With him.

Girlfriend behavior? Maybe. But if I was going to be emotionally reckless, I might as well look hot doing it.

I raised my hand to knock—three polite raps, but there was no answer. Just the hollow thud of knuckles against what was clearly an empty room. I sighed, one hand dropping to my hip, the other already fishing out the keycard I'd semi-legally acquired.

Technically speaking, it wasn't stealing if you charmed it out of someone, right?

Turns out the concierge was a die-hard Moretti Racing fan— and an even bigger Matteo DeLuca fan. One coy smile, a signed cap, and a promised photo later, and I was the proud temporary holder of one crisp white keycard to Room 521.

My heels clicked softly against the tiled floor as I stepped inside. The room was dark except for the golden glow sneaking in through the curtains, casting soft shadows over sleek furniture and that plush, king-sized bed I had *very* specific plans for.

I dropped my suitcase just inside the door, kicked off my shoes, and collapsed face-first into the bed with a dramatic sigh. Matteo's cologne hit me instantly. Something warm and woodsy with just a hint of spice. *God, that scent.* It wrapped around me like a weighted blanket and a secret all at once.

I laid there for a moment, burying my face in the pillow, smiling like an idiot. So okay, the surprise had failed, he wasn't here to be ravished the second I walked in. But I was nothing if not adaptable.

A buzz from my phone pulled me out of my daydream. I flipped it over to find a message from the man himself.

MATTEO:

Pulled into an extra training before my next meeting. Was really hoping to see you tonight but this schedule fucking sucks.

I bit my lip, eyes flicking to my suitcase. A plan formed in less than five seconds.

NICOLA:

Would this make it any better?

I snapped a photo—tasteful, teasing, *devastating*—of the blue lace set I'd slipped on. The one he hadn't seen yet. The one I specifically packed because I had intentions. His reply was nearly instant.

**Matteo:**

*Jesus, warn a man. My phone was on full brightness and Carlos was right next to me.*

I laughed out loud, a full-body kind of laugh.

NICOLA:

Oops. Tell Carlos he's welcome.

MATTEO:

Menace.

No reply for a second.
Then:



I stared at the screen for a long beat, something soft catching in my chest. I hadn't expected to fall this fast. Not after everything. But somehow, even with oceans and circuits and insane schedules between us, he made it feel easy. I rolled onto my back, phone on my stomach, heart somewhere up near the chandelier.

I sorted all my things, hid my suitcase in the closet, then slid on the trousers I had formerly borrowed from Lucia. After she saw them on me in a more awake state, she waved a hand and said, "Those are yours now." I tried to argue but she smiled and mentioned how Alexander loved an excuse to take her shopping.

I decided to head to the track. Might as well stay busy while Matteo was off doing his thing. Practice sessions, team meetings, sponsor obligations—whatever it was, he'd be buried in it. And if I stayed in the hotel room any longer, I'd spiral. The driver opened the town car door just as my phone buzzed in my hand. My father's name lit up the screen. I answered immediately, already smiling.

"*Ciao, Papà*," I said, leaning back against the cool leather seat.

"*Ciao, Tesoro.* Are you busy today?" His voice was calm and warm—unhurried in the way that always soothed my racing thoughts.

"Heading to the track now. Why? What's up?"

"I have a full slate of meetings," he said with a dramatic sigh, "And Monty is sulking at the door like I've abandoned him. Could you take him off my hands for the day?"

I laughed. "Monty needs constant attention or he's rather dramatic."

"He gets it from you."

"I'll pretend that wasn't an insult," I teased, "Of course I'll take him. I'll swing by. Do you have time for a quick coffee before your meetings?"

"For you? Always. Meet me in the executive lounge. Ten minutes?"

"Done. See you soon."

I hung up and smiled to myself. No matter what chaos the team or the world was throwing at him, he always made time for me. And not in the obligatory *I'm-your-dad* way. It was intentional. He wanted to. Maybe that was the reason for my belief in love, albeit a bit dreary. But who could ever achieve the level of love my parents had for each other? It was impossible. Who would drop anything at any time for his family?

The corner of my mind chanted at me a name I tried to ignore. What if he couldn't show up for me when I needed him most? What if I was heartbroken and disappointed just like every other time?

But when I asked my inner self that, I was only met with one thought: *he would show up for me. He always has.*

The executive lounge was quiet early in the day. Mostly staff, a few drivers, some executives in suits murmuring over pastries and espresso. I spotted my father immediately—perfect posture, Moretti Racing polo, leather notebook in front of him, and Monty, his ridiculously pampered boy, curled at his feet like royalty.

"Hey," I said, leaning in to kiss his cheek. He smelled like espresso, cologne, and motor oil. The classic cocktail of the Moretti men.

"Nicola," he said with a proud smile, standing to give me a real hug. "You look rested. Is that...happiness I detect?"

"Don't start," I warned lightly, sliding into the chair across from him.

He raised a brow. "I didn't say anything."

Monty leapt into my lap without ceremony and immediately settled in, tail wagging.

"Traitor," my father muttered, shaking his head, "I feed him, and yet here we are."

"Dogs know where the drama is," I said, sipping the espresso a server placed in front of me. "He thrives in emotionally rich environments."

My father laughed. "So tell me, how are you faring? With the boy...with the event and new role?"

I leaned back, swirling the coffee in the tiny porcelain cup. My father was a kind man, but he also did not beat around the bush. He hit you right on with what was going on. I inherited the trait, with a little less finesse. I jumped right over the 'the boy' comment and into the event that took up most of my working thoughts other than the aforementioned boy. "It's a big event, but everything's running smoothly. Most of the big things are locked in, the press schedule is finalized, and driver's teams have confirmed their commitments. The whole track should be in attendance." I was rather proud of that too. It was rare to get everyone on the same page, or everyone to one event, especially considering that it was post-season. Usually everyone would be jetting off to their preferred vacation spots, or home to their families. But I had good relationships with the teams and the drivers. So between me, Anna, and the boys, getting the drivers to attend had all come together. It felt like nothing short of a miracle, and I was quietly stunned and thankful for my group of friends who had rallied behind me.

He nodded slowly, watching me with that quiet intensity.

"You've grown into this role," he said finally, "I'm glad you asked to join the track this year."

At the beginning of the season, I was so determined to find my place, to make a path for myself. And I had done the damn thing —not just the usual visiting my dad during races but being *important* here, helping make a difference. Now I was heading up the Moretti Foundation and dating a driver. It all felt like some fever dream.

"You taught me well," I smiled. "No one controls my destiny but myself."

His eyes softened. They were his own words he had told me after the breakup when he caught me crying in the living room watching a movie in the middle of the night, which was rare.

I didn't cry, let alone in front of anyone. The last time my father had seen my tears, I had been a child crying over a broken toy, so I'm sure it was jarring to say the least.

"I know I pushed you hard when you came back. I wanted you to succeed, to find your place here. You've always loved the sport so much." He paused and looked a bit sad. "I'm sorry for not seeing that sooner. Your brother never held the same fire you have for racing. I wanted him to want it so much, I think I overlooked you."

"Oh *Papà*, you haven't, I just needed to find my voice first."

"*Tesoro*, you have always had a loud voice." He smiled, really smiled, reaching up crinkling around his eyes.

"I get that from you." I smiled.

"I'm happy as long as you are happy, Nicola. Doing the Moretti name proud."

"But I'm not just here because of the name. I'm good at this, Papà. And I want to be here. Not for the legacy. For *me*."

He reached across the table and took my hand. "I know. And I'm proud of you. Not just because you're succeeding—but because you stayed when it got hard."

I blinked away the sudden sting in my eyes and nodded.

"Matteo's lucky," he added. "Even if he doesn't always realize it."

"Oh, he realizes it," I said with a smirk.

"Are you still feeling confident about announcing at the gala?" he asked, not letting me avoid that particular topic anymore.

I let out a sigh I felt I was holding, then smiled. "We face things head on."

My father chuckled and stood, checking his watch. "I have to go charm investors. But I'll see you at the circuit?"

"I'll be there—with Monty." I scratched behind the dog's ears. "He's got a media interview at noon, apparently."

"Tell him not to say anything controversial this time," he called over his shoulder as he left.

I laughed softly, watching him go.

As I rounded the corner into the paddock hospitality lounge, I spotted two very familiar faces: Lucia—glasses perched on her nose, iPad in one hand, coffee in the other—and Anna—twirling a baby pink pen like she was plotting world domination.

"There she is!" Anna grinned like she knew something I didn't. Honestly? She probably did.

Lucia looked up from her screen and gave me the once-over. "Oh, we're wearing *the* trousers today," she said, all-knowing and smug.

I flicked my hair off my shoulder with dramatic flair. "You mean *my* trousers. They were a gift."

"They were a hand-me-down," she countered. "There's a difference."

"You said Alexander liked spoiling you and that I should stop arguing," I smirked, sliding into the seat beside her. "Also, thank you. I look hot."

"You do," Anna confirmed, sipping her sparkling water with a wink. "And judging by the unhinged messages Matteo was sending

Lucia last night about missing you, I give it about thirty minutes before he starts prowling this place like a lost puppy."

Lucia snorted into her coffee. "He already sent me a picture of Nicola's perfume bottle like it was some kind of sacred relic."

"That's his Roman Empire," Anna said solemnly. "Nicola's scent."

I cackled. "Please. Don't give him ideas. The last thing that man needs is more material for his dramatics."

Lucia's expression softened as she nudged me lightly. "So...how are you really? The last few races have been a blur."

"I'm good." The words came out without hesitation—and for once, they weren't a lie. "Like, scary good. Which is wild because I never thought I'd be this girl. You know, the one who smiles at her phone like a complete idiot at midnight."

"You've got the sparkle," Anna said, narrowing her eyes in a very serious, very best-friend-doctoral sort of way. "Only happens when it's the real deal."

I rolled my eyes, but my heart flipped traitorously in my chest. "Okay, maybe he does give me heartburn and butterflies at the same time."

Lucia leaned in, chin on her hand. "He's good for you."

I nodded, a little softer now. "He really is. And I want to be good for him too."

There was a pause—one of those quiet, golden ones only friends could create—before Anna let out a dreamy sigh. "Ugh, love. It's so annoying."

"Disgusting," Lucia agreed, smiling into her latte.

"Oh hey, I heard some whispers about the Foundation chair stepping down?" Anna asked.

"Oh yeah..." I scratched my temple. "So I kinda forgot to mention...I got a little promotion."

"Oooh how exciting! What's your promotion?" Lucia beamed at me as Anna waited expectantly.

"I was nominated as the new chairwoman of the Moretti Foundation."

"I'm sorry, what?" Lucia screamed.

"Holy shit!" Anna cheered.

"When did this happen? And why didn't we know? And oh my God, have you told Matteo? Because he's gonna lose it! We should throw a party, Anna, start sending invites out! Our girl is a chairwoman!" Lucia was bouncing up and down, out of breath as she rambled out her excitement. "I'm going to hug you now!" she declared and crushed me in a hug before she even finished speaking.

"You sneaky bitch!" Anna shook her head. "When did this happen?"

"Uh, two weeks ago…"

"Nicola Angelica Moretti," Lucia scolded in full mom voice.

"That's not my middle name," I laughed.

"Not the point." Lucia glared, then immediately softened. "I'm so damn proud of you."

"Now you really are a boss ass bitch," Anna added.

We all cracked up at the same time, and for a moment, it didn't matter that we were in the middle of a high-stakes racing weekend, or that we were juggling PR events and sponsorship meetings and a thousand different time zones.

At that moment? We were just three women, sitting in the middle of the chaos, holding each other up.

And damn, it felt good to be known like this.

# 27

# MATTEO

*J*'d been through enough media cycles to know when a question was coming before it was even out of someone's mouth.

The reporter shifted forward in her seat, her eyes gleaming with that particular brand of journalistic glee that came with digging into things that weren't theirs to dig into.

"So, Matteo," she said, the smile too saccharine to be anything but bait, "There've been a few...photos circulating. You and Nicola Moretti looked *very* close after the last race. Is there something you'd like to share with your fans?"

I held her gaze, calm, practiced. A few years ago, I might've fumbled this. Might've joked my way out of it or dodged the question entirely. But now?

Now I just thought of Nicola's text from earlier.

'*Would this make it any better?*' it had read. Attached was a photo that had nearly killed me. She was laid back on the hotel bed in some lacey little thing that definitely did *not* count as clothing. Her legs were crossed, lips parted in a smug little smirk like she knew exactly what it would do to me. Because she did. Because she was evil. Beautiful, smart, funny—and evil.

God, all I wanted was to end this interview, find her, and ruin that set. Slowly. Thoroughly.

I cleared my throat and leaned in, voice even. "I think there's an important conversation to be had about privacy. Drivers—public figures in general—we deal with a lot of intrusion. But sharing personal photos without consent? That's a line no one should cross." My jaw ticked slightly, but I kept it reined in. "Those images were private. They weren't meant for public consumption, and it's disappointing that they were treated like gossip instead of the violation they are."

The room went still. A few reporters nodded—some scribbled notes. I could feel the next question coming, so I lifted a hand and added, "As for my personal life..."

Pause. Deep breath. *Think before you say something that makes your PR team faint.* "...I'll keep most of it personal, because that's what it should be. But I'll also say this"—I glanced at the cameras with a smile that felt a little too honest—"I'm very happy. And very lucky."

There were a few murmurs, some exchanged glances. My answer had just made headlines. Inside, though? Inside, I was replaying the way Nicola looked in that lace, imagining the click of her heels against the marble as she walked toward me later tonight, pretending she didn't know what she'd done.

She knew.

She *always* knew.

And I was already counting the minutes until I could get my hands on her.

Another hand shot up immediately after I answered, this time from a journalist I recognized—British press, notoriously blunt.

"Matteo, does this mean you're officially in a relationship? Or are we still in the *'just friends'* territory you mentioned last month?"

I smiled, letting my tongue rest against the inside of my cheek. "You know," I said, "I think the term *'just friends'* seriously undersells how complicated and interesting people's connections can be."

A few quiet laughs around the room.

"I'm not big on labels, but I'm big on honesty. So if I say I care deeply about someone, that I respect them, that I'm proud to know them—that should count for something."

*And if I say I'm one text away from skipping this whole weekend to pin her against the wall of her suite?*

Probably shouldn't say *that* out loud.

Another voice jumped in—this time from an Italian reporter with a mic branded in Moretti red. "Is it hard, dating someone so closely tied to your team?"

My grin widened. "It's Formula One," I said. "Everything's hard. You learn to compartmentalize."

*Like not thinking about how she looked with her hair up, or how she whispered good luck in my ear like she meant it everywhere.*

Another hand went up, this one more hesitant. "Matteo, with the championship still undecided, and your teammate out of the points, all eyes are on you. How do you stay focused with everything going on—on and off track?"

I nodded slowly, that one grounding me a bit.

"This is my job. My dream. Everything I do is to be better— faster, sharper, smarter. I care deeply about the people in my life, but when I get in the car, it's just me and the circuit. Everything else waits. I'm partial to yoga as some good training prep too."

I sat back as the press officer announced one last question. I kept my expression calm, hands folded loosely on the table. I gave one final nod to the reporters and pushed my chair back, thanking the press officer as I stepped off the platform and into the cooler air of the hallway. The moment the doors swung shut behind me, it felt like I could breathe again—sort of.

"Nice job in there, Starboy," Anna's voice chimed as she fell into step beside me, clipboard in one hand, phone in the other. Her stride was brisk, heels clicking against the polished concrete as we walked toward the paddock offices. "Very diplomatic. The internet's going to eat it up."

I ran a hand through my hair, trying not to look as restless as I felt. "Didn't feel very diplomatic."

"You almost twitched when they mentioned her," she teased, eyes still on her screen. I shot her a glare, but it didn't stick. She was right. I'd almost fidgeted when they brought up the photos. I could still see the curve of Nicola's hips in that pale blue lace every time I blinked. Anna turned the screen of her phone toward me. "Anyway. I've got campaign notes for you. Two shoots are going ahead after some final team approvals—one with Carrera, one with a new upcoming F3 star Serena Kolman. Moretti might be picking her up as an Academy racer."

"Alright sounds good," I muttered, trying to stay focused.

Anna smirked. "You sure are distracted today."

We reached the Moretti team hospitality building, and I lingered at the edge of the sidewalk, tapping my fingers against my thigh. I didn't have another meeting for twenty minutes. Technically, I had time to disappear for a bit. Technically.

Anna raised a brow. "You going to be able to focus the rest of the day, or are you going to spend it texting your not-girlfriend about lingerie until you combust?"

"How do you know about that?" My head spun toward her.

"We went shopping." She rolled her eyes. "Okay get out of here, you're useless to me like this," Anna said, already turning toward her next task. "You've got about nineteen minutes before admin wants you back for a walk-through video. Try not to wrinkle your shirt."

I didn't wait for her to change her mind.

I was already halfway down the stairs, phone in hand, texting Nicola.

MATTEO:

Guess what I'm about to get?

NICOLA:

On my nerves?

MATTEO:

Cheeky.

I've got a small break. About 19 minutes before my next meeting. Please dear God tell me you're on track.

NICOLA:

Location sent.

God help me.

I followed the directions on my phone like it was my new favorite scavenger hunt game. People said hi as I passed, and I smiled and tried to give them a nod of hello or any acknowledgment, but I had a one-track mind. I turned the corner and spotted my fucking kryptonite clad in red heels at the end of the hall.

"Took you long enough," she said, her sunglasses dipping low on her nose as she looked up at me, those blue eyes that filled my dreams making me think of nothing other than getting her alone.

"Fuck, I missed you," I whispered, pulling her into me, burying my head in her neck, kissing along the way. She tried to hold back a giggle at the spot I kissed last. And I let myself fucking bask in that moment. Nicola Moretti *giggling*—who'd have thought?

I mean, I did. I found that spot in Portofino during those sleepless nights. It haunted my thoughts; I wanted to do it again and again.

She pushed my chest with some effort, but it didn't move me in the slightest. She was so fucking cute, it made my head spin.

"DeLuca, we're in public. Our whole big reveal is all planned, don't go mucking it up."

"I don't care," I grunted out, pushing into her again, a moan escaped her as I put a thigh between her legs. Her body reacted before her head caught up. She arched into me, and it was like drugs straight to my veins.

"Matteo, I'm serious!" she seethed at me in that half whisper, half shout. I pulled back with a sigh.

"What about the calm room?" I asked, knowing she had one set up in the Moretti camp and the Belen camp. She glared at me but nodded and slipped out of the cage I'd created around her body, one over the shoulder glance was enough to get my feet moving.

"We're using *your* room," she said before opening the door and I followed her like it was a pavlovian response.

I closed the door behind me, flipping the lock. Mine was one of the few rooms with it. Then I reached out, slipped my hand around her waist and tugged her to me. She crashed into my chest, losing her footing only slightly before I caught her and flipped us. My lips crashed into hers, I needed a fix.

"I've been thinking of that damn lingerie all day. You're pure evil."

She laughed, "It's so easy to get under your skin, DeLuca."

"Please tell me you're in my damn hotel this time."

"Didn't get a room actually."

"I'll book you the one next to me. Pay off whoever is there, it's yours."

"That's okay, I have my own key," she smirked and then paused. "My clothes are already hanging in the closet and everything."

"Where?"

"At yours." She rolled her eyes at me. I let out a half breath.

"Thank fuck," I said kissing her again, punishing this time for being a little brat. Her tongue tasted like espresso and sugar, and it danced with mine. I backed her against the door, before I slid both my arms under her and whispered, "Hold on," hoisting her up. Her legs immediately wrapped around my hips. I was barely thinking anymore; I wanted to live in this moment, be fucking consumed by it.

"I've been losing my damn mind," I rasped, voice rough in the dim glow of the room, my hands gripping her waist like she might disappear if I let go. My thumbs pressed into the soft dip of her hips, and she arched into me, breath catching.

"It's been fourteen days of pure misery without you." I dragged my mouth along the curve of her neck, savoring the way she trembled. "Since I've had you in my arms." Her moan nearly undid me. "And I'm fucking *starved*, Princess."

Everything I'd kept on a leash since the second I saw that photo —the lace, the teasing smile she wore just for me—came crashing down like I'd been holding my breath underwater.

She threaded her fingers through my hair, tugging just enough to make my pulse stutter. I kissed my way down her jaw, over that spot just beneath her ear that made her gasp like I was a sin she shouldn't want this badly.

"You wore it for me," I murmured against her skin, voice low and reverent.

She didn't answer with words—just pressed her chest to mine, the delicate lace of that blue bustier brushing my shirt, and it made my brain short-circuit. My hands glided up her sides, fingertips tracing the boning of the corset, feeling the tremble beneath her breath.

"I did," she whispered finally, her lips grazing mine. "But you better take your time with it. This set's too pretty to rip."

My laugh was half-growl, half-despair. "You're killing me."

She tilted her head, smug and sweet and everything I'd been craving. "You started it."

I backed her toward the couch near the back of the room, slow, savoring every second of this like a man finally letting himself feel again. "Trust me, *Amore*, I plan to finish it too."

She shivered, knees hitting the edge of the couch, and I leaned in—mouth ghosting over hers—as I slid my hands down her thighs. For a moment, I just looked at her. Cheeks flushed, hair tousled, a smile that knocked the breath out of me.

Not just the woman I wanted in my bed—but the one I couldn't stop picturing in my future.

"Matteo," she said softly, fingers catching the hem of my shirt.

I kissed her before she could say anything else. Slow at first. Reverent. Then deeper, hungrier, because I had missed it. Missed *her*.

She tasted sickly sweet. Like something I'd give everything to keep, happily addicted forever.

Clothes were pulled off in a blur of heat and hands and breathless laughter. Every sigh, every soft gasp was mine. I worshiped every inch of her like I'd been waiting my whole life for that moment.

And maybe I had.

Because when she clung to me, nails digging into my back, and whispered my name like a prayer—there was no circuit, no podium, no championship in the world that came close to the way that felt.

Like home.

"I have to tell you something," Nicola whispered between kisses. I paused at her words and pulled back.

"Are you okay?" I asked. It was easy to see her anxiety now, her eyebrows creased, and her eyes looked stormy.

She nodded, and her voice was barely audible. "I got a promotion."

I blinked. She was grinning so wide it was almost painful to look at. "The promotion. It's chairwoman of the board for the Foundation."

My heart stuttered, then pride slammed into me, knocking the air clean out of my lungs. "You're serious?"

She nodded, biting her lip like she was trying to hide her smile. Pointless. It only made me want to kiss her senseless.

"Nic—" Her name broke out of me, rough, and I didn't care. I didn't care about anything except touching her, holding her, making her feel what was storming through me. "You're incredible."

She cocked a brow, smug as ever. "So now I'm technically your boss? Or at least higher up than you."

My voice dipped low. "Well, you've always been better than me. Smarter. Sharper. More stubborn. And now? Officially promoted. Which means"—I dipped to her ear, my lips brushing the shell—"I get to brag I'm dating *the* Nicola Moretti."

Her laugh cut off in a gasp when my hands slipped under her bra, fingers spreading across warm skin.

"Matteo—"

"You have no idea how proud I am of you," I murmured, pressing my forehead to hers. "How lucky I am. I could spend forever telling you, but I'd rather show you."

Her breath hitched, her hands fisted in my shirt as she yanked me down into a kiss. Hungry. Familiar. A year of bickering between us twisted now into something hotter, deeper, unshakable. She wrapped her legs around my waist, pulling me closer with a wicked smile. "Guess you'll have to listen to your boss, then."

I grinned against her mouth, already lost, already hers. "Baby, I'll follow your orders all night."

Her breath stuttered, her nails digging into my shoulders as I mouthed down her throat, then her collarbone, sucking hard enough to mark her. She gasped my name when I bit lightly, my hands already working open the button of her pants.

"Matteo, we need to be quiet—"

"Fuck that," I growled, spreading her legs with my hips, dragging her panties aside so I could slide my fingers against the wet heat waiting for me. "Fuck, baby...already dripping for me."

Her head fell back, a strangled moan tearing out of her as my thumb circled her clit and two fingers pushed inside, stretching her tight around me.

"You get a promotion," I rasped, curling my fingers until she cried out. "And I get the privilege of watching my brilliant, gorgeous girl fall apart on my hand."

She bucked against me, nails clawing my skin, her panting breaths breaking on my name. I pressed my mouth to hers, swallowing every sound as I worked her harder, faster, my free hand gripping her thigh tight.

"Matteo—God, I'm gonna—"

"That's it, Princess. Let go for me."

Her body bowed against mine, and she shattered—trembling, gasping, clenching hard around my fingers. I kept working her through it, kissing her like I'd never stop.

When she finally collapsed against me, trembling and spent, I slid my fingers free and sucked them into my mouth, groaning at the taste of her. Her eyes went wide, cheeks flushed scarlet.

"Promotion looks good on you," I said with a wicked grin. "But I'm not done celebrating yet. Not even close."

Her chest was still heaving when I popped the button on my jeans, her eyes flicking down as I shoved denim and briefs out of the way.

"Matteo," she whispered, breathless, almost warning.

But she was already spreading her legs wider, already tugging me closer. My cock pressed against the damp heat of her panties, and I nearly lost it right there.

"You sure?" I rasped, though my body was already trembling with the need to be inside her.

She bit her lip and nodded, whispering, "Always."

That's all I needed. I hooked my fingers in the lace and dragged the panties aside with a bit more force than I intended, the fabric ripping. I needed her now. I could replace the lace. Hell, I'd buy her hundreds. I sank into her in one hard, desperate thrust, my need to be inside her taking over any rational thought.

"Fuck—Nic." My forehead dropped against hers, a guttural

sound tearing out of me as her tight heat clamped down around me. "You feel...so fucking perfect."

She gasped, nails digging into my back, pulling me deeper. "God, Matteo—move—"

And I did. My hips snapped forward, hard and relentless, the slap of skin on skin echoing in the quiet room. Her moans rose with every thrust.

"You're mine," I growled into her mouth, teeth catching her bottom lip before kissing her hard. "My beautiful girl."

Her hands fisted in my hair, tugging me closer, gasping against my lips. "Yours," she panted. "Always yours."

That undid me. I shifted, angling her hips up so I could hit her deeper, and she cried out, her head falling back. I mouthed down her throat, sucking another mark into her flushed skin, every part of me aching with how badly I needed her to come undone again.

"Matteo—oh God—"

"Yeah, that's it, baby. Take it. Let me feel you squeeze me." My thumb found her clit, circling tight and fast as I fucked her harder. Her thighs locked around my waist, pulling me impossibly closer.

She was trembling, eyes fluttering shut, moans spilling out of her like music. "I'm—fuck—I'm gonna—"

"Come for me," I gritted out, teeth clenched, fighting to hold on as she writhed under me. "Give it to me, Nic. I want all of it."

Her body bowed, every muscle straining as she shattered, pulsing tight around me, her cry muffled when I swallowed it in a kiss. The feel of her squeezing me sent me over the edge—my hips slammed forward one last time, and I spilled deep inside her with a groan that ripped through me.

For a long moment, it was just ragged breaths and the sound of her heartbeat pounding against my chest. I pressed my forehead to hers, still buried inside her, both of us shaking from the high.

"Promotion celebration," I muttered with a weak grin, brushing my lips over hers. "Think we did it justice."

She laughed, breathless, tugging at my hair until I kissed her again, softer this time.

"Matteo?" she whispered against my mouth.

"Yeah, baby?"

"You owe me new lingerie," she sighed, gesturing to the ripped blue lace panties.

I chuckled, kissing her harder, still not ready to let go. "Worth it."

# 28

# NICOLA

The post-season blur was exactly that—a blur. A cocktail of events, confetti, fast cars, and gala planning. Somehow, between the last checkered flag of the season in Abu Dhabi and waking up this morning in a ridiculously posh Roman hotel suite, a whole week had vanished.

Alexander won his sixth world championship in Qatar, just one race before the end, cementing him into a Formula One legend with the most consecutive championship wins.

I still got chills thinking about it. He stood on that podium with his fists in the air, confetti raining down. Lucia cried happy tears in the VIP lounge with Gia asleep on her shoulder. Matteo hoisted Alex on his shoulders at one point like they were drunk frat boys and not elite-level athletes with millions of followers and millions more in endorsements. We all celebrated until the sun came up. Literally. My feet didn't touch a bed until nearly 6:00 a.m., and I don't remember taking off my heels. Or my lashes.

*Worth it.*

I was in Rome for my big post-season event. Everything I had worked on for the last few months the biggest event yet for the Moretti Foundation, glitz and glam, and astronomical fundraising goals. My phone buzzed where it sat beside me, and my heart did that annoying flutter thing it had picked up lately.

MATTEO:

Landing in 2 hrs. Don't start the party without me, Moretti.

NICOLA:

You're lucky I'm waiting at all. I look very good this week.

MATTEO:

Pics or it didn't happen.

I smirked, curling my legs beneath me on the plush white duvet, still in my silk robe. I snapped a mirror selfie—robe slightly off the shoulder, makeup half-done, coffee in hand, lips already glossed. Flirty, but with plausible deniability.

NICOLA:

You'll have to wait and see. Delayed gratification builds character.

MATTEO:

I have enough character. What I don't have is you under me. Would love to remedy that issue tonight.

I bit my lip, heat curling low in my belly.

NICOLA:

You're lucky I like you.

MATTEO:

You just like me, Moretti?

My mind flashed to a few nights ago—those slow, honey-drenched days we'd spent wrapped up in each other like the world outside had ceased to exist. After the chaos of the final race and the whirlwind of champagne-soaked celebrations, Matteo had whisked me away to a quiet villa tucked in the rolling hills of the Italian countryside. No cameras. No schedules. Just us.

We were supposed to stay a weekend, but we dragged it on as long as we could.

We barely left the bed the first day. Sunlight filtered through gauzy white curtains as we stayed tangled in sheets and laughter and whispered promises. His skin smelled like warm cedar and citrus, and I clung to it like oxygen. Every time he touched me, I felt the walls around my heart crack open a little more.

By the third day, I'd insisted we come up for air. "We're starting to forget what clothes feel like," I teased, already pulling a sweater over my messy hair. He groaned in protest from the bed, hand lazily trailing across the sheets where I'd been moments before.

We slipped into town like shadows. Hats pulled low, sunglasses on, fingers brushing secretly under tables and in quiet corners of cobblestone cafes. The village was sleepy and sunlit, nestled between vineyards and olive groves. No one recognized us there. No one cared.

It was bliss.

That night we walked along a quiet dirt path that curved behind the villa, the sky bruised with twilight and the air scented with lavender. He pulled me close under a string of fairy lights draped across the terrace and started to sway, humming a song I didn't know but never wanted to forget.

"Dance with me," he'd said, his voice low and a little shy. My thoughts shouted at me:

*I love you*

*I love you*

*I love you*

I wanted to say it. Every second. Every time he looked at me like I was more than the life we'd both carefully planned around.

But the words *I love you* burned like stars in my throat—bright, brilliant, and terrifying.

So instead, I said it in all the ways I could. In the way I made him coffee in the mornings before he was even awake. In the way I laughed at all his terrible jokes. In the way I kissed him like I didn't care that there was a timer on this bubble we'd built.

But still...every time I looked at him—really looked at him—I wanted to scream it. *I love you, Matteo DeLuca. You reckless, brilliant, maddening man. I love you so much I don't know how to be quiet about it anymore.*

And yet, I did stay quiet. Afraid that if I said it out loud, it would become too real. Too breakable.

Now, back in Rome on the morning of the gala, I could still feel the imprint of those days on my skin. The warmth of him in the quiet. The freedom of loving him in secret.

But secrets had a shelf life—and tonight, we were ready to tell the world.

Before I could spiral into a whole thing about feelings this early in the morning, a knock echoed from the adjoining suite. Anna's voice followed, muffled but chipper, "Nic! Open up. I need caffeine or a stylist. Possibly both."

I padded over and opened the door, grinning as Anna stepped in, wrapped in an oversized Belen Racing hoodie and leggings, looking far too good for someone who probably hadn't slept either.

"Why are you glowing?" she asked, squinting at me like I'd personally offended her with my post-espresso radiance.

"Maybe because I'm about to have a very hot Italian man in my bed tonight?"

She groaned, "Disgusting. But also, go off."

We both collapsed onto the sofa in the corner of the suite. I tossed her one of the croissants from the breakfast spread, which she caught midair with one hand like the PR goddess she was.

"Okay," she said, munching, "Let's go over the plan."

"For?"

"Your first public outing with Matteo. The world's already speculating after those photos leaked. Half the grid knows. The other half suspects. But tonight, you'll go official."

I chewed on my thumbnail. "Are we sure?"

Anna raised a brow. "He's stupid in love with you. Yes."

I sighed dramatically, "Fine. But I'm not doing some cheesy, over-the-top reveal."

"Of course not. I was thinking chic. Classic. Hand in hand, walking into the gala like a sexy power couple who have nothing to hide and everything to celebrate, post a photo together for the fans, and you're golden."

"God, you're good."

She preened. "I know. Also, I already coordinated with Alex's stylist for the press schedule, so I can get you and Matteo a buffer on the red carpet. Just enough time to make it a moment."

I let out a smile and leaned back. "Fine. Operation Public Power Couple it is."

She raised her coffee in salute. "To the hard launch that's about to blow up the internet."

I clinked my coffee cup against hers. Somewhere inside me, nerves fluttered—but they were the good kind. The *'holy shit, this is real'* kind.

Tonight, it was all happening. And against all odds and my former better judgment, I was ready.

Sunlight filtered through the floor-to-ceiling windows of the penthouse suite, golden and generous, as I stood in front of the mirror fastening a delicate gold hoop through one ear. My phone buzzed on the vanity beside me.

MATTEO:

Landed.

Another buzz.

MATTEO:

Don't look too beautiful until I get there, I want
the full effect.

I smiled at the screen, biting my lip to stifle the heat that flushed my cheeks. I typed back quickly.

NICOLA:

You're lucky I even waited for you. I was
considering going solo just to start a scandal.

Three dots appeared. Then vanished. Then it appeared again.

MATTEO:

Scandal is hotter when I'm involved. Save it for
me, Moretti.

I was still grinning when the suite door swung open thirty minutes later. I turned, expecting Matteo alone.

Instead, he walked in surrounded by a full entourage—Lucia, holding little Gianna on her hip, and behind them...two familiar faces.

"Surprise!" Matteo beamed, sweeping into the room like a ray of golden sunlight.

I blinked. "Wait. Are those—?"

"My parents," he said, grinning. "They flew in last night. Lucia and I picked them up this morning, and I might have conspired with your father for the two extra tickets." His eyes sparkled with mischief.

My heart skidded in my chest, "I was wondering about those mystery tickets!" I could feel the emotion welling in my chest, I blinked a few times knowing the pure adoration was there.

Lucia laughed lightly, adjusting Gianna on her hip. "Don't worry, I didn't tell him it was overkill. But I did warn him that showing up to a gala with his entire family might read as overwhelming."

"Hey," Matteo said with mock offense, wrapping an arm around his sister's shoulders. "If we're doing this, we're doing it right."

Gianna let out a squeal at the exact moment Matteo's mother rushed forward and hugged me, tightly, like we'd known each other forever. I barely had time to respond before his father followed, shaking my hand with a warmth that settled somewhere deep in my ribs.

Matteo stood behind them, eyes locked on mine, a lopsided smile tugging at his mouth.

"You didn't have to—" I started.

"I wanted to," he said simply. "They've been asking about you nonstop. Figured if we were going public tonight, it should be with the people who matter most standing beside us."

My chest tightened. And just like that, every fear I had about this becoming too real, too loud, too big—faded. Because there he was, giving me all of himself. His world. His family. His love. He crossed the room to me slowly, hands finding my waist, eyes softening. "Still want to go solo and start a scandal?" he whispered.

I leaned in close, voice low, "I'd rather have your hand in mine DeLuca. You've turned me into a romantic."

His answering smile was the kind that made everything else fall away.

Somehow, being surrounded by the DeLuca family didn't feel overwhelming. Instead, it was easy.

*Being with you is easy.* Matteo's words bounced around in my mind. It felt simple but monumental at the same time. I was slowly getting used to this feeling of being loved, of the people who cared about me actually caring, not using me or talking about me behind my back like in past relationships. Everything with Matteo was bright and new.

I loved him. I loved him so much it felt like it was bursting from me.

With the day to spend together, we left the hotel as a group early and wandered through a quieter corner of the city, where the buildings were sun-washed and crumbling in the way that made everything feel timeless. Matteo held my hand like he didn't care who saw. His thumb traced the inside of my wrist as we walked, like he couldn't help touching me.

We stopped at a quiet café tucked between two ivy-covered buildings. His mother insisted I try the sfogliatelle, claiming no one in Rome made them quite like this. Matteo's father told old stories about Matteo's childhood—how he used to sneak out to race mopeds and once got grounded for spray-painting a makeshift finish line across their driveway.

Matteo groaned, "Papà, seriously?" I laughed so hard I almost choked.

"Tell her about the time you crashed Zio Luca's Vespa into Nonna's tomato cart," Lucia added, stirring sugar into her espresso with a grin.

"Traitors," Matteo muttered under his breath, but his smile betrayed him.

Gianna sat in Matteo's lap, happily smearing apricot jam on his shirt with sticky fingers, and he didn't even flinch. He just kissed the top of her head and whispered something that made her giggle.

Later, as we walked a little behind everyone, Matteo pulled me aside beneath a row of cypress trees. The others kept walking, giving us a few moments of quiet.

He stopped and turned toward me, brushing my hair back from my face. "You okay?" he asked softly.

"More than okay," I said, searching his eyes. "Your family... they're wonderful."

"They already adore you," he said, "Especially my mom. I'm pretty sure she's planning a wedding."

I let out a breathy laugh, but the emotion stirred under my skin. "I just...I didn't expect any of this. I thought tonight would feel scary. Big. Like the start of something I couldn't control."

"And now?"

I looked up at him. "Now it just feels like life. Yours and mine. Crashing together in the best way."

He smiled, but something flickered behind it—something quieter, more intense. His hand dropped to my waist, fingers sliding just beneath the hem of my sweater.

"Nicola," he said softly, "I think I started falling in love with you the first time you told me off at Silverstone."

I blinked, my heart stuttering.

He stepped closer, his forehead brushing mine. "You don't have to say it back. I just wanted you to know."

I bit my lip, heart caught between my ribs. And even though I'd practiced the words in my head a thousand times, they still caught on my tongue like velvet.

He kissed me right there under the sun. I felt it in every part of me—my heart already belonged to him.

# 29

# MATTEO

Nicola was humming under her breath—something slow and off-key—as she swiped a makeup brush across her cheekbone in the mirror. My shirt hung open, bowtie dangling from my neck like I'd already given up on it, and I was sprawled on the end of the bed watching her.

Well, more like pretending to watch the news on mute while really just watching her.

"You're staring," she said without looking over.

"Of course I am," I said, grinning, "It's either you or the recap of Alexander's sixth win. No offense to him, but you've got the better legs."

She rolled her eyes, biting back a smile. "You've seen me put on makeup a thousand times now. You're going to get bored eventually."

"Impossible," I said, "Every version of you is my favorite. Makeup, no makeup, messy bun, just woke up, angry at me for stealing the last towel..."

"You used the towel I hung for *myself*!"

I held my hands up in mock surrender. "Truce. We're about to go public. No towel-related scandals tonight."

She laughed then—really laughed. That soft, bright sound I never got tired of. There was this freeness to her tonight, a softness around the edges I didn't take for granted. She let her guard down like a drawbridge, piece by piece, and it felt like a goddamn honor every time she let me in.

I reached for the champagne chilling on the side table and opened it with a quiet *pop*, pouring two glasses while she disappeared into the bathroom to change.

"Don't look!" she called, just as the door shut behind her.

"As if I could ever look away," I muttered, mostly to myself like the lovesick fool I was.

I adjusted my cufflinks, tugged my collar, and stared at the mirror like it might give me some sort of calm. But all I could think was, '*This is real.*' This life. Her. Somehow, I'd gone from teasing her at press conferences and arguing over team dinners to watching her get ready on the night we'd show the world we were together.

I hadn't planned it, not any of it. But if I had, it still wouldn't have come close to this.

The door creaked open, and she stepped out with her back to me. "Matteo," she said softly, lifting her hair over one shoulder, "Can you...?"

Then she turned.

And I forgot how to breathe.

The dress was red. Not just red—'*stop your heart, set the room on fire*' red. Throwing me back to months ago and teasing her for wearing the team's colors. Little did she know, at the time, it was my favorite color to see on her. By now she had figured that out, the soft knowing smile that reached her eyes, easily told me that. The dress hugged every inch of her like it had been sewn onto her skin, the back dipping low, a trail of tiny buttons leading to the zipper she was asking for help with.

I stood and crossed the room slowly, fingers itching to touch her. Not even out of desire—though, yeah, that was there too—

but because she looked like something out of a dream. And part of me still didn't believe she was real.

"Nicola," I murmured, voice low as I stood behind her.

My fingers moved to the zipper, but I paused.

"You are...you're breathtaking."

She turned slightly, a smile tugging at her mouth. "You're biased."

"I'm not biased. I'm in love with you. That's different."

Her breath caught. I saw it in the mirror. She blinked, just once, before smiling down at her hands.

"I've seen you in team kits and dripping wet in the rain," I said, slowly zipping the dress. "I've seen you angry and exhausted, determined and fierce. But this...this softness? You like letting me see that part of you, you in red." I looked her up and down and let out a whistle.

"I'll never stop being in awe of you," I said, "Not just because you're beautiful. But because you survived a world that tried to flatten you, and you came out sharper, smarter, and somehow still soft where it matters most. You never had to be perfect for me. You just had to be you."

She turned then, facing me fully, and I saw it in her eyes—that thing I'd been feeling for weeks now. Love. Big and blinding and honest.

I cupped her face, pressing my forehead against hers. "I'm not going to pretend like I planned any of this. But being with you—this is the best decision I've ever made."

"I'm glad you stole my towel," she whispered with a laugh.

"I'd steal all your towels if it meant keeping you."

She leaned up, kissed me soft and slow, and I swore the rest of the world dropped away.

"I love you too, *idiot*," she sighed into me. My breath caught. I couldn't hold it anymore. I had to tell her, but I hadn't expected her to say it back, not yet. I knew she felt it too, but Nicola had placed bricks on bricks of walls around her, protecting herself.

Her shields were locked into place, but here she was opening the door, letting me in. For the first time, the future didn't feel so far off. Her hand in mine. Being able to profess to the whole damn world that this whirlwind of a woman was mine. I was one lucky man.

The car ride to the gala passed in a blur of nerves I hadn't expected to feel. Not race-day nerves. This was different. This was personal.

Nicola sat beside me, legs crossed at the ankle, one hand on her lap and the other resting between us, close enough for me to feel the warmth of her skin. The dress shimmered every time the car hit a patch of light, like the night was trying to show her off.

She was calm. Regal, even. But when I reached for her hand, she laced her fingers through mine without hesitation.

"You sure about this?" I asked, my voice low, barely more than a breath between us.

"Yes." Just one word—but it landed like a punch to the chest, knocking the air right out of me. Simple. Certain. So very Moretti of her. Nicola never wavered when she made up her mind. She didn't do things halfway, didn't say yes unless she meant it. And the fact that she was sure about *me*? That I was something she'd chosen with that same unwavering conviction? God, it felt like the biggest honor of my life.

Outside the venue, the cameras were already going wild— flashes popping like fireworks, fans shouting behind barricades, the red carpet glowing under the entrance lights. It was the kind of chaos I was used to...but tonight it felt different.

Because she was beside me.

We stepped out together. Instantly, the sound doubled.

I felt her pause for half a breath, just enough for me to catch the flicker of nerves in her eyes. I squeezed her hand. "Ready to make them all jealous?"

"God, you're annoying," she muttered through a smile.

The press didn't know where to look. I caught at least three jaws drop when they realized Nicola Moretti wasn't just walking beside me—she was *with* me. And I couldn't even pretend to hide it. I kept my hand at the small of her back, touching her waist lightly as we turned toward the cameras, my body angled toward hers like gravity had finally stopped pretending.

We posed for the official shots—her with her practiced elegance, me with the smug grin of a man who knew damn well he'd hit the jackpot.

"You realize this is going to break the internet, right?" she whispered out of the corner of her mouth.

"Good."

She laughed and turned to face me, took my face in her hands and pulled me down, our lips meeting on the red carpet. The sound was worth every headline that would follow.

Inside the gala, everything glittered. Glass chandeliers, champagne towers, black velvet tablecloths. The world of Formula One in its most polished, exclusive form.

We were quickly swarmed—teammates, drivers, media, even some executives doing that fake-sincere '*We always knew!*' routine.

But through it all, I didn't let go of her. Not once.

Eventually we found a quiet pocket near the back of the ballroom, half-hidden by tall floral arrangements and golden candlelight.

I turned toward her. "You were right, you know."

"About?"

"You belong here. More than anyone. And not just because you look like a goddess in that dress."

She laughed softly, "You're ridiculous."

"I'm serious," I said, "You've built your place in this world on your own terms. I'm so proud of you, Nicola."

Her face softened then, the walls coming down like they always did when it was just us. I stepped closer, tucking a strand of hair behind her ear. "You make everything better."

She smiled, blinking slowly like she was trying not to get too emotional.

I stood proudly at Nicola's side, watching her command the room with effortless grace. There was something about the way she moved through the night—confident, elegant, utterly herself— that had everyone leaning in to listen when she spoke. She made it look easy, even though I knew how much she'd once feared this kind of spotlight. Now? She owned it.

My gaze drifted across the ballroom to where our parents were seated together—mine beside hers, sipping wine, deep in conversation. Nicola caught my eye, and we exchanged a look, eyebrows raised and smirks barely contained. *'Look at them. They're actually getting along.'*

I made my way to the next table where my sister sat, her arm slung over the back of her chair as if this glamorous gala was just another Tuesday. Before I could even sit down, a glittering blur launched herself into my lap.

"Zio!" Gianna beamed up at me, her arms wrapping tight around my neck. Her dress sparkled under the chandeliers, a tiny tiara askew in her curls.

"*Ciao, Stellina,*" I said, pressing a kiss to the top of her head. She smelled like sugar and something vaguely floral—probably the glittery lotion Lucia let her wear for special occasions.

She wriggled, then pulled out a tiny purse and opened it with great ceremony. "Wanna see my lip gloss? It's very special. Mommy says it's just chapstick, but I *know* it's fancy."

I nodded solemnly. "Extremely fancy. I don't think I've seen anything that sparkly all night."

She giggled, then looked across the room with a dreamy sigh. "Zia Nicola looks really pretty."

I followed her gaze. Nicola stood near the stage, laughing at something someone said, her red gown catching the light like fire. She was incandescent.

"She really does," I murmured, more to myself than to Gia.

Lucia leaned over, sipping from her wine glass, a smug tilt to her lips. "You know, I really couldn't have planned this better."

I raised a brow. "Planned what?"

She gestured between Nicola and me with her glass. "You falling for my best friend."

I rolled my eyes. "First of all, I knew her *way* before you did. And second of all, you fell for *my* best friend."

She laughed, nudging Alexander with her elbow. "Crazy how that worked out, huh?"

"Yeah, you're welcome for that," I muttered.

Alexander just smirked, looking far too satisfied for someone who claimed he *wasn't* a matchmaker.

And as I sat there with my niece on my lap, my sister smirking at me, and Nicola shining like a flame across the room, I realized something deep in my chest settled. This—*all of this*—was the life I never knew I needed.

The lights dimmed slightly as Nicola stepped onto the stage, the hum of chatter fading into quiet. She stood tall, radiant beneath the soft spotlight, and the room leaned in. I swore she looked straight at me before she spoke, like I was her anchor in a sea of eyes.

"Thank you," she began, voice steady and clear, "For being here tonight, for believing in something bigger than ourselves. The Moretti Foundation was born from the belief that the Formula One community is more than just a sport—it's a family. A global one."

A pause. A breath.

"And tonight, thanks to your generosity, your belief, and your unwavering support, we didn't just meet our fundraising goal. We surpassed it. By over a million euros."

The room erupted in applause, cheers echoing off the vaulted ceilings. My heart swelled. Pride, awe, love. All of it tangled in my chest.

Nicola smiled, emotional but composed. "These funds will support families in need around the world. Many who have been displaced, struggling, or living below the poverty line in the very cities our sport visits each year. From São Paulo to Silverstone, from Las Vegas to Melbourne. Every stop, every story matters. And because of you, we can do more. We *will* do more."

She thanked the teams, the drivers, and the Moretti Foundation members. She was graceful and articulate, her passion shining through every word. But to me, it wasn't just what she said. It was *how* she said it. With her whole heart. Like this mattered more than any legacy or title or spotlight.

Across the table, Alexander grinned and leaned toward Lucia, who murmured something in his ear that I couldn't quite catch. He kissed her temple, pride softening the sharpness of his usual expression.

When Nicola finally stepped down from the stage and returned to the table, the applause still echoing in the background, I rose to meet her. I didn't care that we were in front of half the paddock. I pulled her into my side, arms tight around her waist, and whispered into her hair, "I hope you know how fucking incredible you are."

She looked up at me, eyes a little glassy but still fierce, and smiled. "You're biased."

"Not biased. Just lucky," I murmured, brushing a kiss to her cheek. "So damn lucky."

The rest of the night passed in a blur of goodbyes and congratulations. People clapped me on the back, gave Nicola hugs, and asked about next year's gala. My parents said goodbye to hers like they were old friends. And just before we stepped outside, Mr. Moretti found me.

He extended his hand.

"Matteo," he said, giving me a firm shake. His eyes—always

intense, always measuring—held something softer now. "Welcome to the family."

I didn't have words. Just a quiet nod. A stunned, grateful smile.

Later that night, with Nicola's heels dangling from her fingers and her head resting on my shoulder as we sat in the back of the car, I looked out at the city lights blinking by and thought *This is it. This is everything.*

And somehow, in this wild, fast, unpredictable world—we found each other.

She reached for my hand. I held it tight, ready to spend all the moments with her. Each heart-racing moment with the girl of my dreams.

# EPILOGUE: MATTEO

## About Two Years Later – DeLuca Vineyard, Italy

The sun was setting low over the hills of Tuscany, bathing the vineyard in warm, golden light that glinted off the wine glasses, the stone walls, the rows of grapevines swaying gently in the breeze. It was the kind of evening that felt like a dream.

Nicola stood barefoot in the grass just a few feet away, the hem of her linen dress brushing her ankles, hair pulled into a messy knot at the nape of her neck. She had a glass of red in one hand and was swaying gently to the music playing from the old record player in the courtyard, humming under her breath.

Nearby, Lucia sat on a patio chair with her newest baby girl in her arms—only a few months old, cheeks round as peaches. Alexander hovered close, stealing glances at both his girls like he still couldn't believe his life was real. Gia chased fireflies barefoot, giggling as Nonna called out from the kitchen window that dessert was almost ready.

It was chaos in the warmest, most beautiful way. And all I could do was watch Nicola.

God, I loved her.

"You're staring again," she said without turning around.

"I'm allowed," I said, walking up behind her.

She leaned into me when I wrapped my arms around her waist, resting my chin on her shoulder.

"Are you ever going to let the kids win in the three legged race?" she teased, her voice soft. It was a family tradition: a day of games, competition. One of my favorite days, and I'd not be going easy on any of the kids, no matter how cute they were. Gianna had been my partner this year; at five years old she was a firecracker. But her little legs moved too slow, so I picked her up and ran us across the finish line. It was a mixture of cheers and boos this year. The house was packed with friends. Anna was here with her kids, a few other drivers staying the weekend with their families as well. The DeLuca Vineyard had expanded, my sister's passion project. With all the land, she had cottages built around the vineyard and turned the winery into a mini luxury resort. During the off-season, we let the drivers have first dibs. The DeLuca Vineyard was rather popular these days, much to my mother's happiness. She loved hosting and had cooked enough food for a small village; a permanent smile etched on her as we all gathered together in the sun. I had even convinced Nicola's parents to come down for the day, since it was a *very* special day.

I looked at Nicola, nerves in my stomach at the box pressed into my jacket pocket. I kissed the curve of her neck. "Only if you're the one waiting for me at the finish line."

She turned then, brows raised. "That was dangerously close to cheesy, DeLuca."

"I'm allowed one cheesy line," I said, stepping back just enough to reach into my pocket. "Especially if it comes with this."

Nicola froze as I dropped to one knee in the middle of my family's vineyard, dust clinging to my trousers, the sky going pink and gold behind her.

I held up the box and opened it slowly.

Her eyes filled with tears.

"Nicola Moretti, you're the girl of my dreams," I said quietly, "I love our life and I want to spend every day with you. On the hard days, the magical ones, the quiet ones, and every day in between. I want a life that starts and ends with you—messy and loud and full of people we love. Will you marry me?"

She didn't speak at first. Just stared at me like I'd knocked the air out of her lungs.

Then she laughed—one hand to her chest, the other swiping at her eyes.

"You idiot," she whispered, "Yes. Of course, yes."

I stood and slid the ring onto her finger. It fit like it had been waiting there all along.

Cheers echoed across the lawn. Lucia stood and handed the baby to Alexander so she could throw her arms around us. Gia shouted, "FINALLY!" like she'd been waiting two years for this exact moment. All our friends and family celebrated with us.

And as Nicola leaned into me, her arms wrapped tight around my shoulders, she whispered against my temple. "I love you, *mi amore*."

# ACKNOWLEDGMENTS

It feels surreal to be here, writing acknowledgements for my second novel! Heart Racing was such a wild ride to write. One of my favorite stories in this sparks fly world and writing it was no easy feat. While For The Thrill of It All was bursting to be written, this one was like pulling at a stuck thread. Maybe it was because it felt bigger to me, I wanted to get it right, to do good by Matteo and Nicola. There's something so special about these two for me. They both mask so hard, try to be what they think everyone wants from them, one is icy and one is golden. It was really fun to explore the same coping mechanism and two vastly different outcomes of a person.

To start off, this book would not be what you have today if not for a HUGE group of people.

**First and foremost to my husband** who brought me snacks and meals and Dr. Pepper while I was in my writing cave. Who kept me sane during editing. I would not be able to do what I do without you. You show up for me in every way, you listen to my plot rants and my character development chaos. You go with me to Barnes & Noble at night after work to write in the cafe together. You do it all. I love you so much.

Thank you to you dear reader for embarking on this journey with me, for loving Matteo from book one and begging me for his own book. You FUELED me.

Thank you to my amazing beta readers: Grace, Chloe, Sienna + Bailey. I am so so thankful for you gals! For the love you pour into this series and the reaction memes and chaos commenting.

Thank you to my amazing team of editors who saw this story

in all its forms. Most importantly to Bailey who took this book and helped me make it shine, commenting on vastly misspelled words and said, 'soooo... you didn't mean to say this, RIGHT?' I love you so much, I can't even put into words how amazed I am by you and how much love and care you put into this book. The calls to talk through things that were feeling too big and overwhelming for me, and every single text along the way. Thank you, thank you, thank you. I promise I will get you Dante's book !

Thank you to my dear friend and proofreader Katrina for making this book shine!

To my author friends I have made this year! I am so very thankful for you. Writing can be a lonely task but having a community that understands this niche thing is so very lovely.

Thank you to my family for sharing my wins with me, for showing up for me, coming to events, bringing me food or caffeine mid events. You never fail to make me feel so very loved.

And lastly, to my sweet gremlin. You're the best dog a girl could ask for, thanks for cuddling with me everyday on the couch while I write and guarding the office from the window bench.

# WHAT'S NEXT?

Want to read Lucia + Alexander's story? Click Here: For The Thrill of It All: A Formula One Romance

More Sparks Fly series books are on the way, among other things. Follow Elliana on instagram @authorelliana for the most up to date news and releases.

# ABOUT THE AUTHOR

Elliana Rose is a lover of romcoms, hoarder of books and personal photographer to her German Shepard "Gremlin". When she is not writing she is making bookish graphics and designs for her shop Primrose&CoDesign, reading in the sunshine, and probably dreaming up a new idea.